A Means to an End

Lorraine Stephens

In memory
of
Jessica Katherine

Chapter One

"Oh Mummy, were you bad? Did daddy have to smack your face again?"

Liz was no fool. She understood her marriage was no fairytale, and certainly not what she'd dreamt of as a girl. But those were the words that flipped a switch; she needed to get out, for her and for the three kids that were in the middle of this.

Not long before this, Liz and Frank had separated for the third time; each time before should have been the last, but for Liz, THIS was it. After a six-week stint at the local Women's refuge, she had managed to rent a house for herself and her three children. She was desperately trying to get back to some kind of a normal life.

Liz felt foolish that she had even entertained the belief that the children had been sheltered from the violence, oblivious to the black eyes and the bruised arms, the constant trips to Emergency.

It would be different this time. She would not go back to him again, no matter what he promised. The physical abuse Liz had endured left her bruised and battered, but the psychological abuse left her a broken shell of a woman. It had been like living in a war zone over the past few years. It wasn't fair to her or the children, not knowing from day to day what they would be walking into.

Liz had been brought up in a loving family, the kind of family you bragged about: parents who rarely disagreed, let alone fought in front of her and her brother. Parents who supported each other and had each other's back. Liz had naively believed all marriages were like that. So when she tried to apply what she'd seen as a child to her own marriage, she inadvertently became the peacemaker. She always took Frank's side, even though she knew it was his fault when he had lost another friend, or another job. She hid a lot of things from her parents and friends, and often went without rather than ask for help. It certainly wasn't the marriage she had dreamt of, but Frank gave her three wonderful children, and always the optimist, she just kept hoping that things would improve over time. She never dreamt for one moment of the horrors that would unfold.

They'd been childhood sweethearts from the age of 14. She'd known he was a bit of a bad boy and had been in a bit of trouble with the cops for street drinking and vandalism. In comparison Liz was a goody two shoes. She had wagged the odd day from school, had a couple of drinks at a party while underage, but that was about as bad as it got. What was so attractive about him then, was terrifying now. He had no respect for authority, was very headstrong and would take enormous risks.

She recalled how he'd erupted into anger one night; he'd returned to his car after a night at the pub to find someone had stolen the black external blind he'd had fitted to the back window of his car. They had driven around all night looking for a car with a similar blind. When he found one, he asked Liz to steal it off the car while he waited as the 'getaway driver'. She was petrified and had told him she didn't think she could do it. He got really mad with her and got out the car and stole it right off the car himself, driving off at terrifying speed.

That was the first time he had hit her. He had punched her in the mouth, right there in the car. That should have been the warning sign to get out of this relationship, but she believed what he had said later, that it was her fault for being such a wimp and not helping him. If she loved him, she would have done it.

Frank had always been in and out of work. He was impulsive and had a quick temper that was often the cause of his job losses. When she was younger this impulsiveness and quick temper used to make her feel safe when she was with Frank; he would always stand up for her, wouldn't take any crap from anyone. Him punching a guy to defend her honour seemed romantic back then. When he had money, he was very generous, and he was hard to resist with his European good looks; a head of thick dark hair and eyes that seemed to look into her soul. To Liz he looked like a Spanish conquistador, and she felt the envy of other girl's eyes when she was out with him.

The warning signs had been there from the start, though she had clearly missed them; perhaps even chosen to ignore them. It had felt like love when he insisted on knowing where she was and who she was with every minute of the day. *So protective.* He didn't want to share her with anyone including her friends and family. *So in love with her.* In the beginning it felt wonderful and all-encompassing in the very best way. It was not until much later she understood that it was about power and control, not love.

Frank was the first boy she was intimate with; she had valued her virginity and had been proud to tell Frank that he was her first. But this didn't stop Frank from accusing her of being 'used goods' and of having sex with other guys, no matter how often she told him he was the only one she wanted to be with.

Shortly before Liz turned seventeen she was starting to think their relationship wasn't a healthy one. She no longer had any close girlfriends she could talk to. They had all gotten tired of her not showing up, or making excuses as to why she couldn't go out with them, so in the end they just stopped inviting her along. Confiding in her parents was not an option. Even though they would never tell her openly, it was clear to Liz they didn't really like Frank.

Although Liz had done well at school, she was captivated with the idea of leaving school and getting a job. She had done a bit of part time work and some babysitting and enjoyed having money to spend on clothes and records. And she badly wanted to buy her own car. So, with Franks encouragement and to her parent's disappointment, she left school before graduating.

Her parents desperately tried to talk her out of leaving school. They were hoping she would be the first member of the family to attend university - she certainly had the smarts, they would often tell her. And he knew it too; school was easy. She just didn't have the drive. And while she had a few acquaintances, she didn't seem to fit into any particular group. But with Frank… with Frank, she fitted in perfectly.

Liz was offered a traineeship at a bank. Although her parents were disappointed she was leaving school, they had to admit the job was a good one, with a good career path. But only three months into her new job, to Franks delight and Liz's trepidation, she discovered she was pregnant. And so they did exactly what was expected and what was right, at least back then, and they got married.

***

It was well after midnight when Liz woke to a loud banging at the front door.

'It's meee, Lizzy, lemee in, I just wanna talk to ya, I'm sorry I hurt ya, pleeeease can we just talk abou it. I love ya so much. I can't live wivout you and the kids.'

'Shit,' she said out loud as she got out of bed and stood behind the front door, her heart racing fast in her chest. *No, not again*, she thought to herself. She hoped they might've had a bit more time before he found out where they were living and turn up unannounced.

Liz stood directly behind the locked front door. 'You'll wake the kids, they've got school tomorrow,' she said in a loud whisper. 'Just go home Frank you're drunk, come back tomorrow, I promise I'll talk to you then, please just go away. I don't want to have to call the cops on you, but I will if you don't go away.' She hoped more than expected that he'd take any notice of what she was saying.

His voice dropped to a loud whisper. 'Oh, come on, Lizzy let us in I just wanna talk that's all, I'll be good, I promise. I'm sorry about wha I did. You jus' make me so mad sometimes.'

Her thoughts raced. *I've heard it all before. It won't happen again, it's all my fault because I make him crazy, because I don't tell him where I am going and who I'm with. My friends and family are all against him. But it's not my fault. I know that now. I can't do this again; I won't do this again.* She pleaded with him, 'Please Frank, just go home. Come back tomorrow, I promise I will talk to you then.'

'Oh come on Lizzy, I'm not gonna hurt ya, it's cold out here,' Frank said. His voice was getting louder. His anger was starting to show.

'No Frank. Please go away,' she said in an assertive voice, even though her legs were shaking so much she was having trouble standing up.

With a sigh of relief, she heard his footsteps retreating from the front door, and hopefully heading towards his car. *Maybe he is going to change and start listening to me* she thought. He somehow always managed to find her. The first time she left him, she didn't tell him where they were living, but one night she'd had an attempted break in. Someone had made a lot of noise, rattled the gate, and banged on the windows. Liz and the children were terrified. By the time the police had arrived the intruder was long gone. In retrospect, she understood that the intention had been to spook her and the children; it had to be him. After that night she had trouble sleeping. She would lay in bed awake for hours on high alert, every creek and crack the house made caused her to panic. It was not long after this incident she decided to move back in with Frank; likely his plan all along

The chilling sound of smashing glass hauled Liz out of her reverie. It was coming from somewhere at the back of the house. One of the kids' bedrooms? The laundry she was not sure, but what she was sure of was who. Her pulse quickened.

'Shit. Shit. Shit,' she yelled while quickly scanning around for her phone. She remembered it was sitting on the table next to her bed. Suddenly she heard the terrifying sound of Sarah screaming from her bedroom. Liz ran for her phone, now in a complete panic.

Crying, she dialled 000 and yelled down the phone. '152 Low Street, Pinewoods – I have an AVO against my husband, he's just broken into my house, please hurry. Send the cops NOW!' She did not wait for a response. She ran towards the back of the house, phone still in hand and was confronted by the terrifying sight of Frank standing in the hallway, shot gun in hand, with three trembling children standing in their bedroom doorways looking terrified.

'Please Frank,' she cried, trying to stay calm for the sake of the children 'There's no need for a gun. I'll do whatever you want. Whatever you say. Just tell me what you want. Let's talk about it. There's no need for anyone to get hurt. I swear to God, Frank, I won't leave you again. We can work this out.' From her phone, the emergency responder reported the police were on their way.

She will never forget the look she got from Frank at that moment. The look was pure hatred. He pointed the shot gun at her head and yelled. 'This is your fuckin doing, it's all your fault. You don't get it do ya, ya bitch.'

She was on her knees begging him to stay calm. She pleaded, 'You're frightening the kids. Frank, please put the gun down, we can talk about this.'

She could hear the emergency responder saying the police are two minutes away. By this stage, the kids were screaming and crying. Sarah cried, 'Please Daddy don't hurt Mummy.'

Liz kept her eyes locked on Frank, 'Josh, Molly, Sarah please go back in your rooms, everything will be okay. Daddy and Mummy will sort it out.'

'You heard ya mum, go on get back in your rooms,' ordered Frank.

Liz nodded reassuringly. She will never forget their terrified tearstained faces, but at that moment she needed to distance him from the kids and keep him talking. 'Go on, it will be alright, Mummy and Daddy just need to talk.'

The next thing Liz remembered was waking up in hospital. She had been told she had been in and out of consciousness for 6 days after surgery to release pressure on her swelling brain. The bullet that was meant to kill her had somehow deflected off her head, but it had caused a large crack in her skull and her brain to swell. The neurosurgeon had explained she had what was called a subdural hematoma. They had removed a piece of her skull to relieve the pressure and she would need further surgeries to repair her skull. Her speech and body movements had been affected; at this point there was no guarantee she would ever fully recover her ability to walk and talk. Long-term rehabilitation would be required to rewire her brain signals to her body movements, as well as years of speech therapy.

She has never been back to that house. She couldn't even bring herself to go near the suburb. She had been told that the police officers who attended, even the long serving emergency officers, were physically sick that night when they saw the blood bath. Her three terrified and beautiful children shot in their heads while they crouched together in the corner of one of the bedrooms. Dead. And that cowardly bastard had shot himself. Dead. Why the children? That was the one question that had driven her mad. He had taken me out, why was that not enough for him? He may have despised me, but he loved those kids.

Chapter Two

(Present day)

That was 15 years ago, but the memory is so vivid it could've happened yesterday, often haunting her night after night. The pain never goes away, still suffering from excruciating headaches and insomnia to this day, and enduring years of physical therapy, just to learn how to walk and talk again. If it were not for her parents, Liz believes she would not be here today. They were her rock when she was in her deepest darkest place, there to pull her out and keep her moving forward. She now realised how difficult it would have been for them. They had not only lost their only grandchildren but had almost lost their daughter as well. Somehow, they stayed strong.

Liz remembers her father sitting on the floor holding her as she sobbed. The pain was too much, both physically and emotionally, and Liz felt she just couldn't do it anymore He had let her cry her heart out, and when she was done he told her to blow her nose, get up and put one foot in front of the other. *You just have to keep taking one step at a time sweetheart,* he would say to her over and over. On one occasion, with tears welling in his eyes, he said, 'I won't let him take you from us as well.'

That was a turning point for Liz, a bit of a wake-up call. Those words and the way they were delivered had given her so much strength. She would tell herself over and over to stop feeling sorry for herself. *He failed. You survived. Don't waste your energy on hate. Nothing will ever change what he did. Nothing you do will bring the children back. You have to go on and lead a full life. You have to live your life for your children. You have to be around to tell anyone who wants to hear about what happened to your children. If you can save just one family from the same fate, then your children's deaths were not in vain.* That was the only way she could make any sense of what had happened to her and her children.

Liz tried trauma counselling, grief counselling, anger management and some other more obscure therapies to try to help her even begin to start the healing process. She gives talks about family violence at conferences, training events, refuges, you name it, she's tried it. Maybe she is still wrestling with the guilt for failing to protect her children, or grappling with the age-old question: 'Why didn't I see this coming?' But nothing seems to help her truly understand why she survived when the children lost their lives so cruelly.

There was no handbook on what to do next, but 10 years ago, Liz decided she had to get on with her life. Searching for answers, she decided to go back and finish high school, and then put herself through university. She went from the most helpless feeling in the world, to deciding not to be a victim any longer, by choosing to help others. She completed a double degree in Psychology and Social work and began her career like so many others, working in child protective services. However, it wasn't long before it became clear that, when it came to making the difference she badly wanted to make, her hands were tied; red tape and lack of resources made it nearly impossible. In frustration, she left and joined a not-for-profit agency that offered free counselling services for survivors of sexual abuse, sexual assault and family violence, something she felt deeply passionate about.

It was Friday afternoon just as Liz was packing up to go home for the week when a colleague came into her office with a concerned look on her face.

'Hey, Liz, if you have a minute, can I just run something past you about a client? I know it's Friday afternoon, but I just can't go home with this on my mind.'

'Yep no worries Karen, take a seat and spill.'

Karen sat down opposite Liz. She took off her reading glasses, letting them hang from a chain around her very slim neck. As usual Karen was immaculately turned out in a designer skirt suit, looking more like a businesswoman than a counsellor. Liz had been a little concerned when she first employed Karen that clients may feel intimidated by her perfectionism, but Liz was well off the mark; her clients seem to adore her, and she clearly reciprocated the feelings.

Karen had been married to a highly successful lawyer for over 20 years until recently. Twelve months ago, he told her their marriage was over, and he wanted a divorce so he could marry his much younger colleague. Karen was devastated, and although she did quite well in the divorce settlement, decided to return to work. Still a little fragile, she began a very strict fitness regime, only eating healthy food and running 5 kilometres every day. She obsesses about what she eats, and politely reminds the other members of staff about the unhealthy aspects of their diets. When it's Karen's turn to bring morning tea to their staff meetings it's always something raw and healthy.

Liz suspected, like so many fifty something women in Karen's position, she blames herself for her ex-husband's wandering eyes and hands. Even though Karen is a very experienced and skilful counsellor, she is still a human being with raw emotions and irrational thoughts. Maybe for Karen her regime is about retribution, thought Liz looking at Karen's slim and fit body. *'Look what you have given up, see how fabulous I look; how independent I can be without you.* A metaphorical middle finger in the air. *Once you get over your midlife crisis you will regret leaving me.'* Nonetheless, the agency was lucky to have her as she is a very experienced psychologist, who luckily for them did not need a big fat pay cheque.

The agency had started twenty years ago with one counsellor and a part-time admin assistant. It had grown over time and expanded its services. It had been fortunate in gaining recurring funding from both state and federal governments to offer free counselling services. The biggest issue for Liz was the long waiting list for their services, as although they had secured recurring funding it was never enough to employ the number of counsellors necessary to meet the community's needs.

The agency stretched its finances to employ as many counsellors as the funding could afford them. As a result, they were not able to offer the kind of wages that a psychologist or psychotherapist could earn in private practice. Even so, the agency seemed to attract highly qualified and experienced counsellors. The majority of the counsellors were either young and enthusiastic psychologists just out of Uni and looking for their first job, or at the other end of the spectrum, very experienced psychologist or counsellors who no longer needed the money and wanted to give something back to the community. The combination seemed to work extremely well, offering both the latest theoretical knowledge along with an abundance of experience.

Liz had started as a part time counsellor, but quickly moved up to the team leader role. A couple of years ago, when the previous manager resigned, Liz applied for her job. When she applied for the role, she had suggested to the board of management who oversaw the running of the agency, that she could combine her role as team leader and manager, therefore freeing up a position to employ another counsellor. Although the managers role was an important part of the agency, it had traditionally been filled by an administrator and not a clinician. Liz wanted to change that. She felt confident she could handle both roles, and still work a nine-day fortnight.

The Agency was complicated by the fact that each service was funded by a different government department. The children's counselling service was funded by state government through the department of child protection, whereas the adult counselling service, whilst also funded by the state government, was via the health department. The Indigenous counselling service was funded by the Federal Government and the youth counselling service was a local government project. As a result, each service had different budgets and different reporting requirements.

There were important legal obligations around reporting, finance, insurances duties and the day to day running of the agency. The Clinical team leader had a responsibility for the more difficult cases, as well as supervising the counselling team. Liz was well aware of the importance of both roles but was still keen to combine the roles into one, as she was not yet prepared to give up her clinical duties.

Some would describe Liz as a work-alcoholic, but truth be told, keeping busy for her was essential, as it meant less time to dwell on the past. The board of management agreed to her request but were concerned about the number of hours she would need to put in to perform both roles, so they only agreed if Liz would give up seeing clients. Not happy about this Liz negotiated with the board for a six-month hiatus to wind down her current client list. Although Liz could have passed on most of her clients to other counsellors, there were a few she strongly believed would have felt abandoned by her, and she did not want to add to their distress.

She had also negotiated with the board that she wanted the flexibility to take up new clients from the crisis service they offered, as this was often a service that needed a quick response. The board reluctantly agreed but insisted she report her client load at the monthly board meeting to ensure she was not taking on too much.

The counselling team receive weekly professional supervision from Liz to not only review their current cases but also to check how they are coping with the workload. The team also provide team support to each other. They were incredibly good at taking care of one another. It was not unusual to see two of the counsellors putting on their walking shoes and taking a brisk walk together around the block. Coming back laughing and full of energy. They were all aware how stressful it can be listening day in day out to adults and children who had endured some of the worst abuse imaginable.

Liz had once participated in a research study where a PHD psychology student was conducting research on *The Re-traumatisation of Trauma counsellors*. She was yet to hear any results, but it certainly indicated the toll it can take on a counsellor's own mental health. Learning how to leave it all behind at the office is extremely challenging, but crucial to their own wellbeing.

Karen smoothed down her skirt and took a deep breath. 'Well, I have a new client, Sally, not sure if you know who I mean, you might have seen her in the waiting area. She has a couple of large colourful tattoos, that look like roses are climbing up and down her arms and legs.' Karen said as she moved her hands up and down her arms and legs to demonstrate.

'Ahh, yep, yep, I think I know who you mean, the woman with the long blond hair with the little tuft of pink in the front?'

'Yes that's her,' nods Karen emphatically. She takes a long breath in and blows it out hard and rubs the back of her neck, tears start to well in her eyes. 'Well, I'm not sure where to start, I feel so helpless.'

Liz stays silent and just looks at Karen, raising her eyebrows and giving her a nod of encouragement. Karen takes a moment to formulate what she wants to say in her mind. She gives Liz the condensed version of what Sally her client had told her earlier that day.

Karen explained to Liz that Sally has two children, a 9-year-old boy, Jason from a previous relationship and a 4-year-old daughter Lilly from her current relationship. The current relationship had gone bad, and a separation had occurred 2 months ago. The father of Lilly, Nathan, stayed in the family home because he runs his own trucking business from the premises. Sally moved out into a rental with the children. Sally suspects her estranged husband of sexually abusing their daughter Lilly on access visits. She had asked Karen if Lilly could see Julie, the children's counsellor.

'I know that we normally insist on having both parents' consent to see our children's counsellor,' explained Karen, 'but I doubt he will give his consent.'

'Why does she suspect him?'

Karen described how Lilly did not want to go and see her dad, saying she has a tummy ache and wanting to stay home. They have a temporary agreement where Nathan has Lilly every second weekend, but this can often vary due to Nathans work schedule. They are still going though family court for a permanent arrangement. She also sends her 9-year-old son Jason who is from a previous relationship, but Nathan is the only father he has ever known. Sally feels this offers Lilly a bit of protection, but then feels guilty, as she knows that a 9-year-old should not have the responsibility to protect his sister.

Sally had told Karen that last weekend she had to drag Lilly kicking and screaming out from under her bed. Sally asked her why she didn't want to go to her dads and Lilly said that it was a secret. She wasn't allowed to tell anyone, or she would be in big trouble. Sally immediately became worried and told Lilly that it was alright to tell her, that she wouldn't get into any trouble. Lilly then told Karen they play a secret game where daddy takes all his clothes off and asks Lilly to touch him, and he touches her. Lilly says it's because her daddy tells her she is special. Lilly told Sally that she doesn't want to be special, and she hates the secret game.

Sally said she went straight to the police and reported what Lilly had told her. The police interviewed Lilly. Sally, of course, could not be present during the interview, so she only knows what the police told her. They informed Sally they did not consider Lilly to be a credible witness. They felt she had been coached by Sally about what to say to them. They also did not want to get involved in a custody dispute. They suggested that she go to child protection if she wanted to take this any further.

Sally then went straight to child protection and spoke to the duty officer. Sally suggested they also seemed sceptical as soon as she told them she and her husband were in the process of going through family court for a permanent custody arrangement. They did speak to Lilly on her own but, again, did not seem to want to get too involved. They arranged for Lilly to go to the children's hospital for a physical examination. Sally took Lilly last week, they examined her, but could not find any evidence of any physical interference.

Karen looked straight at Liz and said, 'I don't know but, from what Sally told me Lilly has been saying about her dad, it feels like typical grooming behaviour to me.'

'Okay, well let's make an appointment for Lilly with Julie and see what she has to say. I have every confidence that if there is something going on Julie will find out.'

Karen nodded her agreement and went to arrange the appointment for early next week.

Chapter Three

Justine felt bad about the argument she'd had with her mum earlier that day. *She has to understand that she can't tell me what to do all the time, I am fifteen now and can make up my own mind about what friends I want to hang out with,* she told herself. Justine was well aware that her mum would not like the idea of her having an older boyfriend, or any boyfriend at all for that matter. Her mother would often tell her that you cannot trust boys, they're all after one thing. *'I don't want you to make the same mistakes I did'* Justine repeated out loud to herself in her mother's voice. Justine winced as she recalled how she had yelled back at her mother. *'Oh, I was a mistake, was I? Well, I'm not you. I will never be like you. I can take care of myself.'* Her Mother would just have to get used to her independence, resolved Justine.

If anyone bothered to ask Justine, she would have described her mum as a homebody. She didn't socialise much, as she didn't have many friends. Mostly, she kept pretty much to herself. She liked to read and sew and seemed to enjoy her own company. You would think this might have made her sad and lonely, thought Justine, as she could not imagine life without the company of her friends, but her mum seemed to be quite happy. She would have the radio on in the mornings and Justine would often witness her dancing around to a lively song, singing along in her very untuneful voice. The problem for Justine was, with a mother that was a loner, Justine was the main focus in her life.

It was a quandary for Justine, because she desperately wanted to be grown up and make her own choices, but she also liked the comfort of being taken care of by her mother. She still made her lunch for school every day, washed, ironed, and put away her clothes, tidied her room and changed her sheets every week, like she was still her little girl. She loved her mum, she really did, but sometimes she felt smothered by her.

Justine's mum, Margaret, worked as a cleaner at a local ship building company. She mostly worked the afternoon shift, Monday to Friday. so that meant she was not often there when Justine came home from school. Justine kind of liked it that way, or maybe she was just used to it. She enjoyed the freedom to contact her friends, watch YouTube or TikTok videos, listen to music at high volume, whatever she liked really without her mum asking her to turn it down or ask questions about what she was doing, or did she have homework to do.

They lived in Lake Swan, a suburb that most people would describe as working class. Most of the houses were built around the nineteen sixties and had had little or no modifications since then. You could clearly see the cracks starting to appear in the mortar and the mould spreading on the roof tiles. The houses had been built quickly to keep up with the hordes of migrants emigrating to Australia back then. There seemed to be three or four different facades repeated over and over, all with the same three bedrooms, one-bathroom, combined lounge and dining, kitchen, and laundry. Although modern at the time and built solidly using double brick and tile, they now looked worn-out and a bit run-down.

Money was often tight. Justine didn't get everything she wanted, but she did get everything she needed. Justine knew her mum worked hard to keep food on the table and pay the mortgage, and deep down she respected her for it. But some days she just got sick of hearing about how hard it had been for her after her father left. It wasn't her fault; she didn't ask to be born.

Justine thought her mum still quite pretty, in an older person type of way. But she wished she would just buy some new clothes, have her hair or nails done once in a while. But no, she insisted on making most of her own clothes and it seemed to Justine that her mother had used the same simplicity pattern and the same floral material all her life. Justine would often tell her mum, 'That's not a dress you're wearing, it's a tent,' and her mum would just laugh and roll her eyes and say she doesn't want to be mutton dressed up as lamb. She recently reminded her mother that she was only 37 - hardly mutton!

Justine sometimes teased her mum and threatened to put her details on a dating app. Her mother was horrified at the thought of meeting up with a stranger for a date. Even though Justine had tried to explain the process, she had made it very clear she had no intentions of meeting anyone that way. Justine couldn't understand why her mother lacked so much confidence and was not interested in getting dressed up and going out on dates.

There had been a guy down the road that had been interested once. She had told her mum at the time she thought he was a good-looking guy. She recalled he fixed trucks, or maybe drove trucks for a living, something like that. He would come around and fix things like leaky taps or broken locks. Once, when the gate almost came off its hinges, he fixed it and stayed for dinner. She'd overheard him asking her out to a movie and dinner, but Margaret just mumbled something about not being available and that she doesn't date. Justine would often mock her Mum about that day, but Margaret would just roll her eyes and say he clearly wasn't serious, he was just being polite. Justine was unaware that her mother had decided long ago she was never going to date or get involved with a man ever again.

It wasn't that Margaret didn't want to be in a relationship, she just didn't trust herself to be a good judge of character when it came to men. Although she had told Justine her father had walked out when she was only 18 months old, this wasn't the whole truth. What Justine was not aware of, was that her father had been walked out the door in handcuffs when she was a toddler. Margaret had met Alex when she was only nineteen, he'd seemed so grown up and mature at the time, talking from the outset that he was looking to settle down and start a family. Margaret had not had much experience with boyfriends, as she was always so shy and nervous in social situations.

He had just swept in and smothered Margaret from the beginning, taking control of everything, where they went, what they did, who they saw. Margaret innocently thought this was the way it was meant to be when someone adored you. He would insist she call him as soon as she got home from work to check she was home safely. He didn't like her mixing with her friends after work or catching up with her old school friend. He wanted to spend every minute he could with her. He was sure her parents didn't like him and took every chance to remind her of that. And it was probably true, but Alex didn't particularly endear himself to them either; in and out of work, solemn and borderline rude to them. There was certainly no love lost.

She managed to justify the relationship by telling herself that they did not know him like she did. They did not see the way he adored her, worshiped her she thought. He loved to see her in nice clothes, as long as they weren't too revealing. He bought her jewellery when he could afford it. He even took her out to a fancy restaurant for dinner one night even though he was well out of his comfort zone.

They had been dating for about two years when Margaret found out she was pregnant, he was over the moon and proposed marriage. They married before the baby bump was obvious. That was when the violence started: she didn't keep the house as tidy as his mother, she didn't always have dinner ready when he came home from work.

The first time he hit her she was leaving him and never going back, but he convinced her it would never happen again. He told her in tears how he had witnessed his own father beating his mother and that he'd felt so weak and helpless at the time. He didn't want to be like his father, and begged Margaret to give him another chance. He would change. He promised. He loved her. He wanted her and the baby and would do anything to keep them together. Except of course, get help. Margaret suggested they go to her GP to see if there was any kind of help for Alex's short fuse. He said he would, but not right now: he had too much work on.

This became a familiar routine. He always begged Margaret to forgive him, he said if she left him, he would kill himself as he couldn't live without her and Justine. He was always so sorry, and in between the beatings he could be very loving. But Margaret knew deep-down things would never change. Love shouldn't feel like a prison. She knew she needed to get away, but most of the time she felt pathetic and worthless.

Margaret had been close to her parents, but they were from a generation where marriage was for life. In good times and in bad times, in sickness and in health. They had made it clear, '*she had made her bed*' and she needed to make an effort to keep the marriage together for the sake of the baby. If Margaret had told them about the violence, she was sure they would have insisted she come home, but Margaret was too ashamed to tell them that Alex hit her.

She wondered why they never asked her why she wore a scarf or a high neck jumper in the middle of summer? If they had asked, she may have had the courage to show them the bruises on her neck. She would just stay home when she had a black eye or split lip and fantasize about her and Justine's escape. Luckily, she did not have to wait too long, just two years into the marriage she got the opportunity when Alex was arrested and gaoled for aggravated burglary.

Justine was vastly different from her mother. She loved to get dressed up and go out and have a good time. '*Life is not a dress rehearsal*,' she once told her mum. She had overheard a lady say this at the local coffee shop a few months earlier and thought to herself, 'Wow that's so true, I hadn't looked at life like that before,' and decided that day to live in the moment. She resolved to pass on this revelation to her mum, and she had. However, Margaret had warned Justine at the time that living for today might be okay for the young, but an adult needed to plan for the future. Justine just rolled her eyes at her mum and told her she needed to get a life. At the time Margaret just shook her head and sighed at her daughter. She was well aware of her own short comings; the external scars had long gone but the internal scars were much harder to heal.

She so admired her daughter's confidence though. Margaret was comforted by the thought that her daughter would have a bright future, she had the personality to grab life by the full. Justine was always so optimistic and hopeful; she always saw the best in people. Margaret felt Justine could do anything she wanted to do if she could only focus on something for more than five minutes.

Justine seemed to change her mind every week about what career she wanted. This week she was talking about wanting to leave school at the end of the year and start a hairdressing apprenticeship. Margaret was adamant that she would be staying at school until she graduated from year twelve. If she still wanted to do hairdressing after that, that would be fine, but she wanted her to have options. Margaret did not mind so much that Justine enjoyed herself, but she had warned her many times she needed to concentrate on school as her marks this term seemed to have slipped.

Justine had always been an average student but lately she had found it harder to concentrate. Maybe if she could commit to what she wanted to do she might have more enthusiasm for Maths or English. She just could not understand how finding what X or Y equals or how comparing the opening chapter of a book to the opening scene in a movie was going to help her get a job. She'd told her mum she was trying, but in reality, Justine just didn't' like schoolwork and it was beginning to feel like it was all going over her head. She was too embarrassed to ask questions for fear of being called dumb and she would often daydream about leaving school and getting a job; about having money to get her own place, maybe do some travelling, anything really. She didn't know what her future looked like just yet, but she felt that was OK.

Margaret knew exactly where Justine's rebellious streak came from. She reminded her so much of her sister when she was younger. Exasperated, Margaret often felt at a loss to know what to do with Justine. She tried to control her, but at times it seems that Justine has trouble controlling herself. Margaret was aware Justine had a boyfriend. She'd overheard a conversation between Justine and her friend Sue about a guy named Ben. It was a giddy, intensely spoken conversation, the way girls talk about boys when they're in their teens and they've yet to be tainted by love. At the time Margaret had to bite her tongue not to interfere and tell Justine she was too young to have a boyfriend, and she decided to let it go. She hoped it was just a crush, or a teenage liaison. She stayed quiet, simply praying to a God she didn't believe in that Justine didn't fall into the same traps that she did.

Chapter Four

Justine was late. She'd spent too much time on her hair and make-up. She was petite and pretty, but not a head-turner like her best friend Sue. When Sue walked into a room everyone noticed. Sue wouldn't look out of place on the front cover of Vogue or Vanity Fair, thought Justine.

Justine checked herself in the mirror; she wondered if she had gotten her hazel-green eyes from her father, so different, they were, to her mothers. Justine had been curious lately, wondering about her father, what he looked like, his personality traits: if he was tall or short, his build, but she didn't want to upset her mum by asking too many questions. Her mum always seemed uncomfortable whenever she brought the subject up. So much so, Justine stopped asking. She once watched a movie where a man had had a secret family. She would daydream she was the result of a passionate clandestine dalliance. Maybe, she romanticized, her mother was so heartbroken she couldn't bear to think about him with anyone else. Could she have brothers and sisters somewhere out there? How wonderful would that be, she thought.

Once she was happy with her makeup, she dressed quickly in her favourite skinny leg jeans and a sleeveless checked shirt that tied up in the front of her slim waist. As she walked out the door to Sue's house, she just yelled goodbye to her Mum. She didn't go and find her and hug and kiss her goodbye like she usually would; she was still fuming from their argument earlier. And besides, she didn't want to have to answer a million questions about where she was going, what time she would be home, and a reminder that she had school tomorrow.

***

The days were starting to get darker earlier; winter was setting in. Justine had dressed in a hurry and had forgotten to bring something warm to keep out the cold. Though she was not feeling particularly cold at the moment, but that was the result of the alcohol running through her veins. She still felt the 'buzz' in her head and was feeling immensely happy.

'Just drop me off round the corner, don't want Mum crackin the shits about being in the car with you.'

'But it's cold and gettin dark outside, you'll freeze to death,' Ben said in his sing song kind of way.

'Na I'll be right, just drop me off at the truck bay over there,' Justine said as she pointed to the left. 'All I've got to do is run down the road, jump over the back fence and I'll be home, sweet, I don't want her hearing that clap trap of a car of yours and asking me a million questions about you.'

'Well, the clap trap sure suits you when you wanna a go somewhere,' suggested Ben.

'Yeah yeah, I know, just stop over there, I'll be fine.'

Ben slowed his car down and pulled into a truck bay just a few hundred meters from Justine's street. They chatted for a bit in the car and laughed about the afternoon they had spent with Tony and Sue. Sue was Justine's best friend from school, and they had met Ben and Tony at a party several months ago. Ben and Tony were 18, and Sue and Justine felt so grown up going out with guys that had a car and could legally buy alcohol and get into night clubs.

Justine had been immediately smitten with Ben. He was not the usual bad boy type she was attracted to - quite the opposite. He was tall and geeky, a gentle giant. His skinny legs and long arms made him look a bit gangly and awkward. It was his face that attracted her. It was perfect, she thought. He had intelligent eyes and the most amazing smile she had ever seen; his whole face lit up when he smiled.

Ben lent over to kiss Justine; she could smell the alcohol and cigarette smoke on his breath as he drew closer. 'Gotta go,' she said, 'Mum'll have a total fit if I'm late on a Sunday night.'

Ben murmured agreement against her lips. Justine hadn't introduced him to her mum yet; she wanted to, but she was waiting for the right moment. That's what she told him, anyway. Ben wasn't particularly looking forward to meeting Justine's mother, anyway, but he would just like to get it over with, the looks, the questions about his intentions, he'd been there before with other mum's and dad's, and always found it a bit embarrassing. He really liked Justine; she was fun to be around. He didn't like the sneaking around bit though, meeting Justine at Sue's house, or in the park. He wanted to drive right up to Justine's house and pick her up. Well maybe soon, he just needed to be patient. He didn't want to push it.

Ben had pulled his car off the road and into the truck bay that was located on the left side of the main road that backed onto Justine's Street. He knew Justine's house was just around the corner, but even so, he wasn't happy about just dropping her off at this hour, especially as she'd been drinking and was tipsy.

After one long final kiss Justine leaped out the car. She almost lost her footing on the gravel of the truck bay entrance. 'Whoops,' she said with a big cheeky grin on her face. 'Almost landed on my bum.'

'Take it easy Justy,' Ben warned.

She steadied herself on the car door while she closed it with a thud. Then leaning through the open passenger window, she said with affection, 'See ya next weekend Benny boy, I'll talk to mum promise, maybe you could come over for dinner or something next week.'

'Ok sounds good,' said Ben. 'Are you sure you don't want me to walk you to your house?"

'I'll be fine, worry wart, it's just down the road, the streetlights are on and I have a torch on my phone if I need it,' protested Justine.

'OK, if you're sure, but don't you go and fall over and break your bloody neck. Bye Justy. Love ya,' he yelled as he waved and drove away.

She stood there waving off Ben quite vigorously and blowing kisses until she could no longer see or hear his car in the distance. She loved the way he called her Justy; her mother would be horrified at the shortening of her name, she mused. Although they had only been going out for a few months, she really did like Ben a lot, maybe even loved him, she thought. He seemed perfect, he was smart and unbelievably cute, and he treated her with respect. She had even fantasied about spending the rest of her life with him, signing her name as Justine Thomas all over her English workbook when she was supposed to be taking down notes in class.

By now the alcohol was beginning to wear off, she could feel the cold air on her bare arms. The sun had gone down, and the wind began to whip up. Justine could feel a storm brewing. As she was standing there blowing kisses and waving, a large truck pulled into the truck bay. The truck driver waved back. Justine was a bit embarrassed because the truck driver must have thought she was waving and blowing kisses at him. She hung around the truck bay for a moment while she sent a text to Ben saying 'Missing u already' with a love heart and a crying emoji, and had just started to walk off, as the truck moaned to a stop.

The truck driver jumped down from the truck and enthusiastically jogged over to Justine. 'Hey,' he said, 'bit cold out here,' while rubbing his hands together, blowing on his cupped hands and then rubbing them together again in an over animated way.

'Mmm sure is,' said Justine, just to be polite.

'I'm John by the way,' said the truck driver with a slight hesitation while offering his outstretched hand as a way of introducing himself. Justine took his hand and shook it but for some reason she suspected that was not his real name.

'What's a pretty thing like you doin out in the cold?' He pulled out a rolled cigarette from his top shirt pocket; he waved it in Justine's direction, offering it to her. 'Interested in a smoke?'

Justine noticed that it was a spliff and was tempted; she wasn't particularly looking forward to facing her mum and she was tired of the arguing and feeling guilty just because she wanted to have a bit of fun. She weighed up the risks in her head, hearing Ben's concerned warnings.

'Better not,' she said not too convincingly. 'I should be getting' home, Mum'll be startin' to get worried.'

'Oh come on it's only just gone six. It'll only take five minutes. I've bin on me own all day, it'd be nice t'have a bit-a company that's all,' he said, as he could see Justine starting to waiver. 'Ever had one'a these before?'

'Yeah course.'

'So, ya know what ya missing then. Good stuff is this.'

Justine knew she should go straight home… but maybe she SHOULD let her worry for a bit. *I'm not a child, I can look after myself,* she told herself.

'Oh, go on then,' she said, thinking it might help to keep her chilled out when her mother finally confronted her about being out so late.

'My name is Justine by the way.'

'Nice to meet ya Justine,' he says as he winks his left eye and nods his head.

He lights the joint, smiles at Justine, takes a long pull and then hands it to her. She takes it from him and, taking a puff, she instantly feels herself relax.

'Let's get in the cab it's bloody freezin out ere.' He walked around, climbed the steps and opened the passenger door for Justine to climb up. Then he walked around to the other side to get in himself. He could feel Justine weighing things up, wondering if it's safe to get into the cab with him. He walked back over to her and with a cheeky grin said, 'If ya scared, you can leave the door open.'

'What makes you thinks I'm scared? I'm not worried,' Justine said trying to sound casual.

He walked closer to the passenger side and made a hand gesture for her to get in, like a gentleman holding open a carriage door. Justine smiled and walked over to the door. Before she climbed into the cab she realised she still had her mobile phone in her hand. She moved a bit closer to the truck driver and took a selfie with him and his truck in the background. Something to show her friends at school tomorrow. But also, a bit of insurance. Just in case.

'Don't mind, do you?' Justine says with a smile on her face.

'Nah take as many as you like, I got nothin to hide. Just don't go postin it on bloody Instagram or anything, not sure me girlfriend would be too happy about me talkin to a pretty young thing like you. What are ya, seventeen, eighteen?' It was obvious she was younger, but wanted to flatter her, make her feel grownup.

Justine *was* flattered, and thought about lying, but then said with resignation, 'Na I'm only fifteen.'

Truth be told, he was extremely alarmed by Justine taking his photo. It spooked him. He felt quite unnerved by the idea that she has his photo on her phone. The voices in his head whispered, *what a bitch, just like the other women in your life, they can't be trusted.* A flash of anger appeared across his face, but he quickly masked it with a fake smile. What he wanted to do was grab her phone and delete the photo immediately, and then smash it into little pieces with his boot. Somehow, he regained control and decided to play it cool for now.

As he walked over to his side of the truck, he pulled out his mobile phone and checked for messages. He hadn't received any calls or text messages for over an hour. He had an overwhelming desire to be invisible; to switch his phone off so no one would know his location. Sensing a build-up of panic, he powered his phone off to ease his anxiety. As he climbed into the cab he looked under his seat and checked the pepper spray and hammer he kept hidden there were still in place. This helped to quell his apprehension somewhat and appease the voices. If things got nasty he would be okay.

He was not comfortable carrying a gun or a knife in his cab for protection. So, he chose what he thought was the next best thing: Pepper spray and a hammer. If ever anything go out of hand with a hitchhiker he could reach down under his seat and grab the contents to ward off an attack.

Justine climbed up into the cab and shut the door, 'Ok, hand the smoke over, you hog,' she said with a cheeky grin and an involuntary wrinkle of her nose; the cab smelled quite strongly of foul body odour. 'Bit manky in here,' she said. She noticed the cab was quite roomy and appeared to have what looked like a small bed tucked in behind the seats. He saw Justine looking at the unmade bed and explained that as a long-distance truck driver he often uses the bed to sleep in while on the road. Hotels cost money, and it's much cheaper and way more convenient to kip in the cab.

As she drags calmly on the joint, John told Justine that he was an owner driver and receives contracts to drive all sorts of goods by a haulage company. This suited him as he can choose when and if he wants to do the job. He would usually drive from South to North with a load, and then pick up another load to bring back North to South. This, he said, can often take a few days. Sometimes he'd go interstate, but not that often, as that usually takes over a week and he doesn't like being on the road for that long.

As he talked to her about his work, he tried to put the paranoia out of his head. But the voices keep badgering him with the same question. What is she going to do with your photo? The voices goad him, insist that she's going to post it on Facebook, with comments about what a loser he is, or caption it with something like "this is what a creep looks like LOL". *She's secretly laughing at you, you idiot,* they tell him. *She's going to amuse all her friends with jibes about how pathetic and inadequate you are. You can't trust her. She's just like all the others. She will betray you in the end.*

He tried to calm his terror and quieten the voices by chatting mindlessly to Justine. She started to relax. Looking at him she says with a bit of a giggle, 'You know that I wasn't waving at you or blowing you kisses, my boyfriend just dropped me off and it was him I was saying bye to.'

'Oh, I'm heartbroken,' he says, feigning offence and placing his hand over his heart.

They smoked the last of the joint, while they chatted about the sort of music they liked. Justine was feeling a bit more comfortable; she told him she liked to listen to Lady Gaga and Justin Bieber.

He says, 'Oh, yeah, that song Bad Guy by Billie Irish s' pretty good.'

Justine crumpled over with laughter as she corrected him. 'You mean Billie Eilish,' with an over emphasis on the Eilish, 'yeah I like that one too.'

He tried to make a joke to cover his embarrassment by telling her his favourite song is by Paul Kelly, 'You know, the one that goes,' - singing out of tune - 'I do all the dumb things.' Justine giggled at his attempted joke, and agreed the song should be his personal anthem.

The distrustful and deluded voices in his head continued their attack as the two bantered; they whispered viciously about how pitiful he was, about what a fool Justine was making him look. Try as he might, he couldn't curb the disturbed and obsessive thoughts and cruel jibes.

Suddenly feeling wildly unstable, he needed to take action. He could barely concentrate on anything Justine was saying to him. He tried to compose himself; to get some self-control back. He asked Justine how far she had to walk home. Justine explained she only lived down the road, so not too far to walk. She talked on and on to him about school and home, feeling quite at ease in his cab. But time was ticking by, and he felt like he was a third party in their conversation, only hearing it in an abstract, out of body way.

Justine sighed and said without much conviction, 'I do really need to go. I have school in the morning and Mum's already on my case.'

'Stay a bit longer, I was just enjoyin the conversation,' he says, trying not to sound as desperate as he was feeling. 'Thought ya might like ta get a bit cosy with me?'

Justine roared with laughter, 'You gotta be joking.' The comment was out of her mouth before she had time to think about how unpleasant she had sounded. She attempted to be more compassionate. 'No, look I really need to get goin, Mum'll be waitin, but uh yer, thanks for tha smoke.'

Panic-stricken, the voices in his head tell him *See we told you she was laughing at you. You pathetic waste-of-space, you can't let her just walk away.* A cold sweat washed over his body, alarm and agitation seeping from every pore. When Justine is momentarily distracted, he moved closer to her.

Justine, unaware of his movements reached casually for the door handle. Suddenly she felt the bulk of him as he grabbed her right arm and pulled her closer to him. He muttered something like *not getting away bitch*. Justine screamed as loud as she could at him to let her go. but before she was able to cry out again his exceptionally large and strong hand was covering her mouth and nose. Did he realise she could not breath? She could make only grunting sounds trying to tell him she couldn't breathe. *This can't be happening,* she thought.

Vision blurring, Justine tried to focus on his face, and what she saw there terrified her. His expression had changed. His eyes looked as black as tar and an evil expression had appeared on his face. She was terrified, and she knew she was in horrendous trouble. That this was not going to end well. She tried to look as pleading as she could, silently willing him to let her go. Hoping beyond hope that the sight of her might touch his conscience, his decency. She could hear his ragged breathing. Her heart was thumping and echoing in her ears. Her lungs were straining. Her chest hurt. She was in terrible pain. She was in desperate need of air. Suddenly a wooziness overwhelmed her. She couldn't keep her eyes open. All her strength had been drained. It seemed to take for ever, but in reality, it was only a minute until everything went black.

Chapter Five

Margaret had tried calling Justine at 7:35 and then every thirty minutes after that. By 11pm She decided to call Sue, Justine's best friend. Although she and Justine had had a heated fight earlier that day, it was unlike Justine to hold a grudge, her mother thought as she picked up the phone to call Sue's house. She was certain Justine wouldn't stay out all night just to punish her. She knew Justine was terribly angry when she walked out the door, but this was truly out of character. They'd had plenty of disagreements in the past, both had said things they didn't mean, but they always made up and cleared the air. Justine could be impulsive, but she wasn't malicious.

Margaret apologised for calling so late. Sue's mum confirmed Justine was not there and then offered to wake Sue and ask her if she knew where Justine could be. Margaret hesitated, not wanting to sound overly dramatic, 'Um, well yes please. I'm really sorry to be a bother, but if you wouldn't mind. I'm just little worried.'

'No bother, said Sue's mum, 'I'd do exactly the same thing if I were in your shoes.'

A sleepy Sue came to the phone and apologetically told Margaret that as far as she was aware Justine left the party to go home. She quickly checked her socials; troublingly there were not posts from Justine in the last six hours, which was unlike Justine, especially after a few drinks. But Sue said nothing to Margaret; she didn't want to add to her concern. She told her instead that she was sure she would be back in the morning. Margaret thanked her and said yes, she was sure she would be.

Margaret wasn't sure if she was angry or frightened by the fact that her daughter wasn't home yet. *She has school in the morning*, thought Margaret, and although Justine was not a particularly good student, she liked the social contact of school. She enjoyed meeting up with her mates and discussing what they had done over the weekend.

Margaret knew Justine was getting older and was wanting more freedom – perhaps even needing it - but Margaret wasn't prepared to let her go just yet. Yes, she could be a bit overprotective, yes, she had embarrassed her daughter last month by turning up early to pick her up from party. She just wanted to see who she was hanging out with. Surely, there's no harm in that, justified Margaret to herself, after all she's all I've got. On reflection maybe she had gone a bit too far.

It was the longest night of Margaret's life. She watched each minute tick by, each one feeling like an hour. She had dozed off for a moment a couple of times on the couch and woken to terrifying thoughts and images in her head. Maybe she had been in an accident and was lying somewhere in a ditch, hurt, bleeding and needing her mother. Although they'd had a fight Justine would not have run away, as the police had suggested earlier when she called, she was sure of that. The police had suggested she wait a few more hours and call her friends in the morning before they would take it as a serious missing person's report. It had been rather embarrassing for Margaret during the phone call to the police. She was not able to tell them Justine's new boyfriend's surname, how old he was, were he lived, what school he attended, if in fact he was still in school.

The police had not been terribly concerned, they said 15-year-old girls stay away overnight all the time. From their experience, they're just pushing the boundaries, trying to show their parents they are no longer in charge of them. Especially if there'd been an argument, it was usually a form of punishment. Margaret hoped more than believed that this was the case. She had never considered Justine to be spiteful before; a handful, yes, and sometimes even unreliable… but she firmly believed that her daughter would never intentionally cause her to worry. To be so terrified that she barely slept. No, that wasn't Justine at all. *Let's just see if she turns up for school*, the police had said. Margaret had a sick feeling in her stomach, she knew that something was very, very wrong.

Shortly after watching the clock tick over to 9:15, the school called and confirmed that Justine had not turned up. Margaret had called all her friends. Sue managed to get Ben's mobile number from Tony and had given it to Margaret. Margaret had called Ben and he had told her he had dropped

Justine off at 6pm last night just down the road from her house. He regretfully said that Justine had insisted he drop her off down the road and not at the door. He told Margaret to call the police again and tell them she was definitely heading home when he dropped her off and that she had no intention of staying out all night.

Margaret went down to the police station this time rather than make a call. She had a recent photo of Justine in her hand. Her heart was racing, and she was on the verge of hysteria, but she knew she needed to keep it together, try to stay calm and stick to the facts. She had to convince them that Justine was missing and not a run-away. She wasn't very good at being assertive when dealing with authority, and she hadn't had good experiences with the police in the past. After a severe beating, she had finally found the courage to report her husband for domestic violence. After all, he had tried to kill her. Crying and shaking, she had shown the police sergeant the bruising on her throat where he had strangled her until she lost consciousness; the black eye and split lip spoke for themselves. He had not taken her report very seriously. They ticked their boxes, noting down details and photographing her injuries, but Margaret didn't hear from them again.

Now, as Margaret walked out of the police station 2 hours after arriving, she still felt the police were stuck on the idea that Justine had run away and would come home when she was good and ready, but none-the-less they opened a file. Maybe that was to calm Margaret down and give her some hope. She had told them nothing seemed to be missing from her closet, all her makeup and jewellery was still in her room. They had at least spoken to teachers at her school, and they'd all confirmed what Margaret had been telling the police: that it was out of character for Justine to be absent, and they certainly didn't believe she'd run away. The police now considered Justine as a missing person.

The Police had wanted to know the whereabouts of Justine's father and suggested maybe Justine had run away to her father's house, or that maybe he had discovered Justine's whereabouts and was waiting for her last night. Margaret informed the police that Justine didn't know her father, adding that it was just as well, after everything he'd put his wife through. She wouldn't have run away to his home, or anyone else's for that matter. The police didn't seem to be as sure as Margaret was. Maybe, they proposed, she had found him on Facebook or Instagram or something like that and decided she wanted to get to know him now. Or maybe the fight between mother and daughter had propelled her to look for him, a way to punish her mother.

Margaret informed the police she didn't know where her ex-husband lived and didn't want to. She made it very clear that she also did not want him to know where she was living. She explained she had taken the opportunity to get away from him when he was arrested and jailed for aggravated burglary. She told the police he was a very violent and controlling man and she wanted nothing to do with him now or in the future. Unfortunately, the Police still wanted his full name and said if Justine didn't return soon, they would need to contact him, just to rule out that Justine was not with him.

I don't want him finding out where I live Margaret had begged the Police Sergeant.

The Sergeant had assured Margaret they would not disclose her address to him, but that was little comfort to Margaret. She knew it was likely that if Justine didn't return soon it would hit the media and he would find out where they lived one way of another, and that would be another disaster Margaret would have to face.

The Police took the photo of Justine from Margaret and said they would put it out to all patrols. They had also taken Ben's contact details from her, saying that they would speak to him right away. They told Margaret to go home and wait, they would be in contact with her very soon.

Margaret called work and let them know the situation. Her boss was very kind and understanding. Margaret had worked for her for over 5 years and was the most reliable and hardworking employee she had ever had; She had told Margaret to take what time she needed, and to let her know if the circumstances changed, or if she needed anything. She assured Margaret that Justine would be home soon, that 15-year-old girls can be thoughtless. Margaret was incredibly grateful: although she had plenty of leave and she could rely on some savings in the bank, she needed this job and didn't want to risk her employment.

Margaret tried to stay busy at home, cleaning windows and washing floors, but time seemed to be moving so slowly. At 4pm there was a knock at the door. Her heart missed a beat, even though she knew in her bones it wouldn't be Justine, because she would just bounce apologetically through the door in her usual loud and lively style. Ben introduced himself to Margaret stoically. Sitting at the kitchen table while his cup of tea went cold, he told Margaret the police had come to his work at about lunch time to talk to him.

Ben worked part time at a hardware store while he was studying teaching at university. He went on to tell Margaret how the police had taken him from his work to the station 'to help with their enquiries' and spent the next 2 hours accusing him of who knew what. They had suggested to him that he was dating a 'child' and had asked him if he was some sort of pervert. Then they had proposed he had taken her somewhere against her will for his own pleasures.

He had told them what had happened several times: that he had dropped her off near her house at her insistence, that they had kissed goodbye, and he had driven off, leaving her in the rearview, waving and blowing kisses. But they didn't seem to believe him. They would constantly change tacts, one minute making accusations and treating him like a criminal, and then in the next breath asking him questions as though he was just a witness, helping them to discover Justine's whereabouts. Probably trying to catch him in a lie Ben surmised. He had seen enough cop shows to know that in interrogations police would often ask the same question in different ways trying to get the person to compromise themselves. He also had wondered if they were employing the good cop bad cop approach. Asking him questions like, *'What have you done to her?'* or *'Just tell us where she is?'* Then to his surprise, they asked him questions like *'Did he see anyone suspicious hanging around'* or *'were there any cars parked close by?'*

The only thing that stood out in his mind at the time was a large truck that passed him just after he had dropped Justine off. He had specifically recalled it because the truck had taken up most of the road. It appeared to be slowing down and indicating to turn into the truck bay. He remembered it had a huge steel bull bar on the front. He couldn't recall seeing anyone, or any other cars loitering around the area he had told them.

Before the police ended their questioning, they explained to Ben they were trying to eliminate him from their enquires, and if he had nothing to hide, he would allow them to search his house. He explained he still lived at home with his parents. He believed they would be only too willing to cooperate. He certainly had no objections to the police searching his home. They drove Ben out to his home and had a look around. Once the police were satisfied there were no signs of Justine either being there or had been there recently, they had taken him back to his place of work.

He recounted to Margaret how the police had accused him of having underage sex, which, even if it was consensual, would still be a crime. He assured Margaret, as he did the police, he and Justine were not sleeping together, he knew she was only 15 and he was not stupid. He was studying primary school teaching and would not risk his future career for a few minutes of pleasure, regardless of that fact that he loved Justine. Margaret believed him, but he doubted the police did.

He told Margaret what he had told the police, that he had dropped her off just around the corner, so she could jump over the back fence. That he would never hurt Justine, he really liked her and was very worried about her. He had no idea where she could be. Although he said she was a bit antsy about going home after the argument she'd had with Margaret earlier that day, she had every intention of going home.

Ben showed Margaret a missing person's flyer he and Sue had put together earlier that morning and asked Margaret if it was okay that they start posting the image online across their socials and ask if anyone had seen Justine to call the police. Margaret was so grateful for the help, she felt she was running on empty.

After her disastrous marriage Margaret was not confident she was the best judge of character, however, she liked Ben immediately, and could understand why Justine liked him. He seemed thoughtful, honest, and gentle; all the things Margaret's ex was not. He was working and studying and seemed to genuinely care about Justine. She wished Justine had felt comfortable to introduce Ben to her. She knew this was mostly her fault, as she would often tell Justine that boys were trouble, and not to get involved with anyone as she would just get hurt. Had she been too hard on Justine, was it all her fault?

Chapter Six

Margaret hadn't slept much that night and refused to take anything to help, as this would only make her feel fuzzy and drowsy, and she wanted to stay alert. She had just put the phone down from the police. They didn't have any new information for her, but they were clearly going through the process for proof of life. They told Margaret they had checked all the hospitals and were checking with public transport to see if anyone matching her description had gotten on a bus or train and would be viewing all CCTV footage at the local stations. They would continue to knock on doors looking for witnesses, as well as do a sweep search for evidence. Her phone and social media accounts would be viewed along with her bank records. Margaret listened carefully to what they were telling her. She told them she really did appreciate the lengths they were going to, to find her daughter.

The Police had quickly ruled out Justine's father: he was back in prison doing a 10 year stretch for possession and supply of class A drugs. Margaret was relieved, at least she didn't have to deal with him knowing her whereabouts, as well as Justine's disappearance. The police also let Margaret know that Justine's picture would be in the newspapers and there would be a story on the news tonight, asking if anyone had seen her, and as a result to expect the press to be camped on her doorstep by morning They wanted to confirm what Justine was wearing the day she went missing. They let Margaret know to prepare for the 'circus' that often happens once they go to the media. But given the lack of information this was the logical next step.

The police also suggested a press conference might help bring about a breakthrough. They wanted Margaret to make an appeal via the media for Justine to come home. It was the last thing that Margaret wanted to do, but if it helped get Justine back, she would do it. The police would let her know when it was arranged.

Margaret phoned her sister in Queensland to let her know Justine had gone missing. She did not want her to hear about it on the news or read it in the newspaper. Justine's sister wanted to fly over immediately to support Margaret at this time, but Margaret insisted she didn't need to come over, that she was coping well. Anyway, she told her sister, Justine would likely walk through the door like nothing had happened once the story goes out, once she realises how worried Margaret is about her.

'If you're sure Maggie,' her sister said, sounding worried, 'you know I'm here if you need me. I'm only a quick flight away and can be there when and if you need me.'

'I really appreciate the offer, but you know what she's like, just thoughtless sometimes.'

Margaret put the phone down, wanting more than believing what she had said to her sister was true.

The Police had called later that day to let Margaret know the media appeal had been arranged for tomorrow at 10am. She needed to be at the police station by 9am so they could discuss what would happen and arrange transport. Margaret called her boss at work to let her know she still needed time off work. She wrote 9am police station in her diary, not because she might forget, but because it felt like she was doing something.

Just before 9am the police arrive to escort Margaret to the station. She hadn't slept much and looked at least 10 years older than she had last week. She didn't know what to wear; Justine would have laughed at her outfit, it was her usual floral tent of a dress. The police assured Margaret they would do most of the talking, all she needed to do at the end was make her appeal for Justine to come home, if she was up to it.

The police told her the media would try to ask questions, trying to get some 'juicy' bits of information from her. She was told to ignore all questions. This helped ease Margaret's nerves; public speaking wasn't her thing. She had been practising all day yesterday in front of the mirror. She had written down what she wanted to say and had rehearsed it over and over again until she was happy with it.

The police had informed the media of the what, the where and the when, in regard to Justine's disappearance. They went on to say that at this stage it was a missing person enquiry, but that they were increasingly concerned for Justine's welfare, as she had not been seen or used her phone or social media at all since last being seen. The phone appeared to have been either switched off, run out of battery or she was not in a position to answer it around 7:30pm the day she had disappeared, as a phone call to Justine's phone at 7:35pm went unanswered, they reported. A recent photo of Justine had been distributed to the media. The police had arranged for a mannequin to be dressed in similar clothing to what Justine was wearing the afternoon she went missing in easy view for the media to video or photograph for their reports.

Then it was Margaret's turn to speak. Her entire body was trembling. The police had told her to look directly into the camera and ignore everything else. Try not to break down emotionally, they had advised, this can make the abductor feel more powerful. She'd practiced and practiced, but it had been of little help. As she started to speak, her voice cracked, and her mind went blank. Visibly shaking she pleaded for Justine to come home as the tears spilled down her cheeks.

The Sergeant took her hand and gave it a squeeze, taking over the circus. He told the media that was all, and reminded the public if anyone saw anything, had dash camera footage or had any further information to call crime stoppers. Camera flashes went off while the media yelled out questions to Margaret about her husband's criminal record. Could he be involved in Justine's disappearance? Did she think she was still alive? Margaret did not really hear much of what was being yelled at her, her head felt like it was full of cottonwool. The Police just stood her up and led her out of the room and told the media they were not answering any questions at this time.

The police Sergeant told Margaret she had done a good job, but it didn't feel like it to her. She told him she had wanted to say so much more. She had wanted to tell the media it was out of character for Justine to run away, that if someone was holding on to her please let her go. That Justine was all she'd had, and she loved her very much. But she'd just become too overwhelmed and all that had come out between tears, was a blurb about please come home.

Reassuringly, he told her 'I've had to deal with the media a lot in my job and I never get used to it. In hindsight there's always something I meant to say and didn't, so don't beat yourself up, you did a great job under difficult circumstances.'

This did not make Margaret feel much better but at least it was done, and she could go home.

***

It had been just over two weeks since Justine had gone missing; Margaret had returned to work on the morning shift – she needed to occupy her mind, which whirled with dark possibilities when left to its own devices. The appeal via the media had initially created a lot of interest from the public, but nothing useful according to the police. A few had reported seeing a truck in the area, but nothing concrete. When Detective Sergeant Andrews and Detective Constable McDonald turned up at her work that morning, an hour into her shift, with very grim looks on their faces, Margaret knew instinctively before they uttered the words, what they were going to say.

The detectives escorted Margaret into a meeting room and asked her to sit down. She noticed a box of tissues and a solitary glass of water had been placed on the end of a large highly polished wooden meeting room table. She suddenly felt small and vulnerable. *It's funny the way your mind works* thought Margaret as she followed the detectives into the room and sat down. She truly felt sorry for the detectives, knowing they were about to deliver bad news to her. She wondered how often they'd had to deliver this kind of bad news to people, and if they ever got used to it. The DS pulled his chair close to Margaret. She was still holding her cleaning cloth in her hand.

'Margaret, I am so very sorry to have to tell you, but a female body had been found matching the description of Justine,' DS Andrews said solemnly.

'A dead body?' asked Margaret in almost a whisper.

'Yes, I'm afraid so,' said the DS as he looked directly into Margaret's terrified eyes.

Margaret's head began to swim, she felt her heart pounding like a loud drum in her ears, the detectives' voices seemed to bounce off the walls and echo around the room. Tears began to well in her eyes.

'But you can't be sure that it is Justine,' Margaret managed to say with some hope.

'No, but the body has been in the water for some time, the medical examiner thinks about two weeks, which would fit with Justine's disappearance,' said the DS gravely.

'Water? What water?' said Margaret starting to shake with panic while wringing the cleaning cloth into a tight knot

37

'There's a lake that is about two kilometres down the track off the truck bay he explained. 'A couple of teenagers were there riding their bikes near the lake, when they saw the body floating in the water.'

'She'd been there all this time, in the freezing cold water?' Margaret cried as tears started to escape from her eyes. She shoved the cleaning cloth in her pocket and tried to wipe the escaping tears with the back of her hand.

The DS handed Margaret a tissue from the box on the table and nodded his head.

'Why? Why would someone do that to my little girl?' She whimpered to no one in particular. Tears began to flow uncontrollably.

The DS handed Margaret the box of tissues.

'We don't know yet Margaret, but we'll do everything we can do to find out.'

Margaret had felt almost numb, but she could no longer contain herself. Her baby being out there in the dark, alone in the icy water and so close to home was enough to send Margaret over the edge. The Detective sat close to her while she sobbed. She absently reached for a tissue and wiped her puffy eyes. She could not bear it any longer. She didn't want to know any more details, she tried to remove the image in her head and picture Justine the way she looked the last time she saw her.

'I need to call my boss. I need to go home,' she said shakily.

The DS reached out and held Margaret's shaking hands. 'I've already asked security to call your boss and inform her you need to leave work. I'm sorry Margaret but we need you to accompany us to identify the body, we need to be sure that it is Justine.'

'Oh,' was all that Margaret could manage to say, before the flood of tears began again. She wondered if it would ever stop.

The detectives reminded Margaret that the body had been in the water for some time, and warned Margaret that the process would be very traumatising for her. They tried, as gently as possible, to explain what the body would look like: bloated, discoloured and in a state of decomposition. That the creatures of the lake had started to aid that process of decomposition. What they didn't describe was the way the eye sockets were now merely fleshy grey holes; that the body of her daughter no longer looked human in the way a mother would be expecting.

They asked if Justine had anything that could identify her without Margaret having to go through the trauma of viewing the body, especially if it turned out not to be her. Margaret told the detectives that Justine had a very distinctive birthmark. It was almost like the shape of Australia on the inside of her upper right leg. They had often joked about the birthmark and used it as a map to point to areas on her birthmark where they might like to go for a holiday.

On the drive to the state mortuary the detectives suggested that the medical examiner could take a photograph of the inside right leg and show this to Margaret, and she could identify the body as Justine or not via the birthmark if she preferred.

'Is that what usually happens?' Margaret asked, wanting to be guided. Wanting these decisions to be made for her.

'In these scenarios, yes. It's not uncommon,' the Detective replied. 'It can save a lot of pain and trauma for the family members, and it means loved ones can be remembered as they were, not as they died."

Margaret nodded her agreement with silent tears. Together they waited an agonizing 30 minutes at the state mortuary for the medical examiner to take the photographs. The ME approached Margaret with two photos and two clear plastic bags containing what looked like clothing and jewellery. When they revealed the photos, Margaret fell to her knees keening; she knew immediately that it was her baby girl lying in there. They showed her the jewellery found on the body and Margaret nodded her head in confirmation that it belonged to Justine. The necklace was a gold chain with a diamanté heart Justine had bought with some babysitting money just before Christmas and was her current favourite.

It was definitely like the one Justine had been wearing, Margaret confirmed. However, there was no doubt about the ring - it had been Margaret's mother's eternity ring, she would have recognised it anywhere. The clothing was also Justine's, it was her favourite striped sleeveless shirt, she had been wearing the day she walked out the door to her friend Sue's house. There was no doubt in her mind, her little girl was never going to walk through the front door again. Never going to grow up, get a job, marry, have children. Margaret's future dreams abruptly ended that day.

Margaret had asked the detectives a barrage of questions. *What happened? How did she die? Would it have been quick? Was she assaulted?* She wasn't sure she really wanted to know, but not knowing was worse. The detectives informed Margaret they would know more once the autopsy had been completed.

Chapter Seven

Liz slept late on Saturday morning, she'd had another sleepless night, not dropping off to sleep until about 4 O'clock. It was such a luxury to be able to sleep late on the weekends and allow her mind and body to rejuvenate. Years ago, her therapist had helped her to change her thinking about sleep deprivation. Stop worrying about sleep hours lost, she had told her, look at it as extra hours gained to think and process things. Funnily enough it did help; when she stopped worrying about it, sleep seemed to come a little easier.

Thoughts of Lilly played on her mind. Stories of children in danger always had an immediate effect on her. In an instant, she was right back to the night her children were taken from her. Even after all the therapy she had done, and her understanding of the cycle of violence, she had still never gotten over the guilt and sickening feeling that she should have done more to protect her children. It was her job to keep them safe and she had failed. If she could save other children maybe she could make up for failure. The grief was still suffocating, but since becoming a social worker she could see a future where she mattered again.

Getting out of bed in the mornings was often a painful struggle for Liz. She completed her usual thirty minutes of stretching and strengthening exercises, put together for her by her physiotherapist. She loathed having to do it every day but was told it would keep her from further surgery. She'd had so much surgery in the last fifteen years she was prepared to do whatever it took to prevent going under the surgeons' knife again.

She smothered sunscreen over her face and tied her unruly red hair into a ponytail, a gift from her mother, along with the sprinkle of freckles on her pale cheeks. To look at her now, no one would ever suspect that her wild and vibrant hair covered a mass of scars.

She put on her walking shoes and walked the two kilometres to the local shopping hub. Although her walking had greatly improved since she left hospital, her gait was still noticeably clumsy. She bought the weekend newspaper and went to her favourite café for an indulgent and sugar laced morning tea. As she walked in the door the familiar smell of coffee hit her. The waitress behind the counter knew Liz as a regular Saturday morning customer and had already rung up her order for coffee before she reached the counter: a large extra hot skinny cappuccino. All the waitress needed to know was which muffin Liz wanted this morning. Liz could hear the familiar whooshing sound like a steam train leaving the station. The steam rose high above the head of the busy Barista as she juggled mugs, jugs, and hot milk like a magician. The usual sound of clattering utensils, scraping of chairs and tables along with the hum of conversations held a certain comfort. The usual obstacle course of haphazardly parked prams and shopping bags were all part of the Saturday morning ritual.

After she completed her order, she sat down at her usual table and started to read the newspaper. She immediately wished she hadn't. The headline seemed to scream at her: *Body of Young Girl Found Murdered and Dumped in Lake*. Oh god thought Liz, another parent grieving for their dead child, violently taken from them. Though very disturbed by the headlines, she couldn't take her eyes off the article. She read that a fifteen-year-old girl named Justine from the town of Lake Swan had been found dumped in a lake two weeks after she went missing. Liz knew the small town of Lake Swan, because it was only about 30 minutes from where she had grown up. The article had asked if anyone had seen Justine or anything suspicious in the area to contact crime stoppers. There was a picture of Justine on the front page, she looked so happy in the photo, it just broke Liz's heart. She took a sip of her coffee and turned the pages trying to find a positive story in the newspaper. She gave up after five minutes, finished her coffee and muffin and left.

Later that night Liz switched on the television to watch the 7 O'clock news. The leading story of course was the murder of Justine. The journalists had found some early footage of Justine when she was about ten years old in a school play, which was heart wrenchingly innocent. Some of Justine's friends had been interviewed and were crying into the camera, telling the reported what a good friend Justine had been, how happy and lively she was. Then the report has switched to footage of Justine's mother looking very distressed and tired, supported by a woman to walk into her home. After the story it gave the number of crime stoppers and asked if anyone had any information to call the number. Liz switched off the television and picked up her book, trying to busy her mind with something else.

Early on Sunday morning after another restless night tossing and turning with thoughts of helpless children, she took Buster her golden retriever for a long walk in the park. Weekends were always difficult for Liz; she tried to stay busy or socialise with friends, but seeing families going about their day often brought it home to Liz that she would never have that again. Mothers pushing babies on swings, dads teaching their children to ride bikes would make Liz smile, but it was often a sad smile. *'Come on get a grip'* she said to herself *'the sun is shining, and the roses need de-heading.'*

Her garden was her pride and joy, she spent many hours pottering around in her vegetable patch, filling up the bird bath with water to encourage the birds and the bees to visit. The garden gave her a sense of peace and tranquillity that she often needed at the end of a difficult day, or over the weekend.

Liz worked a nine-day fortnight, having every second Friday off, though she would often go into work on her day off, citing that she just needed to catch up on paperwork, and it was easier to do it at her work desk than at home. Most of the staff would mockingly give her a hard time about coming in on her day off but understood her feelings of loneliness.

Chapter Eight

A kind young police officer escorted Margaret home after she had flatly refused to go to the hospital or her GP. The officer stayed with her for a while and suggested Margaret might like to call a friend or relative to come over or stay with her. Margaret's parents had been dead for a number of years, and she only had her sister in Queensland now. She knew she should call her again, that she'd be on the first flight, but she just couldn't even begin to comprehend how to have that conversation. The police officer, sensing Margaret's resistance, suggested perhaps a neighbour? Margaret agreed, much to the relief of the young PC. June had been her neighbour for over fourteen years. They were friendly enough but didn't socialise together. June was an elderly lady and would be comforting at a time like this.

The young police officer went next door to find June and explain the circumstances. Not knowing what else to do Margaret put the kettle on, took out three cups ready to make tea. She started to rummage in the pantry for biscuits, then forgot what she was doing and started straightening up the cans on the shelf. It was not until she heard the kettle boil that she remembered what she was in the pantry for. The tears started again. She already felt such complete exhaustion from her previous outburst, her brain felt clogged and heavy. As June and the police officer knocked and entered her house, she wiped away her tears and got on with making the tea.

Margaret didn't really know much about June, although they'd been neighbours for years. They'd share vegetables from their gardens when both had grown too much for their own use, and chat about the weather and neighbourhood gossip. Margaret knew that June would always keep an eye out for Justine if she was working early or late; she knew June didn't have any children and that her husband had been killed in the Vietnam war.

After drinking their tea, the young police officer left to go back to the station. June refilled the kettle and with extraordinarily little effort started to make sandwiches for their lunch. Although Margaret did not feel hungry, she surprisingly felt comforted with someone taking care of her for a change.

While making lunch June told Margaret that although she didn't know what it is like to lose a child, she understood what it felt like to lose the one person that you think you can't live your life without. As June begun to butter the bread, she explained that her husband had died as a result of the Vietnam war, but not during the war. June was a student nurse when she met Will. Will was what most people imagined when they thought of a country boy. He was a bit of a larrikin. He liked to have a beer and a joke with his mates. June recalled it was love at first site for her, he was so handsome and polite. They were married within a year of meeting each other. Only three years into their marriage Australia had entered into the Vietnam war and Will was called up to serve.

'He came home from Vietnam though didn't he?' Questioned Margaret

'Oh yes he came home,' said June, her back to Margaret as she was cutting up tomatoes, 'but it wasn't the same Will that had left the year before.'

He had been discharged twelve months later on medical grounds, June went on to explain to Margaret. He had been diagnosed with post-traumatic stress disorder, he had panic attacks, nightmares and suffered from depression. 'I was a nurse,' said June, 'so I knew a bit about what he was suffering from, but I just couldn't seem to help him deal with his demons. He kept telling me that I would be better off without him, that I was young enough to meet someone else and start again. We tried to have children, but it just didn't happen for us. I was hoping children might bring some happiness into his life. One day he went out and didn't come home. He'd hung himself.' June had finished cutting the sandwiches and turned around to look at Margaret with tears streaming down her face. 'You know,' said June. 'It's the strangest feeling, the contradictions you experience. Before they diagnosed his illness I was constantly screaming at anyone that would listen - there is something wrong with him, he is not well, he needs medical help. Yet, after they confirmed that yes, he was genuinely unwell, I didn't want to hear it. I wanted to cover my ears and pretend that the love of my life wasn't seriously ill.'

Margaret nodded her agreement and confided in June that she knew exactly what she meant. 'When Justine first went missing and the police suggested she may have run away, I was adamant, I wouldn't even contemplate it, she would never run away. I was actually hoping she's been in an accident, that she was lying in a ditch someplace or in hospital unconscious somewhere. When there were no reports of accidents involving 15-year-old girls, and as the days dragged on, I was trying to convince myself that maybe she had run away because I was too strict with her. I didn't want to invite the alternative into my mind, because that option was unimaginable. But somewhere within the deep depths of the pit of my stomach I feared the worst. I kept trying to push the feeling down, but I knew, I just knew, she wasn't coming home.'

'I can't even imagine how hard this has been for you Margaret, not knowing for weeks where your daughter was, trying to stay hopeful, but fearing in your heart that she was not coming home.'

'Oh June, Margaret said tearfully. 'Our last words to each other were so awful. I told her I didn't want her to make the same mistakes I did. Then she yelled back and asked me if she was one of my mistakes. I wish I had told her that she was the best thing that ever happened to me,'

'We all say things we don't mean in the heat of the moment; she would have known that. Try to think about the good conversations, the fun times, eventually it will become easier I promise,' consoled June.

They embraced each other, both trying to comfort the other. Margaret felt a closeness to June she had not felt before.

June whispered in Margaret's ear. 'I no longer take anything for granted, because in a blink of an eye your whole life can change.'

Later that day after June had gone home, Margaret phoned her sister and told her the terrible news. She didn't want her to hear about Justine on the 6 O'clock news. Margaret's sister immediately arranged to travel over and planned to be there by tomorrow night. Although they had never been very close, Margaret appreciated the support she offered.

Chapter Nine

The autopsy report was in on Justine. Detective Sergeant Harry Andrews called his team together.

'Well, I think we can rule the mother out as a suspect.' One of their theories before they had found Justine's body was that Justine had come home and she and her mother had argued, and it had gotten out of hand. Although Margaret appeared to be a caring and loving mother, she did seem to be a bit secretive and controlling.

'Seems we won't need to be digging up the back garden after all,' he told the team.

The autopsy report had come back with a couple of interesting results. What had unquestionably ruled Margaret out as a suspect for DS Andrews was that they had found evidence of sexual assault. Unfortunately, the body had been in the water too long for any trace DNA evidence to be useful. The cause of death appeared to be asphyxia, they believed she was strangled with her own shirt, as it was found still tightly wound around her neck. She was dead before she was put into the water; there was no fluid in her lungs. The report also found alcohol and quite a high level of cannabis in her blood suggesting she had been drinking and using marijuana in some form or other close to the time of her death.

Ben had admitted to alcohol being available at the party he and Justine had attended - after all, most of the party goers were of legal age. He'd admitted to having a couple of light beers, but that was all. He was adamant he'd been okay to drive. When he'd been questioned about Justine's drinking, he reluctantly confirmed Justine and her friend Susan had been drinking some cheap sparkling wine. He'd suggested Susan and Justine had consumed an entire bottle. At the time DS Andrews had let the comment go, but in the back of his mind he wondered if Ben had encouraged Justine to drink alcohol. Maybe get her nice and drunk so he could take advantage of her later. He fervently denied any drug taking by himself or anyone he knew at the party. *Well, that seems to be a lie* thought DS Andrews.

Initially they had ruled the boyfriend out; he'd been given an iron clad alibi by both parents, everyone confirming that he'd arrived home and spoken to both of them the night of the party. But parents, DS Andrew knew, had been known to lie for their children. Although a small town like Lake Swan didn't have CCTV cameras on its streets, Moretown, where Ben lived, did have a set of traffic lights with a camera. They were able to see what time Ben had driven through the lights on his way home from Lake Swan after he said he dropped of Justine. This did not provide much time to rape, murder and dispose of her body in the lake. But maybe he was smarter than they'd given him credit for.

What if he had driven home with Justine's body in his car, knowing that the traffic camera would pick him up and back up his story? And then he either convinced his parents to tell the police he had come straight home and not gone out again… or he waited until the next day to dispose of the body. Both were possible, even if they had holes thought the DS. Besides, stranger murders were rare, and much more difficult to solve. In his experience it was usually someone the victim knew and trusted. And at the moment they didn't have any other suspects or lines of enquiry to pursue.

DS Andrews decided to bring Ben back in for questioning, but this time as a suspect, and not a witness. *Let's push a bit harder, shake him up a bit* thought the DS, *see what he has to say now that we've found the body.* Ben was humiliatingly dragged out during a shift at work in handcuffs. They didn't even let him change from his work uniform. His work colleagues staring and whispering, clearly thinking he must be guilty. His boss yelled to Ben that he would call his mum and dad and let them know the police had taken him away for questioning. Ben had been informed he was under arrest for the rape and murder of Justine. They told him that he was not obliged to say anything unless he wished to do so, but whatever he did say would be recorded and may later be given in evidence, or words to that effect. Ben's ears felt like they were stuffed with cottonwool; after the words 'rape' and 'murder', he heard nothing.

They sat him in the back of the car and asked him if they could search his work locker. Ben, still in shock, agreed, saying he had nothing to hide.

He couldn't stop his legs from shaking, his mind racing, tears welling in his eyes. He kept thinking about the last time he saw Justine smiling, waving, and blowing kisses to him. She was so happy, so lively, so sweet. How could she be dead? *It can't be her* he thought.

He was left in the back of the car for what seemed to be hours, but in reality, it was probably more like 10 minutes. The police returned to the car and drove him to the police station in silence. Ben felt like he was in a nightmare. He still couldn't believe what the police had told him. How could someone so young be alive one minute and then dead the next? It didn't make sense. She couldn't be dead. He didn't want to believe it.

He needed to try and keep himself together, keep his thoughts clear. How could they even contemplate it could be him? It all seemed so surreal to Ben. He was finally uncuffed at the station. The shock of what he had been told about Justine was starting to sink in. He would never see Justine again. Never hear her laugh or hold her hand.

In a mind fog he was fingerprinted, photographed, and asked to sign something he thought was a list of his possessions. He was shaking so much he could hardly sign his name, let alone read and comprehend the document. He was asked some questions about his mental health, but he was on autopilot and responded robotically with yeses and no's he assumed in the right place. He was cautioned again and told he could call a relative or friend. He was also informed he could have a lawyer present. Ben nodded his understanding to the Sergeant, but looked very confused, like he was not really processing what was being said. He was escorted down the corridor and placed in an interview room with a desk and 4 chairs.

He'd walked into the room like he was in a trance. He sat down when told, without questioning. A uniformed officer gave Ben a bottle of water, and then held up a bunch of keys in front of Ben and asked him as he held each key one by one which one was Ben's car key. Ben nodded when the officer held up the right key. The officer then informed Ben due to the seriousness of the crime they had the authority to search his car, and that someone would be back soon to interview him. He was then left in the room on his own to contemplate what had just happened. He was really scared. He knew that innocent people went to jail. He just kept telling himself he had nothing to hide, he had done nothing wrong.

After what seemed like hours two plain clothes police officers came into the room, sat down opposite Ben and switched on a video recorder and introduced themselves as DS Harry Andrews and DC Ian McDonald. Ben was aware of who they were, as he had already spoken to them when Justine had gone missing. They had been a lot friendlier back then. Now they were both all business, cold and solemn. They asked Ben to repeat his full name and address for the tape and asked him if he knew why he was here. DS Harry Andrews reminded Ben he could have a lawyer present if he thought he needed one. The 'needed one' was said with a suggestive tone that only guilty people would need a lawyer present.

It had been at least an hour since Ben's arrest and the fog in his brain had started to clear. In fact, he was quite angry. While the police were wasting their time questioning him like a criminal, the real murderer or murderers were still out there, possibly hurting someone else.

Ben wasn't stupid, he'd seen these sorts of interviews on television where the accused didn't request a lawyer because they had stated that they had nothing to hide, then said things that were twisted around by the police. He wasn't going to take any chances. He looked directly as DS Andrews and told him yes, he did indeed want a lawyer present. He didn't have a lawyer, did not know of any lawyers, but he wanted one all the same. Ben also said that he was ready to make a phone call. He wanted to call his parents to arrange for a lawyer. He knew they couldn't afford one – not a good one, anyway - but sometimes you have to trust your gut feelings. Ben had some savings in the bank and decided that having a lawyer present was far more important than buying a new car.

The DS looked a bit frustrated and let out a long sigh, but suspended the video recorder and left the room. He came back and plugged in a phone and then the DS and the DC both left Ben alone to make his phone call. He called his mother's mobile phone; she answered before it had even rung. She was very distressed and worried about him. She had told him that both she and his father were at the police station, that they had come straight down as soon as Ben's boss had called. She was upset because they wouldn't tell her anything or let them see him, "they're treating you like a criminal," she sobbed.

Ben's parents knew their son couldn't have done anything to Justine. He was such a kind and gentle young man. They couldn't understand why he had been arrested. He tried to calm his mother down. He assured her that he was okay, and she had nothing to worry about because he had done nothing wrong. But he would like them to find a criminal lawyer for him all the same.

'Do you really think that's necessary?' She asked. 'Lawyers are so expensive, just tell the police what happened, then we can all go home.'

Ben explained that he wanted representation, as he wasn't sure of his rights or what he should or shouldn't do. He told her that he had some savings and hopefully he wouldn't need a lawyer for long, just until this was cleared up.

'Okay, my sweet, don't worry, just leave it with us, we'll sort it out,' she told him that she loved him and then hung up. It was a small town with only two Law firms that mostly specialised in family law. Ben's father had dealt with one firm when he had a worker's compensation claim turned down by his company. The Lawyer had negotiated a decent settlement that Ben's father had been happy with. He called the same firm and spoke to a young Lawyer named Nicole. He gave her a brief update with what he knew. He explained that Ben had been arrested and that he was innocent. She was happy to represent Ben for now, but she said if it got more serious, she would call in one of her more experienced colleagues. She explained the fee structure and Ben's father agreed and asked if Nicole could come straight down to the station.

Chapter Ten

Liz had had a long and exhausting day, but she'd discovered something quite remarkable about one of her clients that had given her a bit of a lift in spirits. Jeffrey, one of her long-term clients, who had been diagnosed with dissociative identity disorder (DDI), or what used to be referred to as multiple personality disorder many years ago, had been in earlier that day. He attended weekly visits and was a survivor of some of the most awful childhood sexual abuse Liz had heard of. It always astonished her just how resilient and resourceful survivors could be. The session had been a difficult one, exploring the 'who is to blame question'. It was so common for survivors to blame themselves for the abuse, as if they just let it happen. Resulting sadly, in taking the anger out on themselves.

Last year Liz recalled a male client had disclosed with self-disgust, that while he was being fondled by his abuser, he'd got an erection. Therefore, he must have encouraged and enjoyed the abuse. The self-hatred had played out over the years with alcohol and drug abuse, along with many hospitalisations for suicide attempts. Liz had explained to him that the body has an automated reaction to touch. His response was a perfectly normal human reaction; it absolutely did not mean he'd enjoyed or encouraged the abuse.

The man had broken down in tears during the session, telling Liz a huge weight had been lifted off his shoulders. For most of his life he'd felt ashamed and revolted by his actions. He now understood the shame and disgust were no longer his to hold onto. With Liz's help and a few more sessions, he was able to direct the hatred and disgust towards the right person, his abuser.

Jeffrey was another survivor who blamed himself for the abuse. From their very first session Jeffrey had insisted on only using one appointment card, always asking Liz to write the appointment time and date in pencil on the back of the card, and then after the session rubbing out the old time and date and entering a new time and date for the next session; something about saving trees, he'd said with a smile. But today Liz had realised that was how he'd kept track of his attendance, in his body as Jeffrey. Even if one of the other persona's that he carried with him had turned up for the session, and he'd had no memory of it, he would still know someone turned up to the session by the new date on the back of the card.

Today the Angry Jeffrey had marched into her office, and ten minutes later had stormed out of the session without making another appointment. So, the old appointment card would've still had today's time and date on the back. Liz had realised by the apologetic phone call from Jeffrey later that afternoon, he'd assumed no one had shown up to the appointment. Liz explained to Jeffrey he had not missed the appointment. The Angry one had turned up to the session but had failed to make another appointment for next week.

The Angry-one would appear occasionally during a session, especially when they were exploring the abuse, but Liz had always managed to get Jeffrey back in charge by the end of the session. She had named this persona the Angry-one, because unlike most of his 'others', the Angry-one had refused to tell Liz his name.

Jeffrey had clearly developed his own coping strategies for making and keeping appointments so he could fit into a world that did not often recognise the struggles that people with mental illnesses had to endure. She made another appointment for him for the following week, and Jeffrey had written it on the back of his rather dog-eared appointment card.

Liz had just finished her last appointment for the day when Julie, the children's counsellor, and Karen, her senior counsellor, asked for an urgent meeting.

'Look at this,' Julie said as she handed Liz a childlike drawing. She explained that Lilly had drawn the picture during their session today. Liz looked at the drawing in horror. It appeared to be a man with an erect penis with drips coming out of the end. Julie recounted that when she asked Lilly what the picture was, she'd said it was her daddy with no clothes on. When asked her about the drips, she'd said, 'Oh that's just the *eggy stuff* that comes out of daddy's willie sometimes when he rubs it like this,' Julie repeated, demonstrating with her hand an up and down rubbing motion.

Julie also worked part time with the children at the local women's refuge. She was used to seeing children's drawings of knives with blood dripping off them, or broken bodies with tears running down their faces. But this was distressing, even for her. She was very concerned.

'Well if you're concerned, then I'm concerned,' said Liz emphatically.

Karen recounted to Liz what had taken place in her session with Lilly's mother. She described how she had met with Lilly's mother Sally while Lilly had a session with Julie. Sally had told her that she is ready to run with Lilly. If she can't get any help from the police or child protection, then she will pack up what she can carry and get the hell out of this state. She said she would move to a different country if she had to, to protect her daughter. Karen had told her that this was not a good idea: taking a child across state lines without the consent of the other parent would be bad enough, but taking a child overseas is paramount to kidnapping in the eyes of the law. Karen had informed her that the consequences could be disastrous if she got caught. She could do prison time and lose custody of Lilly to Nathan.

But Sally was undeterred. She was willing to take the risk to protect her daughter. She had then said something that frightened Karen. *I'd never let him get custody'* her look was chilling, *'this can't go on. I won't continue to drag a screaming and terrified child out from under her bed and try to reassure her that it will be okay, when she knows it's not going to be okay.'*

'What did you tell her?' Asked Liz

Karen told Liz that given the pressure Sally was under. she'd thought the meeting had gone better than expected. She'd assured Sally they would be contacting child protection and provided a report on what they had learnt from Lilly. Julie would begin working on protective behaviours with Lilly. Karen had also suggested Sally talk to her GP, explain the circumstances and request a medical certificate for Lilly to keep her home this weekend. After the weekend he would be away at work anyway, driving trucks interstate. Sally seemed to be reassured with this plan for now but said she would not hesitate to run if she had to.

After the meeting Liz sat quietly in her office contemplating what she'd just heard. *Oh God I just feel so helpless* she said out loud while hugging herself. Lilly is four years old, the same age as Liz's youngest daughter Molly was when she was murdered by her father. *I couldn't even protect my own children, so how the hell am I going to protect this one?*

'There must be something you can do to protect Lilly, come on Liz think,' she'd whispered to herself.

They could put in some stop gap measures, but this wasn't going to be resolved unless the police or child protection got involved, and that was out of her control. It sickened her to think she was sitting on her hands while another child was being groomed for abuse. It wasn't just the age thing. She knew Lilly would tug at her heartstrings for being the same age as Molly was when she died. But it was more than that. It wasn't often Liz got a chance to protect a child from abuse. Her clients were mostly seeking help as a result of the of abuse; They were wounded and broken already after spending years haunted by the exploitation and manipulation of their perpetrators. So rarely did she get a chance to protect a child from a predator. She knew she had to do something.

Chapter Eleven

Ben had been escorted to a holding cell and told he needed to wait there until his lawyer arrived. He didn't have his watch or phone so was unaware of how long he had been waiting, but it seemed like hours. Finally, an officer came into the cell and informed Ben that his lawyer had arrived and escorted her into his cell. She asked for privacy and the officer left them alone, informing them they had five minutes. The Lawyer introduced herself to Ben as Nicole Harrison.

'Call me Nic,' she said as she thrust her right hand towards him. She could see Ben was distressed, his eyes puffy and red. She'd had a brief conversation with his parents and assured him she understood this had all come as quite a shock to him. Not just the fact that Justine had been found raped and murdered, but that the police suspected Ben of the heinous crime.

Nic asked Ben what he had told the police and what had happened so far. Ben brought her up to speed as fast and concisely as he could. He told her he'd been questioned as a witness when Justine had first gone missing. He'd nothing to do with Justine's death, he could not even bring himself to say rape and murder. He described how he'd dropped her off near her home after the party and went straight home, and that was the last time he'd seen her. He'd been as shocked as everyone else when he heard she's gone missing.

'And your parents can corroborate the time you got home?'

Ben nodded his head.

'Okay good. Look Ben don't answer any more questions you don't have to. Sometimes the only evidence the police have against you is what you've told them in your interview. Let's just see what evidence the police actually have before you give them anything else. Okay?'

'But if I don't answer their questions, won't it make me look guilty?' questioned Ben.

"It doesn't matter what the police think, it's what they can prove. It's their job to investigate and find any evidence that you have committed a crime. They have the burden of proof, not you, Ben. You have the right to silence, and you should exercise that right. You can always tell your side later if you have anything to add.'

Ben nodded his silent understanding.

The officer arrived to escort Ben and Nic to the interview room. Though still emotional, Ben felt a little more confident in the situation now that he was in the hands of a lawyer.

Ben did as he'd been advised. He confirmed his name, birthdate, address and that he was under arrest, but refused to answer any other questions, or provide any further details when asked about the murder. When the police asked him a question, he just answered it with no comment. They had tried a number of different angles to goad Ben into giving an answer. DS Andrews had suggested Ben had not meant to kill Justine; it had been a terrible accident. They'd had consensual sex and then Justine had cried rape, and Ben had panicked, knowing his teaching career would be non-existent if it came out. DS Andrews said they believed it was not a planned murder, as the body had been left in a shallow lake, only being held down by some of the larger rocks that had been collected from around the water's edge.

The rocks had been stuffed haphazardly into an old single bed sheet that Justine had been wrapped in. The rocks were obviously put there to try to keep the body from surfacing, but their weight was insufficient. As soon as the gasses were produced as part of the decomposition process, the body resurfaced. It had been quite easy to spot from the shore of the lake, as it hadn't been taken very far in. It had seemed to them like an unexpected and hastily thought-out plan. From their experience with previous murders, this was not the work of a calculated and practised killer. If Ben would just tell them what happened, his remorse and confession would be taken into consideration. He would not be putting Justine's mother through a long, drawn-out trial. Surely he didn't want to do that to Margaret.

It was tough not to respond with outrage, but Ben sat firm and tight lipped. After a frustrating 45 minutes of "no comment", and the police asking their questions or introducing their scenarios, it was clear to the Police they were not going to get any more information. Nic had asked the police what evidence they had found in Ben's car, his locker or at his home to suggest he had disposed of a body. The Police had to admit they had nothing. She then asked the police what evidence they had that Ben hadn't gone straight home after dropping off Justine. The police again had admitted they had very little evidence, other than the traffic light camera's that actually supported Ben's story. And Nic reminded them that Ben had an alibi from his parents for the time that Justine would have gone missing. Nic told the police she was tired of the questioning of her client, she felt she had given the police long enough to present their side. It was clear they had no evidence that Ben had been involved in Justine's murder.

Nic checked her watch and then looked up at the clock on the wall making a bit of a show of it.

'How long has my client been held in custody Detective Sergeant?' Asked Nic. She had spoken to Ben's parents on her way into the station, so she knew damn well it was getting close of six hours. She also knew The DS would need to get approval to hold Ben for a further six hours, and he would need something concrete to hold him in custody. 'Do you have any evidence my client has committed a crime? Either charge my client or let him go,' Nic said in the most authoritative tone she could muster.

DS Andrews looked directly at Ben and told him he was free to go. 'But don't think this is the end of it, we'll be watching you,' he'd said in an irritated voice. 'Oh, and by the way, we've impounded your car for further analysis, so you won't have your wheels for a while, sorry about that.' The tone was the least sorry one Ben had ever heard.

Ben collected his things and signed some paperwork. He thanked Nic for her help. She had given him her card and told him to call her if he needed her. She hoped rather than expected that that wouldn't be the case. In her experience once the Police had a suspicion they were like a dog with a bone. Ben's parents were still waiting at the station. They had a brief conversation with Nic and thanked her for helping their son at such short notice. 'All in a day's work' Nicole had informed them with a wry smile. Ben got a big teary hug from his mum and a slap on the back from his dad. They left the station immediately; they could not get out of that place faster enough for Ben's liking.

Chapter Twelve

The next morning Ben borrowed his mother's little lime green Hyundai, squashing his 6-foot 3-inch body into the small front seat. With barely any forethought, he drove straight to Margaret's house. He was nervous; surely by now she knew he'd been questioned as a suspect? But when she opened the door she smiled and welcomed him into her home.

He didn't know what to say, except, 'I didn't do it.'

Margaret could see Ben's distress simmer just below a very teary surface, so she did what any mother would do and enfolded him into a hug, guiding him into the house. She introduced Ben to her sister Joy, who had taken the red eye and had arrived from over east about an hour ago. They were having a cup of tea and invited Ben to sit with them.

'I'm so sorry' said Ben as he drew his hands down his face. 'It's all my fault, I should've dropped her off here. I'll never forgive myself.'

'It's not your fault Ben,' said Margaret kindly. 'I'm the one to blame, I shouldn't have been so controlling, if I'd just been calmer about things she wouldn't have felt the need to hide things from me.'

'Oh, listen to the two of you, just stop it,' said Joy, frustrated. 'Neither of you are to blame, the only person to blame is the monster who killed her.'

He told them about the police interview and how they'd accused him. How they had suggested he and Justine had had consensual sex and she panicked and cried rape and he killed her to cover it up. He told them he had to engage a lawyer to help him. He'd never been in trouble before, not even a speeding ticket.

'They're just doing their job, I suppose,' said Joy. 'They have to rule everyone out.'

After they had finished their tea, Ben suggested that they go out to the lake. He wanted to see the place where they had found Justine and leave some flowers. Ben waited for Margaret and Joy to change into something more suitable; it'd been raining on and off for weeks and the ground around the lake could get quite muddy. They all piled into the tiny lime green car. Ben explained to Joy and Margaret the police were holding his car for further investigation and he wasn't sure how long it would be before he got it back. Margaret felt so sorry for Ben, he was clearly terribly upset and doing his best to hold it all in.

The sun was desperately trying to break through the clouds as they approached the lake. The large gum trees were whispering to each other as their branches swayed in the light breeze. Ben felt an eery unease. It was obvious where Justine had been found; aside from the police tape that was dancing in the breeze, slackly strewn around a couple of large gum trees, there was a sea of colourful bouquets near the entrance which made all three visitors catch their breath. Teddy bears and candles were scattered amongst the blooms; ribbons and cards had been tied to bushes and trees, and even a few photographs had been propped in amongst them, mostly of Justine when she was in primary school.

'Oh my,' breathed Margaret. All other words escaped her.

Ben smiled and felt a shiver tingle up his spine; Justine had been so loved, and he was glad to see that people wanted to show their love this way. One of Justine's teachers was there leaving some flowers and walked over to Margaret to give her a hug.

'Oh Margaret. We just can't believe it. We just expect her to walk through the classroom door. I am so sorry, she was a delightful young girl,' the woman said as she released Margaret from an embrace. They spoke about Justine and school, acknowledging that Justine was not the best student in the class, but she was always the first to put up her hand if someone needed help. 'She will be so missed,' said her teacher choking back tears.

Margaret remembered Justine's first day at school with a smile. Justine had come home so excited. When Margaret had asked her how her first day had been she had said, 'Great!' and excitedly showed Margaret the reading book she had made in class that day, a handmade little thing covered in wonky childlike letters. Justine read from the first page to Margaret with a proud smile: *A for Apple. Apple is red.* Margaret could see how Justine had almost stayed in the lines to colour the apple a bright red. Then she turned to the next page. *'B for Ball. A ball is round,'* she read out loud with a grin, and then the third and final page, *'C for Cat. Cat is black.'* Then she looked straight at Margaret and said with a very serious look on her face: *'See, I can read and write; I don't need to go to school anymore.'*

Margaret's reminiscing was disturbed by a gaggle of loud chatty girls arriving to leave a teddy bear with a big red bow around its neck, probably from school, she reasoned. The girl was saying to her friends that she had heard the police had arrested 'the boyfriend'. Poor Ben, thought Margaret, he's going to have to put up with a lot of gossip and innuendos.

'Sorry to ask you Margaret, but do you know when the funeral will be? It's just that I'm sure a lot of the staff and students would like to attend,' said Justine's English teacher apologetically.

Margaret explained that Justine's body hadn't been released yet and she was unsure how long it would be before she could start to make plans, but assured her that as soon as she had a date, she would advise the school. This got Margaret thinking about a funeral – something she'd shoved to the back of her mind until now - and she wondered what Justine would have wanted; to be cremated, or buried? What music would she like played? Obviously this topic had never come up in conversation before. Maybe she could ask Sue, her daughter's best friend, what music she liked. She wondered how well she knew her daughter after all.

Of course, when Justine was small Margaret knew everything about her, they were so close. They would often go out for coffee, Justine sipping cream-topped hot chocolate while Margaret sipped her flat white. They would go to the movies together, alternating between kid's movies and old classics. Sometimes, as a treat, Margaret would even take Justine to the nail salon, and they'd choose a colour for each other to have on their toenails. But lately they hadn't spent a lot of time together and when they did, they'd seemed to be at logger heads most of the time.

Margaret was again snapped out of her thoughts, this time by Ben. Ben said he was ready to go if she and Joy were. He looked at Margaret and whispered that they are all saying he did it. She gave him a very public hug hoping that it might stem the gossip of his guilt.

Ben dropped Joy and Margaret off. He explained that he couldn't stay as he had a shift at work in an hour and a Uni assignment to finish. He'd thought about requesting an extension, given the circumstances, but found that keeping busy was better than moping around with too much time to think.

Margaret put the kettle on to make tea, while Joy went to change her damp shoes. There was a message flashing on the answering machine. Margaret pushed the button to listen to the message. It was from the Police; they had said that Justine's body would be released tomorrow, and could she advise them what funeral directors she wanted to collect the body. The only funeral directors that Margaret was aware of was a local family business, which she quite liked the idea of, in as much as she could like the idea of her daughter's funeral. Somehow it seemed more intimate. She told the police that she'd call the local funeral home and passed along their name. When Joy came into the kitchen Margaret told her about the phone call. A funeral needed to be planned. Where to start?

Joy suggested that they get out a pen and paper and start making a list. Joy asked Margaret what type of funeral she wanted for Justine. One thing was certain in Margaret's mind: Justine wouldn't want anything religious; she'd want something light, something fun, with a celebrant leading the sermon who could deliver this whilst honouring who Justine had been; who could truly allow them to all celebrate her life.

Joy suggested they use the internet and google celebrants. They were both surprised by how many they had to choose from. After about an hour Margaret was feeling quite exhausted, but with delight in her voice she said to Joy, 'I think I've found the right one for Justine, take a look at her picture and what she says on her website.' Margaret read, *my commitment is to help you say farewell to your loved ones in a uniquely and individual way that stays true to who the dearly departed was in life.*

'Oh, that's perfect,' said Joy. 'She looks just like the type of celebrant Justine would have approved of. We need to meet with her.'

The celebrant's name was Francesca Worldly and Margaret thought she looked like Mother Earth, so peaceful and spiritual. Joy thought she looked more like someone who would hover over a crystal ball and tell you your future, but what did that matter, for the first time since she arrived Joy saw a spark in Margaret. They arranged to meet with Francesca the day after tomorrow at Margaret's home.

***

Francesca was a rare breed. She had a motherly presence about her. Her language was eccentric yet intimate. She called Margaret 'blossom' or 'petal' when she spoke to her and she said odd things to Margaret like, '*Beauty, hope and inspiration can grow from grief*', and '*nothing is so strong as gentleness, and nothing is so gentle as real strength.*' Margaret wasn't sure she understood *what* she was saying but she liked the *way* she said it.

Although Francesca's style was unique, she clearly knew her stuff. She had made some suggestions to Margaret about where to start. Think about what she wanted to dress Justine in, and maybe get a few outfits out and see how they made her feel. Look through Justine's music collection and photos in preparation, but don't make any snap decisions: there was no hurry. Take your time and try to enjoy the experience, she had suggested. Margaret doubted she would enjoy the experience, but she appreciated the suggestions.

Burying Justine in the dark cold ground was not an option, she would have hated that. Margaret decided she would have Justine cremated. That way she could keep her close to her for now and could think about where to scatter her ashes later. Justine was always someone so full of life and enthusiasm, and a rose garden in a cemetery just seemed a bit too sedate for her.

Although Francesca had advised her to take it slowly, Margaret felt overwhelmed by all the decisions and things she needed to do. But she did need to start somewhere. An outfit for Justine was something she felt confident she could tick off the very long list of things to do. Joy suggested they have some lunch and then they could both go to Justine's room and go through her clothes together, unless Margaret wanted to do it on her own. Margaret turned to Joy and gave her a hug and it was very clear that she valued her help and her opinions and couldn't possibly do this without her.

After lunch Margaret and Joy sat down on Justine's bed and looked around her room. It was cluttered with a paradoxical mix of plush toys, handbags and sneakers. Her dresser was covered with perfumes, creams, makeup and nail polishes and her walls were covered with posters of her favourite pop stars. Margaret was not sure if it was a typical teenager's bedroom, but it did seem to reflect a person that was somewhere between a child and an adult.

Margaret started to tidy up and put things in the right place, wanting to make it look nice for Justine, it helped her feel like she was still a mother.

Once she was satisfied, she opened her wardrobe and felt a wave of emotion. She reached out and touched her school uniforms which were hanging limply between her raincoat and a pair of jeans. She had a strong desire to grab the clothes and smell them to see if she could still smell her baby girl. She sat down on Justine's bed.

'I'm not sure I can do this,' She whispered to Joy.

Joy reached out and squeezed her hand, 'Let's just sit here for a moment.'

Margaret grabbed one of Justine's stuffed toys and hugged it to her chest. It was a well-worn soft floppy dog Justine had had since she was an infant. The tears rolled down her face.

'I'll be okay in a moment,' she said to Joy.

Joy reached over and handed Margaret a tissue.

'Take as long as you need,' she said, 'We don't have to do this today.' Margaret wiped away her tears and blew her nose, knowing that tomorrow wouldn't be any easier. And besides, what else was she going to do? She just had to accept the tears were going to come.

After a deep breath she got up off the bed and walked to the wardrobe and took out two of Justine's favourite dresses.

'She looked so lovely in this one,' she said to Joy.

It was a soft salmon pink with black straps that crossed over at the back. The bodice was decorated in tiny roses and the skirt of the dress flowed beautifully as she walked. Justine had worn it when Sue's mum had re-married earlier that year, and had been so excited to go to her first wedding. Although it was only a small wedding in the local park, the reception had been in one of the local restored historical manner houses. Margaret had waited up for her, wanting to hear all about it. Justine had floated through the front door and started dancing around the lounge room, saying that if she ever got married she would hold her reception in the same house. She thought it was the most romantic setting ever. They had spent the next hour talking, as Justine went through all the details, and did not go to bed until well after midnight.

The second dress was the one she had worn to her friend's 15th birthday, only a few weeks ago. At the time Margaret wanted to comment to Justine about how low cut the front was but knew she would just get the look. So, in the end she just said, *You look very nice dear.*

'Mmm I think the pink one,' Margaret said to Joy with a private smile on her face.

'Good choice,' said Joy while nodding her head.

Margaret felt shattered after the experience of finding the right dress, she didn't know how she was going to get through all the other decisions she would be required to make. Joy seemed to sense her concerns and told Margaret she was going to call her husband Bill and her workplace and advise them she would be staying a little longer. Margaret felt overwhelmed with emotion. She and Joy had not been close, but when she needed her older sister the most, she was there for her. Margaret said with relief. 'Well, I'll need to go shopping, my cupboards are bare.'

Chapter Thirteen

It was Monday. Monday nights Liz always went to her parents' house for dinner. They had both retired some years ago and had downsized from the family home Liz had grown up in. It had always been her father's dream to own a house close to the ocean. He was a keen fisherman and loved to go out just after dawn and fish until the evening breeze came in. They lived in a large coastal town called Moretown, a 30-minute drive from Liz's home. Just about the right distance -not to close that they lived in each other pockets, but not too far for regular weekly visits. Sometimes Liz stayed over if she'd had a few glasses of wine, but today she was keen to get home early and jump on the computer to do a bit of research.

Her parents' home had a warm and friendly feel to it. Her mother always had something sweet and delicious baking in the oven, and it wasn't unusual to find sewing patterns and new swatches of fabric strewn about the place. *Shop bought clothes just don't fit me* she would constantly tell Liz. The lounge room was fitted out for comfort, not style. A solid wood coffee table with a spread of magazines sat between two overstuffed couches. Every shelf and cabinet held clusters of family photos. Liz could and often did spend ages looking at the photos of her children. They had not always been out on display. For a while they'd been hidden away in a cupboard for fear it would dredge up the past and upset Liz, but now she would hold them close and remember something fun, something good. It had taken years and a bucket load of positive energy to erase the last memories she had of her children faces the night they died.

There were photos of her parents' other grandchildren. Fortunately, her brother had met and married a wonderful woman and they'd had two adorable children a couple of years after her parents had lost their world. They had been a wonderful surprise. Her parents had often teased him that there was a world full of women out there that were missing out on a wonderful loving husband; it took him a while before he finally snagged one.

Liz's brother Paul was extremely bright, he had won a maths competition in his third year of high school that was open to university students. Liz had often joked that Paul had gotten her share of brains as well as his own. He had been diagnosed with autism when he was a teenager, which seemed to explain a lot of his quirks and his discomfort in social situations. Liz adored her nephew and niece. They would often stay over during school holidays, providing a shining light to her after years of darkness.

The conversation at the dinner table was about the recently discovered body of a young girl in Lake Swan. Lake Swan was an older town, Semi-rural about a 30-minute drive east from Liz's parents' home. Liz's mum was appalled that such a horrible thing had happened anywhere, but in a small town, where everyone knows each other, it affects the whole town she told them. Lake Swan was a lovely pioneer town first settled in 1834 and had a long history of dairy farming. Like a lot of the old towns, the main highway ran right through the middle and the housing was simply and haphazardly constructed around it. The highway is the main highway that connects the south to the north of Western Australia. Unfortunately, it meant high levels of traffic, including large trucks that are constantly flowing through the town centre.

Lake Swan used to be the epicentre for the area until about twenty years ago. Fortunately for the residents, the train still runs twice a day to the city, but little other services were left. Twenty years ago, it had the only hospital and high school for the entire area, as well as most of the government services. Families from Moretown had to drive or catch a bus to get there for most of their needs. But people had started to discover the beautiful coastal hide-away of Moretown in ever increasing numbers, including Liz's parents.

The wonderful coastline, with its small islands, help to protect the beaches for young children to learn to swim, as well as offering some great scuba diving sites. There were also some less protected beaches that offered great waves for those who like to surf. Moretown also had a low and wide estuary where three rivers flowed into it before reaching the ocean and this made for a great foreshore area for families to have a barbeque or picnic. Or, to the envy of Liz's dad, an extensive view from the window of your holiday mansion, if you had a million dollars or two to spare. It was no wonder the population had swelled from around ten thousand to eighty thousand in the last twenty years.

'Do you know when and where the funeral will be held?' Liz asked.

'No dear,' said her mother. 'There was nothing about a funeral in the local paper, why, do you think you might like to attend?'

Liz often attended funerals when it involved a child who had been murdered if it was within an easy distance for her to travel. She felt a profound need as a parent of murdered children to show some solidarity. It was also her way to express the disappointment that children are still being murdered in a civilised world. She had attended seven over the last ten years. This one would make it eight; far too many in Liz's mind.

'Yes, I was thinking I might,' said Liz to her mother.

Liz's mother didn't say anything, she just nodded and looked at her with a sad expression which spoke volumes.

Liz said her goodbyes with hugs and kisses to her parents and promises to go to the movies or do something fun with them soon.

Walking into the office on Tuesday morning, Liz took a quick glance at the central diary. Everyone had a busy day. The diary was always fully booked, with many more waiting for an appointment. Liz couldn't remember a time when they didn't have a long waiting list. It wasn't the work that caused the most stress for Liz, it was that bloody waiting list. She understood only too well the amount of courage it took for survivors to pick up the phone and ask for help, only to be told that they had to wait for an appointment. It saddened her that they couldn't provide an immediate response to everyone that phoned. Although the service had eight very experienced and efficient counsellors, it was never enough to satisfy the community's needs.

She had one client first thing, then she noted it was her turn as the duty officer. She would be required to return calls to new client referrals or crisis calls. She also had two individual supervision sessions with her team booked in. She told herself she must also get to that report for the health department today, it was due next week. It was part of the funding requirements, and the last thing she wanted to do was put at risk any of their current funding. She made herself a cup of coffee and took it into her counselling room to prepare for her first session.

After the session, as Liz was finishing up her notes, she suddenly became
aware of a commotion outside her office door. The session she was nota-
rising had been a tough one, and it took her a second or two to tune into
the sound. Claire, the receptionist knocked on her door and walked in looking very distressed. She told Liz that one of her clients, Pam, had just turned
up without an appointment and wanted to come and say goodbye to Liz.
She said it with strong emphasis on the *goodbye*.

'Oh, okay,' said Liz, 'let her come in.'

Liz's client walked in looking very sombre. She could see she had a cath-
eter poking out from under a large band-aide on the back of her hand. In a
very defiant tone, she had informed Liz that she had tried to kill herself last
night, but clearly had not been successful. Her teenage daughter had found
her and called an ambulance. She had just walked out of the hospital that
morning against the doctor's advice and called a taxi. She had come here
first to say goodbye to Liz, and to thank her for all she had tried to do for
her, before she was going to finish the job and do it properly this time. She
informed Liz that she had an area picked out in the bush where no one
would find her. She had a hose and duct tape stored in the boot of her car,
and she had downloaded all her favourite songs on her phone to listen to.
All she had to do now was go and get her car and buy a bottle of Jim Beam.
She had a solid plan and this time she would succeed.

Liz thought to herself, '*Then why are you here? Why have you come to say goodbye? Is this your last ditched attempt to ask for help?*' Though Liz would never ask
her that. Instead, Liz asked her a different question.

'Do you want to die, or do you just want things to be different?' Liz had
asked this question to suicidal clients or on duty calls many times, and only
one person had ever said that they wanted to die. When he had said to her
that he wanted to die she had told him that unfortunately she couldn't help
him with that, and she had contacted a mental health crisis service. She suspected that he was hoping his response might get him an appointment
sooner with their service, but it had the opposite effect. She explained to
him that clients needed to be stable to come into counselling, that he needed
to be assessed by the local mental health crisis team. He would need to work
with them until his mental health was robust enough to start counselling,
and then she would be happy to make him an appointment.

A tear escaped from Pam's eye. There was no doubt she had been asked
the question before, too.

'If things were different, then I wouldn't want to die, but they're not, are they? I can't keep putting my children through this, it's not fair on them, they would be far better off without me.'

Then Liz said something to her that she rarely said, only when it was absolutely necessary, when it was life or death. She didn't like using guilt, but when you're desperate, you have to use desperate measures.

'Do you love your kids?' After a nod from Pam, she said those dreadful but necessary words. 'Well, they will spend the rest of their lives thinking that you didn't love them enough to stick around when things got tough.'

Liz knew this was a cruel and unfair thing to say to a parent, especially one that already felt bad about themselves. She only ever used this tactic as a last resort. She committed to herself to apologise to Pam later, but for now she had to stay stoic. Pam took a deep breath and disclosed to Liz that she had lost her way, she could not find the pathway out of her current situation. Liz spoke gently to Pam for a while asking her about what had happened that had shifted her into this dark space, because she had been doing so well lately.

It seemed that she had lost another job due to an explosive outburst with her boss. Pam didn't do well with dictatorial bosses, particularly the type that bullied her and wouldn't listen to her point of view. The only way she knew to protect herself was to be loud and angry, because quiet and subservient hadn't helped her in the past. This was no surprise, given her history of childhood sexual abuse, where she had been made to feel powerless and utterly worthless. After some convincing she allowed Liz to call her psychiatrist, who had been treating her for years.

Liz left the room so that she could speak to the psych alone. After about 10 minutes Pam emerged from the room and said that her psychiatrist wanted to speak to Liz. Liz had spoken to Pam's Psychiatrist many times before. They had worked together on Pam's recovery. The Psychiatrist told Liz that she was very worried about Pam's mental health, and she could get her a bed immediately in a private mental health hospital in the city, if Liz could arrange to get her there. Liz said that she would make the arrangements to get her there and then confirm with her once it was all in place.

Liz phoned the local mental health services only to be told that they don't do transport. To Liz's horror they'd suggested to just pop her in a taxi, like she was attending a function. Next, she phoned the ambulance services only to be told that they do emergencies, and this was not an emergency. Liz got off the phone feeling frustrated; she had a client that was clearly in distress, she had a bed waiting for her in a specialist psychiatric hospital but there was no service to help get her there. There was no way she was going to let Pam drive herself there. Liz looked in her diary with a sense of resignation. She re-scheduled her two supervision sessions to later in the week, swapped duty with Karen and accepted that she would just have to work back late to complete her report.

She drove Pam to her home so that she could pack a bag. Spoke briefly to a neighbour, who was happy to look out for the girls after school. Pam's girls were sixteen and seventeen and pretty independent: they'd had little choice. Pam then left a heartfelt note for her two teenage children telling them she loved them, and that was why she was getting some help. She apologised for what she had put them thorough last night, and to call her as soon as they got home from school.

This had not been the first time that Pam had attempted suicide and probably wouldn't be the last. It was very hard for her children to understand why this kept happening. They knew their mother had been abused as a child but didn't know the extent of it. Pam's history of abuse was horrendous. She had been abused by a paedophile ring for years. It was a wonder that she'd made it this far. Liz drove her the 100 kilometres or so to the hospital herself. This was not what the agency had been funded for, but what else could she do? Luckily, Pam slept most of the way as she was clearly exhausted and was probably still a little drowsy from whatever drugs they had given her the night before in emergency.

It was late in the afternoon by the time she got back to the office. She had caught up with Karen and Julie for an update on Sally and Lilly. Sally was doing okay at the moment. Her ex-husband was currently on a long-haul job and was still on the road. Lilly, it seemed was very bright, and was picking up the protective behaviour training very quickly. Julie had sent an interim report to the department of child protection, with a recommendation that Lilly only have supervised access visits with her father but was yet to hear back from them. She would give them a call if she had not heard back from them by next week.

Satisfied, Liz walked into her office and closed the door. She took a deep breath and blew it out slowly. Lilly was safe for now. That meant she had a bit of breathing space to put her plan into action. Although things were okay at the moment, she needed to be prepared for action if needed. She would also keep an eye on Facebook for any mention of a funeral date for Justine. She hoped it would be soon.

Liz sat down at her desk and fired up her computer and started working on the statistics for the report. Her counsellors provided their statistics to her each month, and she entered them on to a spreadsheet she kept for the purpose of reporting. The figures were always alarming, how many sessions they were providing, how many clients they saw, demographics such as postcode, gender, age, nationality, the average number of sessions per client, how many and how long people were on their waiting list. It never seemed to change, as soon as they finished with one client there were so many more waiting desperately to fill that spot.

Liz had to complete reports for each different service they offered. The children's service, the adult service, the youth service, the indigenous service, the Domestic violence service, each service was funded through a different government department, therefore required different criteria and statistics. The budgets for each service had to be reported separately to ensure taxpayer's money was appropriately spent. Rent, insurances, training, administration and management had to be split with the correct percentage charged to reflect the number of hours and clients each service delivered. It was exhausting but necessary to continue their funding and to keep each service running.

Liz was disturbed by the sound of a vacuum cleaner. Once again, she would be the last person in the building. It was quite eery when all the lights had been switched off. The building was a community building with a number of other not-for-profit agencies working from different suites. Although the agency would have loved their own building, the rent here was very low. It also gave their clients some anonymity if a neighbour, friend or a relative saw their car in the car park.

Liz stretched her arms and arched her back, sore from sitting at her computer for hours. It was time to go home. The rest of the report could wait for the morning, it just needed a few finishing touches. She shut down her computer and got up from her desk. The first few steps were always the most painful, making her feel a hundred years old. Thankfully no one was around to see her as she held onto the back of her chair for support. Embarrassed about the way she walked, it was certainly more painful than she made it look.

Liz felt around the edge of the overhead cupboard in the reception area for the keys the receptionist hid there. This was the security method she employed to protect the agency from theft. It felt a bit cloak and dagger, but there was the cash box that held the petty cash (to purchase tea supplies, often holding the large sum of twenty dollars, thought Liz with amusement). Liz unlocked the drawer that held all of the office keys and took the key to the filing room. She unlocked the room and went to the filing cabinets and pulled files on Lilly and Sally.

This was not unusual for Liz, as she would often review files. A bit of a spot check. Mainly to check the counsellors were using the right conventions in their note taking. Their files were often subpoenaed by Lawyers or the courts once charges had been laid, particularly if the counsellor was the first person the client had disclosed sexual abuse to. It was crucial the information in the files did not do more harm to the client. It was important to use such syntax as *'she recalled'* or *'he explained'* or *'she said'*. Unless the perpetrator had been to court and found guilty the notes could not present the information as a fact.

It was also better for the notes to be brief, with just enough information to refresh the counsellor's memory of what they were working on, or if *homework* had been set for the client. Unfortunately, Liz had learnt about diligent note taking the hard way. In the early days as a counsellor one of her clients had told her that every Monday and Wednesday her perpetrator, who was also her landlord, would demand sex in payment for rent. This had been noted by Liz in her file notes as a fact: that the landlord only ever demanded sex on Mondays and Wednesdays. When it went to court the client had said her landlord had demanded sex on different days. As a result, the defence Lawyer was able to suggest she was lying, that she was in fact making it up as, she had told Liz one thing and the courts another, suggesting it didn't actually happen at all. Liz realised rather quickly her notes contained too much detail, they were too specific. She should have just noted that her client had recalled her landlord had demanded sex in lieu of rent.

Cases like that often-had little evidence and relied on, 'he said she said'. Children were disbelieved and often thought to be making it up. Whereas the perpetrators were seen as pillars in the community. Women were vilified for being an unmarried mother. What chance did she have? He was believed and found not guilty. Liz has never forgiven herself for that error and would never make it again.

Though things had changed in recent years, particularly since the prosecution of a number of priest's, who were also previously deemed pillars of the community. A lot of victims of abuse were vindicated. But ever since this experience Liz has been pedantic about file notes, and audited files on a regular basis. She opened the files on Lilly and Sally and read through the details. She then took out her little black notebook she kept in her handbag and began writing.

Chapter Fourteen

After Joy had made her phone calls to her boss and her husband, she and Margaret went to the supermarket.

'What do you feel like for dinner?' asked Joy. 'The fish looks nice.'

'Um, yep sounds good.' Margaret said with amusement. Same old Joy, she would ask you a question, and before you could respond she would answer it herself.

As they were leaving the supermarket, Joy suggested they go into the liquor store and grab a couple of bottles of wine. Margaret wasn't a big drinker, in fact she hardly drank at all, not because she didn't like a drink - if she went out to dinner she wouldn't hesitate to have a glass of wine or two - mostly it was because she couldn't afford to buy alcohol when Justine was a baby, and now that she can, it just did not occur to her to buy a bottle of wine.

'What sort of wine do you like?' asked Joy. Before Margaret had a chance to answer her, Joy went into a story of how she usually drank Sauvignon Blanc from New Zealand, but recently had discovered the Riesling from the great southern area in Western Australia was fabulous. She had mistakenly thought Rieslings were a sweet wine, but had attended a wine tasting event with her work colleagues and had been convinced to taste a Riesling. To her surprise the Riesling had not been sweet at all, she had found it to be quite a dry wine, but with a crispy and fruity flavour. Margaret smiled and told Margaret whatever she chose would be fine with her.

Joy put the fish in the oven to cook while Margaret started chopping vegetables to make a tossed salad. Joy managed to find a couple of wine glasses tucked away in Margaret's display cabinet and poured herself and Margaret a glass each. Margaret took a sip and looked at the glass,

'Good Lord, I haven't used these glasses in years, they were a wedding present from Auntie Angela.'

Joy sighed, 'Poor old Auntie Angela, at least the cancer took her quickly. She was in terrible pain towards the end, but refused to die in hospital, wanted to be in her own bed in her own home. I sometimes found it hard to believe that Auntie Angela and Mum were sisters, they were so different.'

'Yes, they seemed to have completely different memories and experiences from their childhood. Mum seemed to blame everything that ever went wrong in her life on someone else, yet Auntie Angela was so independent and responsible.' Joy refilled their glasses while Margaret continued. 'A bit like us in a way, I mean that we're quite different.'

'In what way are we so different?' asked Joy.

Margaret took a large sip from her glass and feeling slightly fuzzy in the head, and with a bit of Dutch courage under her belt said, 'Well, you were always their favourite, you could do no wrong, whereas me, I was the black sheep.'

'Their favourite?' Laughed Joy. 'What gave you that impression?! They were much harder on me than on you. I always had to take you with me, had to look after you, make sure their precious little girl was safe. Did you know that mum had three miscarriages after me? She thought she'd never have another child until you came along. They wrapped you up in cotton-wool like you'd break at the slightest bump. "Don't let her swing too high, don't let her climb trees, don't let her fall down and hurt herself." God, if I ever came home and you had a cut or a bruise I got into such trouble.'

'I never realised,' said Margaret. 'I just thought you were bossy, that you didn't like me, that you didn't want me to have any fun.'

'Well now you know better. To me it felt like you were the golden child, and I didn't matter. Looking back that was probably why I rebelled against mum and dad's rules. Undoubtedly just craving attention.'

'I'm so sorry Joy,' said Margaret feeling genuinely remorseful for all the years she had thought unkindly towards her.

'Hey, remember when I went on my first date with a boy, and you tagged along?' said Joy.

'Tagged along?' said Margaret indignantly. 'It wasn't my idea. Mum and dad told me I had to go with you, I wasn't supposed to let you out of my sight. But you made me walk ten paces in front of you, and then when I turned around you'd gone. I had to stay at the park for hours, because I was too scared to go home without you.'

'Oh yeah,' said Joy with amusement. 'I'd forgotten that part. I remember now! We went down to the trampolines, we were meeting his mates there. After we had bounced for about half an hour, we had fish and chips and then he walked me home. What was his name… Sam? Scott? Something like that. He was quite sweet.'

'I waited for hours in the park for you to walk past. Then I followed you down the street and into the house, luckily Mum didn't ask me anything about the afternoon, she just assumed I was with you the whole time.'

Margaret and Joy continued to reminisce about their childhood, laughing into the early hours of the morning before they decided they should go to bed. Margaret felt the huge gap between her and Joy had closed somewhat. Maybe something good had come out of this tragedy.

The next morning Margaret received the news that Justine's body had been released to the local undertaker. She and Joy made an appointment to meet with them later that day to discuss the arrangements. She brought the pink dress with her. They picked out a simple coffin and booked the large chapel in the crematorium for Friday week. Margaret anticipated this would give her time to organise everything else.

When she and Joy got home there was a car in her driveway, with two people sitting inside. As they got out of their car Margaret recognised them both. She hoped DS Andrews and DC McDonald had not been waiting too long. She invited them in and put the kettle on. The detectives regrettably did not have any new leads or any new information. Initially, when the story was headline news, they'd had a rush of calls to the crime stopper call centre, but that had now dried up. They had followed up on all the calls, even the nutters and time-wasters. They described a caller who they'd termed The Ouija Board Psychic who had been talking to Justine through his spirit guide. Margaret apologised, even though she did not have anything to apologise for.

DS Andrews and DC McDonald conveyed their frustration. Someone must have seen something, even something they think is insignificant can often break a case. Young girls just don't go missing from a main street without someone seeing something. They wanted to do a reenactment using an actress or someone that looked like Justine. They would get her to walk home from where Ben had dropped her off. They wanted to do this on Sunday, the same day of the week and at the same time she would have been there, in the hope it might jog someone's memory. Especially if someone does a regular activity at the same time each week like, put out the rubbish, or take their dog for a walk. It would also be filmed and put on the news.

They wanted to warn Margaret and give her as much notice as possible. Seeing a look alike would be distressing, but they were hoping she could help them with the accuracy of the clothes and Justine's looks and mannerisms. Margaret agreed immediately, saying she would do whatever it takes to help find her daughter's killer. She told the detectives that the funeral was booked for next Friday. The reenactment was arranged for the Sunday after the funeral. Margaret saw the detectives to the door and thanked them for their perseverance. Joy and Margaret ate dinner and decided to have an early night. It had been an exhausting day, and after last night they both needed a good night's sleep.

As arranged, Francesca Worldly arrived the next morning to discuss the service. She floated in like a brightly coloured kite, the scent that wafted in her wake was warm and spicy. Francesca was a large woman with a mess of black curly hair tied up on the top of her head, trying desperately to escape the scrunchie that held it precariously in place. She did not wear a lot of makeup, except for her ruby red lipstick and her brightly coloured fingernails. She took out a note pad from her oversized handbag and motioned Margaret and Joy to follow her into the garden.

'I like to work outside if I can,' she explained. 'It helps to free my thinking and inspire me.' They all sat down on the garden chairs. Although the sun had come out it was still quite fresh. Joy went to make tea.

'Well petal, tell me about your beautiful girl, what was she into? What were her likes and dislikes? What music did she listen to? What books did she like to read? What television shows did she watch? I want to know her.'

Francesca listened intently, asking questions and taking notes. When Margaret described Justine as a *bit of a social butterfly*, Francesca suddenly said, 'Oh yes, yes, that speaks to me. *Butterfly*. Oh, I like it – I think that should be the theme, what do you think blossom?'

Although Margaret did not particularly like being referred to as flora, she really did like Francesca. Her style appeared to be quite playful and flamboyant. Margaret knew instantly that Justine would have liked her. She couldn't have cared less for a 'theme', but she truly knew this woman's heart was in the right place, so she nodded her agreement, offering a little side-smile to Joy as she did so.

Francesca confirmed she was available Friday week. She knew the facilities at the crematorium well, as she had conducted many of her funerals there. She had suggested that Margaret and Joy put together a collection of photographs of Justine and set them to her favourite music to be displayed in a sort of slideshow style on the big video screen inside the crematorium.

Margaret explained to Francesca that she wasn't terribly confident with computers, it was Justine who used to help her when she needed to send an email or look up something, and although Joy used a computer at her work, she was not sure she had the experience to put together the photos to music.

Francesca listened very calmly to their protests about their lack of computer skills. She told Margaret that although most people thought of her as a bit ditzy, she was actually a wiz on a computer. She told Margaret for a small fee she could put it together for her. All she needed was the photos in chronological order and the music a few days before the funeral, and she would do the rest. Margaret was very relieved. She told Francesca she wanted an open invitation to the funeral. She explained that Justine's school had already indicated the staff and students wanted to attend. Francesca suggested that Margaret could put the invitation on Facebook, and for the older folk put an advert in the local newspaper. Francesca had come well prepared and was able to provide Margaret with a couple of examples she had previously used. Margaret could manage the newspaper, and she would get Ben or Sue to help her with Facebook invites.

Francesca also asked Margaret if she wanted to speak at the funeral. Margaret's initial reaction was no, she did not think she could manage it. Francesca suggested that she not make any decisions about that today, she had time to think about it, but recommended she start to put together what she might like to say, if she decided she were able. If she could not speak, then someone else could always speak on her behalf. They had agreed to meet again early next week to go over the plan they had put together.

After Francesca had left, Margaret thought with a sigh, *where do I start?* Joy suggested they focus on one thing at a time. It was so good to have Joy here - she didn't know what she'd do without her.

'Ok let's have lunch and then I'll get out the photo albums, the photos I have on the computer and my phone,' said Margaret.

Chapter Fifteen

It was good to be home after a busy day. Liz was grateful she only had to reheat frozen leftovers for dinner. She fed Buster while she waited for her dinner to heat up. Minced Roo meat, pasta and vegetables was woofed down in a microsecond, like he hadn't been fed for a month. Liz took her plate to her study, sat down in her chair and with Buster now lying at her feet she turned on her computer. Buster must have been having a vivid dream, as he kept moaning and moving his legs in a running motion, probably chasing the neighbourhood cat. She'd been keeping an eye on Lake Swan's High School Facebook page hoping for an announcement of the time and date of a funeral for Justine. She planned to attend the funeral regardless of whether or not she went through with her plan.

She had managed to attend the funeral of her own children. The family had delayed it for three weeks so she could be there. Although still battered and bruised and taken directly there from hospital in a wheelchair, she was so thankful to her family for giving her the opportunity to say her final goodbyes. It had been a private funeral, only family and close friends. It had been pitiful, looking at those three tiny little white coffins being carried by her heartbroken family.

Frank's parents showed up looking like ghosts of themselves. It didn't help that they were dressed in black, it seemed to emphasize their pale skin and listlessness. Liz didn't talk to them. She was still struggling to put two words together, and she didn't have the energy to spare, however they did exchange a look of despair. In that look Liz tried to convey that it wasn't their fault, and she didn't blame then; after all, they had lost a child too, as well as their grandchildren. But she knew deep down they had accepted some responsibility and felt guilty, because after all, he was their son, and his behaviour had been entrenched long before she had been on the scene.

Liz noticed that Justine's funeral had been announced for Friday and it was an open invitation. The funeral service was at the Lake Swan crematorium at 10am, with a wake back at the family's home. Liz couldn't believe her luck; this would fit perfectly into her plan. The invitation had said not to wear black. It has asked people who attended to wear a colour of the rainbow. It had also stated this was a celebration of Justine's short life, so please don't bring flowers, bring balloons, in any colour of the rainbow. Wow, she really admired Justine's family for their courage to say goodbye to their loved one in such an upbeat way.

Liz did a search for true crime documentaries and was surprised by how many options she had to choose from on both commercial and non-commercial television networks. One looked particularly interesting, as it had seven separate 40 minutes episodes about how the killer got caught by the police. Liz thought she might watch the first one and see how interesting it was. Before she realised, two hours had gone by and she had watched four episodes back-to-back, and easily would've watched more, except it was getting late and her body was crying out in pain from sitting for too long.

During her marathon true-crime session she'd taken down some notes in her little black notebook. A number of killers had gotten caught by a member of the public noticing something that was out of place, like a car parked near the scene at an unusual time, or someone acting suspiciously. Once the police had a suspect in their sights, it seemed they would often track them by CCTV camera images picking up their movements or their car's movements. Another useful device to track a person's movement was their mobile phone. In most instances the killer had a personal connection to their victim. Although the 'stranger danger' communication warnings were still important, in most instances it was the people closest to victims that were the untrustworthy one's. The most difficult murders to solve were the random killings where the perpetrator had no personal relationship to the victim, but these were rare.

With Buster at her heels, she went to her bedroom to look in her wardrobe for something that might pass as colourful. What she noticed with astonishment was how incredibly drab and colourless her clothes were. It seemed that most of her clothes were black, grey, white or navy blue. Was she still dressing like she was in mourning? What was she afraid of, that by adding some brightness to her wardrobe she might be seen to no longer be grieving for her children?

'This has to change,' Liz said to Buster, as she leant down to give him a scratch behind his ears. 'I'm going to need to go shopping.' Buster wagged his tail in agreement.

At the top of her wardrobe were a number of boxes that contained wigs and head scarves. She pulled them down to take a look. She had not touched them in years, and just the sight of them made her feel nauseous. She recalled how she had requested they shave her entire head for her multiple surgeries. It was far easier to cover her head with a wig or a scarf than to try to cover a bald spot each time she had gone under the surgeon's knife. She had bought herself a couple of wigs, both vastly different to her own red curly hair. She told herself at the time it was a good opportunity to see what she looked like with different coloured hair; to try on someone new. But in reality she just wanted to be anonymous. Her red hair was recognisable, and she just didn't want to be looked on with pity by strangers: that poor mother who had lost all her children. She pulled out her favourite wig, a sleek blond bob with cool tones. She had wondered at the time if it were true that blonds had more fun, but soon realised that blond or not, nothing would bring her joy for a long time.

Walking into the office the following day, Liz was greeted by the smiling face of the receptionist, Claire. Liz told her she planned to go clothes shopping in her lunch break today, so she might be a bit late getting back. She'd remembered seeing the perfect dress for Justine's funeral in one of the department stores. The dress had a large rainbow skirt and was bright purple at the top, very un-Liz, but apparently very Justine.

Upon arriving at the store at lunch time, Liz was relieved to see the dress available and in her size. She put the dress on in the changing room, swung around a few times and looked in the mirror. She laughed to herself. She wouldn't look out of place in the Pride March but might attract a bit of attention at a funeral. The last thing she wanted was to be memorable, or to steal the thunder of a dead teenager.

Hanging the rainbow dress back up, she selected and tried on a lovely fitted dress that was patterned haphazardly with geometrical coloured shapes. Varying shades of blue, green and yellow - colourful enough to meet the brief, but not extraordinary. She wouldn't stand out in this dress. It was a bit more than she would normally pay for a single item of clothing, and she wasn't in the habit of spoiling herself. Liz couldn't count how many times had she advised a client to go out and spoil themselves or to do something nice for themselves because they deserved it. *Well, I need to listen to my own advice once in a while.*

Liz went back to the office. Her next appointment was with a client called Janet. She'd had a lot of difficulty persuading Janet to open up to her, but it was early days, and trust was always an issue for survivors. She had told Janet last week they were going to attempt some 'inner child' work today if she felt up to it.

Liz was pleasantly surprised when she had actually turned up. In her experience clients like Janet seemed to just want to pick at the festering wound, then leave it alone to scab over again. She was hoping that by Janet attending the appointment, it maybe meant that she was ready to rip the scab off and explore the open wound. Janet was the mother of a young girl who was the same age as she was when her grandfather had sexually abused her. This had been the catalyst for her reaching out for counselling. The memories had stated to resurface in the form of flashbacks and wouldn't go away.

Liz went through a progressive relaxation process with Janet. They had agreed on a signal for Janet to use if she wanted to stop at any time, and she was encouraged to if things became too much. It was important to the process that Janet felt in control. Liz then went through a process of connecting Janet to her inner child.

Janet had trouble finding her at first, but eventually placed both her hands lowdown on her stomach. 'Little Janet' seemed to be about four years old. Liz was just asking her a series of questions about what she was doing and how she was feeling, when she was taken aback by one of Janet's remarks.

Janet blurted out in a very spiteful voice. 'I hate her.'

Trying to keep the disbelief out of her voice, Liz asked Janet why she hated her four-year-old self and was not surprised by her response.

'Because she's such a show off. She's just a little flirt. She twirled her skirt and showed her knickers. It was all her fault. She asked for it. She deserved what she got, and I hate her,' Janet spat.

'But Janet this is what four-year-old girls do. They dance around and twirl their skirts. They are not being sexual. Only an adult would sexualise the behaviour. What about your own daughter? If she twirled her skirt and accidently showed her knickers, would you think she was being sexual and flirting with an adult?'

With tears in her eyes Janet's response didn't surprise Liz. 'That's completely different,' she argued. Of course, her own daughter would not be flirting, because she is a good and lovable little girl, and little Janet… well she was just dirty, bad, and unlovable.

Liz looked at Janet. A tear had started to escape. 'Is little Janet really unlovable?'

With Janet still holding herself and now crying, she admitted for the first time that little Janet just wanted to be loved by her grandfather. She did not want the abuse. Liz had explained that survivors often look back at childhood memories through the eyes of an adult and interpret things differently to the reality of what had actually happened. After booking another appointment for next week, Liz sent Janet home with some very specific homework to do. She was to connect with little Janet and be kind to her. Maybe even try to play a game with her if she felt up to it. Janet left the office feeling a little lighter, and quietly confident she could do what she had been tasked to do.

Liz finished typing up her notes then she went to the central filing room and locked away the file. She then knocked on Karen's open office door. Liz was keen to get an update from Karen on how Sally and Lilly were doing, and whether Karen had had a response from child protection yet.

Karen informed Liz that she hadn't heard back from child protection, so she would give them a call tomorrow morning. She also informed Liz that Sally was still talking about running with Lilly but had not done anything so far. Sally had mentioned to Karen that her husband had been acting a bit weird lately; nonargumentative, almost placid. When she told him Lilly was still not well enough for access that weekend, he didn't demand to see her or even asked her for evidence like a doctor's certificate. He'd just accepted her word over the phone, and said it was okay and he could wait until after his next road trip. Sally had said this was not like Nathan at all, and although she was relieved, she was unnerved and suspicious that maybe he had a hidden agenda. Maybe he had something on her, because it was so unlike him to be accommodating, and to give up so easily.

What could he have on you? Karen had asked Sally. Sally had shrugged her shoulders and said she had no idea, but she was wary. She went on to say that he's a cagey little bastard, and she didn't trust him as far as she could throw him. Karen had suggested to Sally that maybe there was a simpler explanation. That Nathan had met someone and was keen to spend the weekend alone with her and child free. Sally hoped more than believed that that could explain Nathan's strange but amenable attitude.

Although Karen still felt a little uneasy about the situation, she told Karen she was happy with the progress of the protective behaviours training that Julie was accomplishing with Lilly. Lilly had been much happier and quite confident since seeing Julie. She was becoming a lot more outspoken, even her kindy teacher had commented on her newfound confidence. *Okay* thought Liz, *we have a little bit of breathing space, but the situation still feels like it is on a knifes edge, because it is all dependent on the whims of Nathan.* She still felt the need to continue with her plan.

Chapter Sixteen

Family night had been changed to Tuesday this week, because the family wanted to mark a special birthday. Josh, Liz's son, would have turned 21 today, had he been allowed to live. The family tried whenever possible to celebrate all of Liz's late children's birthdays. As silly as it sounded, in the early years after the children's murders the family still bought birthday cards, and had a birthday party, but over the years, as emotions became less raw, less intense, they'd started getting together for dinner and had a birthday cake for dessert. This was a milestone birthday for any young adult, and the family wanted to honour it.

Liz hadn't kept a lot of the children's things. Having to pick up and run several times, she'd become pragmatic about possessions. If it was not necessary, it stayed behind. However, she knew the importance of the children's comfort toys in times of trauma and there was always room in the bag for them. After their deaths she could not compel herself to leave them behind.

Josh's comfort toy had been a cloth rabbits' head attached to a small blanket square with a satin ribbon boarder. He'd become very attached to this toy when he was a baby. Liz hadn't realised the strength of the attachment until one day when Josh was about 18 months old. He'd been in trouble for drawing on the freshly painted walls of his bedroom and had been told in no uncertain terms what he had done was very naughty. In tears, he'd immediately gone to fetch bunny. He popped his left thumb straight into his mouth while hugging bunny and rubbing the silky boarder of the blanket square with his right thumb. Liz had found him about 10 minutes later fast asleep on the lounge room floor, with his thumb still in his mouth and a tight hold on bunny. After that bunny went everywhere with him. As long as he had bunny he would sleep anywhere.

Although Liz always referred to the toy as bunny, she remembered that Josh had his own name for the toy. He called it Dah. She recalled with fondness that he would say, '*Where my Dah*' when he was looking for bunny, but if Liz called it Dah he would look at her like he didn't know what she was referring to. Dah had been in the washing machine so many times it was more holes than Bunny. And each time it was in the washing machine, Josh would sit in front of the washing machine and wait for Dah to be washed, and then sit on the lawn under the washing line waiting for Dah to dry. He would often complain that Dah smelt funny after a wash. He had been told that sometimes bunny needed to be washed just like Josh needed a bath. He seemed to accept the explanation. Heaven forbid if she ever lost bunny, as there was no backup.

When Josh got to about five, he seemed to need bunny less and less, and luckily for Liz his thumb sucking seemed to stop when bunny was not in his hand. By around eight, other toys had become more important and Liz had managed to put bunny out of sight and out of mind. At the time, her intention was to keep bunny safe so that she could embarrass him on his 21st birthday by returning his comfort toy to him and telling the many hilarious stories that involved bunny and Josh.

Liz put bunny in her handbag along with a 21st birthday card and a bottle of Champagne she had bought earlier and drove to her parent's house for dinner. She had also packed a small overnight bag just in case she was too tired to drive home. After several glasses of Champagne and a lot of tears and laughter, she was glad that she had thought to pack a bag. She went to the spare bedroom and tried to sleep.

With so many thoughts rolling around in her head, she couldn't sleep. After about thirty frustrating minutes she gave up. She put her reading glasses on, plumped up the pillows and sat up in bed. Pulling her old cardigan around her shoulders, she opened her laptop and took out her little black notebook from her handbag. She logged on to her laptop and opened up google chrome and then went to google maps. She put the address she had written in her notebook straight into google maps and a map appeared with a red arrow directing her to the address. On the right-hand side of the page was a clear photo of the house. She then changed the scene to satellite view and clicked on the little yellow man icon at the bottom right side of the screen. It showed the house and the surroundings very clearly and she was able to manipulate the view up and down the street looking at the images of all the properties close by.

She noted that the date the images were captured was about two years old, so things may look a bit different today. She couldn't see any CCTV cameras on the house or at any of the neighbouring properties. But of course, that could be different now too, so she still needed to take a look herself. There appeared to be a walking path that went around the block, and a children's park around the corner with a small car park. She made some notes in her notebook and closed down her computer.

Sleep escaped Liz until the early hours of the morning. Four hours sleep was better than none. She showered and dressed, said her goodbyes to her mother and father and went to work. Thankfully, she noted in her diary today was an administration day only, no client's booked for a session. Grateful for small mercies, as she was really struggling to focus.

Liz had been asked to write a letter for a client for an up-and-coming court case. He had been charged with a drug offence, and she had agreed to write a letter of support to the court. Liz knew that she needed to be incredibly careful about what she said, and how she said it. She did not want to tell a judge *how to suck eggs,* but she wanted to explain that her client had been receiving counselling for past trauma related to alleged sexual abuse, and that his behaviour was consistent with others who had also been traumatised by childhood sexual abuse.

What she really wanted to say was that he needed rehab and not a jail sentence, but she knew she had to trust that the judge would read between the lines of her support letter. She addressed the letter to her client, giving him the choice of presenting the letter to the judge. It was important to provide clients who'd had little choices in the past with the power to make choices for themselves.

As soon as Liz got home, she changed into her walking clothes, put on her runners, grabbed a hat and sunglasses, and went to get Buster. He was there waiting for her in the laundry wagging his tail so excitedly that his entire body was moving back and forth. Liz had installed a doggy door in the back door that led to the laundry, so that when she is at work she can leave Buster in the backyard all day. It provided Buster with protection if it rained, and the freedom to hole up in the laundry if it was cold. She suspected, however, that he spent a lot more of his time asleep in the laundry than in the backyard playing.

Buster had not seen Liz since yesterday evening, but you would think it had been a year by his overtly excited reaction. She gave him a good belly rub. How nice it was to be welcomed home so enthusiastically, it often lifted her spirits. She spoke to Buster like he could understand her every word. She told him she was going to take him for a walk to a new area. Lots of new sniffing opportunities, but they would need to take the car to get there. She put Buster in the car and drove to the little children's park she had seen on google maps last night. She got out of her car, put on her hat and sunglasses, and then got Buster out of the car and put on his lead.

She started walking around the neighbourhood like any ordinary person taking their dog for a walk. Unfortunately for Liz her gait was stiff and ungainly and therefore didn't give her the look of an ordinary person. She didn't want to look suspicious or standout, but there wasn't a lot she could do about the way she walked. She let Buster do lots of sniffing, giving her time to look around, while hopefully not attracting too much attention.

Not a lot appeared to have changed since the google map images had been taken. But looking at a map and seeing the real thing was quite different. It was hard to believe she had just minutes ago left behind a bustling town. There was a distinct feeling of tranquillity in this semi-rural area. The sun filtered through the trees to give the area a lazy rustic atmosphere. Liz could smell the fresh minty odour from the large peppermint trees that gave plenty of shade to the undergrowth of ferns. The bird life was delightful. Liz could see willy wagtails wagging their tails on the ground looking for a feed, while overhead butcher birds were flying, magpies were singing, and little blue wrens were busy flying from bush to bush. If this trip had been for any other reason, other than to scout the area, it would have been very pleasant.

Thankfully, there were no obvious signs of any CCTV cameras on properties she had walked past. There were no shops or businesses in the area, it was purely housing. The housing estate was on large plots of land, most of the properties were at least half an acre in area. There were also a number of vacant plots that had no housing at all. Liz got to the address she had been looking for. Her heart started to race, and her breathing escalated. Just relax she told herself, as she slowed down her breathing. She was just taking her dog for a walk, after all.

The house was on a property that looked to be at least an acre in size. The garden was not well kept. The whole property appeared to be uncared for and neglected. There seemed to be a lot of overgrown plants and weeds that looked very dry and spindly springing out all over the place. Liz noticed a large truck parked outside a huge shed that was towards the back of the property and adjacent to the house.

This was definitely the property she'd been looking for. There was just the cab of a large haulage truck with no trailer parked in the driveway. Even so, it still looked enormous and towering. The truck, by contrast, looked exceptionally clean and shiny. Clearly the truck was well maintained by its owner. In fact, it looked out of place parked on an unmaintained gravelly limestone driveway, which was littered with potholes and rocks. The truck sparkled in the vestiges of the sunlight, set against the backdrop of a dilapidated dump of a shed. It was quite bizarre. It looked like a mirage, like it had magically appeared and would disappear at midnight.

It appeared that very little maintenance had been done to the property in some time. The house was difficult to see from the road, surrounded by a couple of large overhanging trees. She peered through the branches, trying to check out the outdoor lighting. There appeared to be a couple of rusted and corroded security lights covered in spiderwebs on the wall of the house and shed. The question was, did they still work, and if they did, how sensitive were they?

While Buster was busy sniffing a fence post, she took out her notebook and quickly wrote down the registration number of the truck and the position of the security lights. She did not take any photos because she had deliberately left her mobile phone at home. Although she wasn't doing anything illegal, all the true crime documentaries she had watched suggested that cops seemed to catch criminals as a result of their mobile phone location data. She definitely didn't want to leave a trail.

From where she stood there appeared to be no movement in the house, although it was difficult to see if anyone was home through the trees, though there was an old car parked in the open car port next to the house, so it was possible. Liz kept walking down the street until she found the left turn she'd seen on the map, she took the turn and walked back down the street that ran behind the property she had been looking at. Unfortunately, she couldn't see anything from the back.

There was a high fence separating the two properties. The house that was now in front of her had a beautiful well-kept cottage garden with an abundance of colourful flowers. Clearly these were people who spent a lot of time outdoors, so she'd need to be careful. The houses were not close to each other, given they were both on about an acre of land, so she doubted they could overhear, or see what went on in each other's homes. As she continued along the road all the houses seemed to be quite separate from each other, with large gardens and trees that gave each home a certain amount of privacy from one another. Liz and Buster walked back to her car at the park and got in and went home.

The next day after work Liz went to a cash machine and withdrew $300. Then she did the same as she had the previous afternoon: she went home to get Buster, changed her clothes, and drove her car to the same children's park as yesterday and went for walk with her dog. This time, as she went a bit closer to the properties edge, she noticed the old car that had been parked in the carport yesterday was not there. However the truck was still parked in the same position. 'Hmm,' said Liz to Buster, 'I wonder if the owner of the house has gone out?'

Her question was soon answered. As she was standing there with Buster, the old car pulled into the driveway. Momentarily frozen with fear, her body began to tremble, and she had to breath in hard to hold onto the contents of her stomach. To hide her face, Liz quickly crouched down and turned to give Buster a pat. This also disguised the fact that her hands were trembling uncontrollably. She pretended Buster had got his legs caught up in the lead, 'Oh you silly dog what have you done now?' she said out loud as she was pretending to untangle him. She told herself *just act normally, you are just a person taking a dog for a walk, there is no need to feel afraid.*

While she was squatting down, she watched the occupant of the car open the car door and get out; her first true sighting of Sally's ex, Nathan. He went to the boot of the car and opened it, lifting out what appeared to be a pretty heavy box. He looked quite fit, interestingly not what she had expected a truck driver to look like. She had expected a short scruffy man with a large belly, in unkept clothes. He was of average height with neat dark hair. There was nothing that really stood out about him.

He was wearing dark sunglasses so she couldn't see what his eyes looked like. She imagined them to be cold and cruel. His appearance was average, like someone you might walk past in the street every day and not take much notice of. But then again, most perpetrators don't have a sign on their forehead to identify them, and they certainly don't all look like monsters. Fighting the urge to confront him, she felt a shiver go up and down her spine. She wanted to yell at him that he was pathetic and no better than a bottom feeding scum sucker who lurks in the hidden depth of a grimy pond, but this would have been an insult to the scum sucker, she thought with hatred.

Nathan had been to the bottle shop. She could clearly see the heavy box he was carrying under his arm was a carton of beer. He walked straight from the car to the house. There appeared to be a side door directly next to the carport for easy access into what she supposed would be the kitchen. He didn't look around and seemed to be quite focused on getting inside the house as quickly as possible. Liz felt quite confident he hadn't taken any notice of her or Buster squatting there.

As she stood up the anger was burning inside her, it took all her strength to casually walk up the street at an easy pace. She let Buster sniff as many trees as he wanted while she tried to quell her rage. She still felt a queasiness in her stomach, and her heart was still racing from the experience of seeing Nathan, but any neighbour looking out their window would just see a lady walking sluggishly with her dog. She remembered with amusement a comment from one of the true crime documentaries she'd been watching. Someone had remarked that when the police say *nothing to see here,* it usually meant there was. She turned left and walked back to her car, feeling that the afternoon had been somewhat a success.

Chapter Seventeen

Margaret stood up, stretched her back and went to put the kettle on for another cup of tea. She looked at the clock - they'd been looking through photos for over two hours. There were three groups so far. The 'yes' pile, the 'no' pile and the 'maybe' pile. Margaret doubted the maybes would get a run, given the yes group had far too many already, and would probably need further culling. Her daughter was so lovely it was tempting to put all the photos in the yes pile.

'Oh, look at this one Maggie,' cooed Joy. 'She was such a pretty baby. You know you're still young enough to have another baby if you met someone. Mother's today are just starting their families at 40.'

'Don't be ridiculous Joy, that's never going to happen.' Though secretly Margaret had wished Justine hadn't grown up as an only child. She would have loved more children, but she'd never met anyone. She had accepted long ago it would just be her and Justine, until Justine met someone and had children of her own. 'It's last thing I'm thinking about right now Joy, and besides, I've not been on a date for years, I wouldn't even know where or how to start,' said Margaret.

'Well, there's that nice chap down the street, John I think he said his name was. I met him briefly when he left some flowers the other day, he seemed genuinely concerned about you. He asked me if there was anything he could do. He said he sometimes fixes things for you. He made me promise to call him anytime if you needed anything.' Joy said with a smile.

'Oh, he's just being polite Joy, nothing more,' said Margaret.

'Well, I got the distinct impression he'd like it to be more than just friends.' Joy said as she raised her eyebrows.

Margaret quickly changed the subject by picking up a very cute photo of Justine in a ballet costume and clutched it to her chest and smiled. She held it out to Joy showing her a photo of three-year-old Justine dressed in a pink tutu, ballet stockings and slippers, her hair tied up in a bun on the top of her head. Her hands held above her head in an awkward prayer like position and her knees splayed and bent. She looked like she was about to do a very clumsy pirouette.

Occasionally parents were allowed to stay and watch the ballet lesson. Justine was in the pre-school class with half a dozen other three- and four-year olds. The older girls love to help the little ones with their stances and steps. On one particular occasion, when the parents were allowed to attend, the ballet teacher had instructed the kids to be butterflies. They were running around flapping their arms laughing and enjoying the experience. Then the teacher had turned and looked directly towards Justine and said, 'Not an elephant, Justine.'

It hadn't seemed to bother Justine one little bit, she just kept flapping, laughing, and running around with the other girls, but Margaret was shocked. Justine was quite stocky for a three-year-old, with strong muscly leg, and yes, she was probably stomping more than gliding, but she was only three. At the time Margaret just smiled and said nothing, but on the inside she was seething. Especially when the other ballet mums giggled at the comment. It was not long after that incident, she told Joy with a smile, that Justine switched to Gymnastics.

Margaret and Joy had recalled family events, reminisced about their childhood, laughed, and cried with each photo of Justine. But after another exhausting hour, they had managed to cull the photos to around fifty. Totally spent, Margaret said she was going to have a lie down. She woke two hours later to voices coming from the kitchen. Ben and Sue had come over to see how Margaret was coping, and June from next door was also in the kitchen making tea for everyone.

Ben and Sue were only too happy to help out with Facebook. Firstly, they helped Margaret to shut down Justine's Facebook page, and then they both put the open invitation to the funeral on their own pages and said they would ask the school to do the same. June volunteered to take care of the advert in the local paper, hardcopy and on-line.

Margaret couldn't believe how kind and helpful everyone was being. It was hard for her to ask or accept help from anybody, as she never wanted to rely on anyone ever again. But she had to admit to herself it was lovely having people around, mucking in and helping. June had brought over a meat pie she had just baked for Joy and Margaret to have for dinner. Margaret insisted that they all to stay to dinner and went about putting on some vegetables. They all protested at the invitation, they didn't want to cause Margaret any extra stress, but she explained that keeping busy was helpful, and being able to talk about Justine to her friends was precious.

While eating dinner, they talked, laughed, and reminisced about Justine. It was therapeutic talking about Justine with a group of people who knew her and loved her. Margaret told the others that yesterday when she and Joy went to the funeral directors, she had noticed Christine, one of Justine's friends' mothers had crossed the street to avoid talking to her. Margaret had been a bit upset at the time, but on reflection she realised Christine's avoidance was not because she didn't care. She just didn't know what to say, and probably feared upsetting Margaret. Margaret confessed sheepishly she may have done the same thing herself in the past if the roles were reversed.

June knew exactly what Margaret was talking about. When her husband had committed suicide, she experienced people feigning ignorance. They would avoid the subject altogether, by saying things like *you're looking well June,* rather than saying *I'm sorry to hear about your husband.*

'I think people thought I'd fall apart at the mention of his name, and yes, maybe it would have brought some tears. But some people are so uncomfortable with tears, they think it's their fault, that they have upset you, but it is just a normal part of grieving. I wanted to talk about him. Oh, God look, it still makes me cry.' June said as she wiped hey eyes. 'I still want to talk about him and remember him. He was a good man, and I'll always love him.' They all nodded in unison and smiled at June. They understood only too well what she was saying.

On Wednesday Francesca floated into Margaret's home to pick up the photos and the background music Margaret had selected for the funeral. Margaret was quite pleased with herself for having the photos and the music all selected and ready to go. However, she was not so pleased with her efforts to write Justine's eulogy for the funeral. She had not gotten very far. She had written her thank you's to everyone for coming, but that was it.

Francesca had told her kindly that she still had plenty of time and not to panic. Just write from your heart. It didn't have to be eloquent, whimsical, or grammatically correct, it just needed to be her personal heartfelt farewell to her daughter, whatever that was. Margaret made a personal commitment to have it written well before the morning of the funeral.

Francesca had a surprise for Margaret. She was beaming with delight as she told Margaret and Joy about the butterfly lady. Francesca had a dear friend called Katherine, but most people referred to her as the butterfly lady. Her friend had a garden with a number of plants she thought were called swan plants. It seemed the swan plants were particularly attractive to butterflies to lay their eggs. When they were still chrysalids Katherine would remove them from the swan plant and take them into her greenhouse and tie them with a little piece of cotton to a branch she had placed there just for this purpose. She watches for the chrysalids to turn black, as this is the indicator they are about to break out of their cocoon and become butterflies.

When the butterfly first appears, they are very vulnerable to birds or any creatures that would like to snack on a butterfly. She had told Francesca it takes about four to five hours for the butterfly to dry their wings and be a confident flyer, but until then they were weak and defenceless. So, she provides a safe place for the chrysalids to turn into butterflies and then she lets them go. Francesca told Margaret she had spoken to Katherine about Justine's funeral and wondered if she had any butterflies they could release on the day.

Excitedly Francesca told Margaret her friend was likely to have around forty to fifty butterflies ready to be released and that she would keep them for Francesca to collect on Friday. Katherine would make small individual paper boxes for the release. They could give the boxes to Justine's friends and family after the service to release the butterflies in unison, if that was okay with Margaret of course. Margaret was delighted with the image of butterflies being emancipated. It was exactly what Justine would have wanted.

Chapter Eighteen

It was the morning of the funeral. Margaret had had little sleep, but surprisingly felt energetic. Maybe it was the relief from finally finishing her eulogy in the early hours of the morning. June had been an absolute trooper. She had been baking all week and had cooked enough sausage rolls, pies, quiches, and cakes to feed an army. After dropping off the baked goods she had gone back to her kitchen to start preparing the mountain of sandwiches she intended to bring. Margaret and Joy were busy putting out plates, cups, saucers, and glasses ready for the wake. They were unsure how many people would come back after the funeral, but they wanted to be well prepared in case everyone turned up.

Balloons and cardboard cut-outs of butterflies had been hung precariously from light fittings, and ceiling fans around the room. Margaret was wearing a lovely, fitted dress. The bodice hugged her trim waist and the long drop-waisted skirt flowed as she moved. Her cleaning job had certainly kept her fit over the years. Pieces of watermelon, purple grapes, oranges, and lemons adorned the dress. Justine would have undoubtedly approved mused Margaret. Joy had helped Margaret with her hair and make-up, it had taken 10 years off her. Joy had found a new dress with tiny little butterflies in the pattern. Margaret looked around the room with a satisfied smile.

The limousine arrived. Margaret would have been just as happy to take a taxi, but it had been part of the funeral package. Joy's husband Bill had arrived early that morning, having taken the red eye flight so he could attend and support Joy and Margaret. Bill's employers were not terribly understanding, they'd only allowed him to take the two bereavement days he was entitled to under the workplace law. Fortunately, the funeral was on a Friday, so it meant he could fly out Thursday night and arrive early Friday morning, and at least he could stay the weekend and not have to fly back until Monday afternoon. Joy was so thankful to see her husband; he'd always had a calming effect on her. Nothing seemed to stress him too much. He was tall and slim, with a very gentle and quiet nature. Although only fifty, he looked more like sixty. He had thin greying hair that scarcely covered his balding head, and he had a way of stooping that made him appear fragile. The stooping had probably become habit as Joy was only just over 5 foot, and Bill was over six foot tall. He had not been well for the last four or five years, and this had also aged him beyond his years.

Bill had proved his usefulness almost immediately. Margaret had been fussing that she just didn't know where everyone was going to sit. Although her backyard was spacious, she only had seating for six. Bill had suggested that they ask her neighbours if they could borrow any outside tables and chairs they could spare for the day. She'd smiled at him and said, *well you're not just a pretty face*. He grinned back at her and held out an imaginary skirt and did an overacted curtsey in her direction. They both had a bit of a chuckle.

Margaret had not known Bill all that well, and it wasn't just the kilometres between them that had caused the distance. Both were introverts. Margaret had thought about picking up the phone and calling him on his birthday, but it never went beyond a thought. It was much easier to just send a card, that way she didn't have to worry about how she would hold a conversation with him. How silly she'd been.

The neighbours were only too happy to assist with the extra furniture and helped carry it over and set it up. They had also insisted on helping to decorate the garden. Although the garden was neat and tidy, you wouldn't describe it as warm and inviting. The grass was regularly mowed, and the hedges were carefully trimmed, but it lacked any colour other than shades of greens. The neighbours brought over potted plants with colourful pansies, geraniums, and other plants that Margaret didn't know the names of. They placed them on the patio, and along the fence line. Margaret couldn't believe the difference it made. It looked so welcoming. After the funeral she promised herself she would add colour to the garden.

Margaret stopped suddenly. Fear had crept into her eyes. 'Oh, Joy what if no one shows up? I just want to give her a really good send-off.'

'That's not going to happen Maggie, you're worrying about nothing.' Joy flinched inwardly at the clumsy use of those words to her sister. 'I'm sorry.

Look if no one shows up, which I doubt, at least all the important people will be there.'

Margaret nodded with a half-smile to Joy. She reached out her arms and embraced her sister.

'Thank you. I don't think I could have done this without you Joy.'

'That's what big sisters are for.' Joy whispered as she held Margaret tighter.

As they released each other they both said in unison *you look lovely* then laughed at the harmony of words. They held hands and walked towards the limousine, with Bill following closely behind. Margaret felt a little more robust as she left her home with her sister at her side.

As the limousine pulled up at the crematorium Margaret could see a mass of colour. Balloons were tied to people's wrists, their cars, baby strollers, fence posts, just about everywhere the eye could see. There must have been hundreds of people gathered outside. It was a bit surreal. It suddenly hit her: she was here to say goodbye to her baby. Maybe it was the build-up, with so much to do and think about, she hadn't allowed herself to think too deeply about the finality of the situation. She was never going to see her baby again. She wouldn't see her get her first job, get married, have her own children. The emptiness suddenly consumed her. A dark cloud descended on her shoulders and sucked out all her newfound energy. Feeling panicked, she wasn't sure she could get out of the limo and face anyone. Maybe she should have taken the sedatives her doctor had prescribed.

Francesca was already there waiting for Margaret to arrive in a silky, flowing and brightly coloured sari with matching pants. She had a beautiful rainbow scarf wound around her head, with large butterfly earrings that glided every time she moved her head. By the look on her face, Francesca sensed Margaret was feeling anxious. She reached in to help her out of the car putting her arms around her and whispering in her ear that she felt Justine's spirit all around her, holding her up and guiding her. She told her that Justine would be forever young, and that she believed Justine was at peace with that.

Although Margaret was not a spiritual person, the words of comfort did seem to help her regain enough energy to get out of the limo. She was already fighting back tears, one or two had already managed to escape, but after those words she could no longer hold them back. She had a good cry in Francesca's arms.

She managed to pull herself together, blew her nose and attempted to fix her make-up with a tissue. It was a lost cause. The smudged mascara had given her the look of a frightened panda. She took a deep breath and walked towards the crowd of people.

There were people from the funeral parlour holding baskets and giving out clips of rosemary with a small card. They were asking everyone to fill out the small card with their names and condolences for Margaret. Had they brought enough cards? There were hundreds of people gathered around and chatting to each other, and although the crematorium was a large building, Margaret doubted they would all fit in. Looking around, she hardly knew any of the faces. There were a lot of pupils from Justine's school with their families, along with teachers and who she supposed were support staff.

Francesca had told her a group of people from Compassionate Friends were there. She explained that they gather once a year and walk in remembrance of children they had lost, holding photos or wearing tee shirts with the names or pictures of their loved one, as a sort of personal Remembrance Day.

Margaret looked over and smiled at the group, and they returned a knowing smile; suddenly she didn't feel so alone. Tears were beginning to escape again, so she took out a clean tissue from her handbag and quickly walked into the crematorium. There was some rather dreary music playing. Two members from the funeral parlour were waiting by the side of the coffin. The coffin had been placed front and centre and was covered in a carpet of brightly coloured hibiscus and frangipani, Justine's favourite flowers. Francesca had assured her that before they start, she would have the music changed to something more suitable for Justine. Margaret, Joy, and Bill sat down on the first bench to the right of the coffin. She just wanted a quiet moment with them both to gather her thoughts. She'd already decided she wouldn't speak. She couldn't possibly put two words together in front of all these people. Her thoughts were racing a mile a minute, matching her heartbeat. She reluctantly had given her eulogy to Francesca and asked that Francesca deliver it for her.

After a minute or two, the crowd started to gather in the crematorium. She could hear whispering, sniffles, and coughing, though it was extremely quiet for such a large crowd. She turned around and noticed the crematorium was completely full. Some people were standing at the back of the room, while others had to stand outside. Ben and his parents were sitting a few rows behind her. She smiled at Ben, and he gave her a nod. She could see he had been crying by the rings around his puffy red eyes.

The first piece of music that Margaret had selected was now playing. The song was 'Forever Young' by Alphaville. Margaret had not realised until she had done a bit of research that the original song had been written and sung by Bob Dylan, but she really loved the Alphaville version and so had Justine. In the background on a large screen the photos Margaret and Joy had selected were rolling through a slide show.

The first photo was of Margaret holding Justine just minutes after she was born. She could still remember that newborn baby smell. It was followed by a procession of other baby photos in all sorts of settings. Then Justine as a toddler. Justine dressed up as a fairy. A photo of Justine in her ballet tutu as well as one in her gymnastics leotard. Margaret smiled, her first day at school was immortalised by her wearing a uniform that was so big it lasted two more years. She looked so tiny and fragile, thought Margaret, with a huge backpack sitting on her shoulders and smiling right into the camera looking so excited to be starting school. It was hard for Margaret to pinpoint the exact moment she had become grown up, but the photo of her in a bikini at the beach with her friends seemed to show her in a different light. She looked so self-assured and uncomplicated. Actually, Margaret mused, she just looked so happy. She and Joy struggled to stem the flow of tears as the lyrics kept repeating the painfully poignant lie. The sniffling and sobbing had increased, and the rustling of tissues became almost deafening.

With a bit of relief, the music changed to a more up-beat song. Margaret had chosen 'Always Something There to Remind Me' Although written by Hal David and Burt Bacharach and had been performed over the years by many artists. It was the version by Naked Eyes that Margaret had preferred. She had heard it on the radio one day when Justine was still just missing. She remembered singing along to the lyrics at the top of her voice while crying uncontrollably.

The photos continued rolling through right up until the week before Justine had gone missing. The more up-beat music seemed to lighten the mood and help stem the flow of tears. She could hear people humming along as the snuffling seemed to diminish just a little.

Margaret already felt exhausted, and there hadn't even been any dialogue yet. Francesca welcomed everyone and thanked them for coming. She acknowledged they were all here to celebrate the life of Justine, who had been tragically taken from them far too young. She went on to talk about Justine, and the beautiful young person she was. She announced that Margaret had written some words but was unable to deliver them herself at the moment, so Francesca would speak on Margaret's behalf.

Margaret had started her speech with a line inspired by Shakespeare. 'Justine how do I love thee, let me count the ways' and then went on to described how Justine was loved, by not only Margaret but an entire town.

Margaret had so many humorous stories about Justine, but she wanted to find one that would be pertinent for today. Margaret had decided to write about the moment when she thought Justine had first understood the meaning of death. She described a time when Justine was about two years old. Their dog had unfortunately died that day. Little Justine had asked where her dog was and was told by Margaret that sadly Rusty the kelpie had died and gone to heaven. Little Justine seemed to be satisfied by that and didn't ask any more questions about the dog. But the very next day when Justine asked, 'Where's Rusty?' Margaret had reminded her, '*Remember Justine, I told you that Rusty had died and was in heaven.*' Justine responded with, 'What again!' There was an outburst of laughter from the gathering, and Margaret smiled as she remembered the day and Justine's innocent response, clearly, she had not understood what dying had meant. Margaret had then surprised herself by writing a poem to end her eulogy. There was not a dry eye in the room as the poem ended with the lines,

> *I carry you in my heart every day.*
> *I treasure the time we spent together in every way.*
> *You are the light in my darkest hour.*
> *Goodbye, my darling my little flower.*

Francesca asked those who wanted to say goodbye or place a piece of rosemary on the coffin were welcome to come up now. The music that Margaret had selected for this moment was Somewhere Over the Rainbow, sung by Eva Cassidy. It was a beautiful rendition, just Eva's tender voice and her guitar.

It was the end of the formalities. Margaret's last choice of music pulsed out. As the coffin slipped behind the curtain, and people started to head outside, the famous rift by Jimmy Page and the gravelly voice of Robert Plant from Led Zepplin's Stairway to Heaven sang out. 'Nice one,' Bill had commented with a sad smile. Francesca asked everyone to wait outside, as she had one more task to be completed before people left. She handed out small cardboard boxes to the pupils from Justine's school, as well as to Margaret and Joy. Bill had waved his hand away, preferring to stand in the background. Inside each box were two or three butterflies, supplied by Katherine, the butterfly lady. Francesca had previously asked everyone not to let their balloon go, as this wasn't good for the environment, she explained she had something else planned to symbolise Justine's release from this world and into the next. She then said to the crowd that had gathered outside:

'Life takes us on a journey. At times it is smooth and other times it is bumpy, and sometimes it is like climbing a mountain, but the death of a child is surely the hardest of all to grapple with. So please join Margaret and Joy in the letting go of butterflies to mark Justine's release from this world.'

She then asked those that had been given cardboard boxes to take off the lid and allow the butterflies to escape from the confines and into the bright blue sky. Although some had to be coaxed and encouraged by finger poke or two, it was a wonderful sight to see fifty brightly coloured orange and black butterflies taking off and flying for the first time. The crowd of people just stood there in astonishment, watching the flowing and twisting butterflies as they zigged and zagged in the air.

Margaret would tell people later that at that moment she felt Justine's spirit go. Maybe it was just relief that the funeral was over, but whatever it was, it helped her feel Justine was now free. Although Margaret's life would always be defined by before Justine's death and after Justine's death, Justine's passing had to mean something. It had to draw a line in the sand. A new start.

People started to come up to Margaret and tell how beautiful the service was, and how sorry they were for her loss. Although feeling both physically and emotionally drained, she reminded them that everyone was most welcome to come to her home for something to eat and drink.

Chapter Nineteen

Liz had completed her daily stretching; the movement helping to reduce the discomfort and keep her body supple. She really paid for it if she was complacent or lazy, with painful stiffness and excruciating leg cramps.

It was Friday. She was supposed to work a nine-day fortnight, with every second Friday off, but had a bit of a reputation for coming in on her day off. Claire, the receptionist-come-office Manager would always say the same thing while raising her eyes to the ceiling with a smile planted on her face: '*Go home, relax, put your feet up we can manage very well without you for one day.*' With a guilty smile Liz would acknowledge that she knew the office would run very smoothly without her, and she was well aware she was not indispensable, but she may as well be here catching up on paperwork than sitting at home brooding.

But today was different. She was definitely taking her day off.

After a long hot shower, she put on the brightly coloured dress she had bought for the funeral. She took out the blond wig from the box in her wardrobe and gave it a good comb. Next she put on the foundation that the girl in the chemist had assured her it would completely cover her freckles. She applied the rest of her make-up and pinned her own hair close against her head. She placed the blond wig on her head and checked herself in the mirror, pleased to see that the girl at the chemist was right: not a freckle to been seen. 'I'd hardly recognise myself,' she said to Buster who had been following her around all morning.

It was a strange feeling. Liz was not ordinarily one that looked for thrills, but she did feel somewhat exhilarated. She had stopped feeling angry a long time ago because it was destroying her. At some point you have to move forward. But this was different, she was fighting back, standing up for the vulnerable. I can do something to protect the innocent.

The funeral was at 10 O'clock. At 9 she picked up her large blue handbag and her pink jacket. None of her neighbours were outside in their gardens. Although her car was parked in the garage, and she had direct access from her kitchen into the garage, she still didn't want anyone in the neighbourhood seeing her in her disguise. She got in her car and drove about twenty minutes to a large shopping centre, where she parked her car. She had purposely left her mobile phone at home so that her movements could not be traced.

There was a phone at the Taxi stand to call for a car. She was aware that most Taxis had video cameras installed for safety reasons, but she was quietly confident her disguise was good enough that she would not be recognised, if it ever came to the notice of the police.

She sat in the back of the grey sedan hoping this might diminish the chances of a conversation while travelling, but as it turned out, the driver was a bit of a talker. She had told him where she wanted to be dropped off. He was aware of the funeral that was on today. He made a number of comments about how terrible it was, that young girls were not safe anywhere anymore. He said he couldn't imagine what the parents must be going through. He told Liz that he was the father of three girls and if anyone ever harmed a hair on their heads he would kill them with his bare hands.

Liz was only half listening to what he was saying when he asked her if she was a relative. She told him she was just an acquaintance of the family. They arrived about fifteen minutes before the start of the funeral. Liz paid the driver, who had introduced himself as Ken, with the cash she had withdrawn yesterday, giving him a substantial tip. He asked if she needed a lift back after the funeral. She told him she had intended going to the wake and yes she needed a ride. He gave her his business card and said to call him when she was ready to be picked up. Liz remembered she had left her mobile phone at home, so she wouldn't be able to call him. With relief, just as she was about to tell him she couldn't because she didn't have a phone, she a saw a phone box across the road from the crematorium.

Liz walked to where most people were waiting for the funeral to start. There were at lease a hundred people holding balloons and wearing colourful outfits. While she was standing there a young man dressed in a black suit gave her a sprig of rosemary. Then he handed her a small card about twice the size of a standard business card. He asked her to write her name on the card and any wishes she wanted to write for the family of the deceased. Liz took the rosemary and the card and when he walked away, she put the card into her handbag. She had no intention of using it.

Even if Liz hadn't been seeing picture after picture of Justine's mother in the newspapers and on the nightly news, Liz could've spotted her instantly simply by the number of people walking up to her and telling how sorry they were for her loss. There didn't seem to be a father present, though this wasn't a surprise, as the funeral notice had identified Margaret as the mother and had not provided a father's name. There was another lady with Justine's mother, maybe it was her partner, thought Liz. As she moved a little closer she could overhear what was being said. Margaret introduced Joy as her sister. Liz had a quick peep over her shoulder and felt a bit silly, of course she could now see the resemblance.

While Liz was standing there looking around, she noticed a large group of people. To her horror the group included people she knew. The group was from Compassionate Friends. Liz had attended several activities with the group, including the walk of remembrance almost every year for the past 15 years. She was not close friends with Sarah, one of the members, but she knew her well enough to say hello and have a quick chat if they ran into each other. This would be a good test for her disguise.

The call came for everyone to make their way to the entrance of the crematorium for the start of the proceedings. Sarah was walking directly to where Liz was standing. Liz had her dark sunglasses on, and to her delight Sarah walked straight past her without a hint of recognition. Thank God for sunny days, Liz thought as she exhaled a large breath she hadn't realised she had been holding. Although Sarah had been a bit distracted as she spoke to the person she was walking in with, Liz was sure she was in the clear. Sarah, it seemed, had no idea it was Liz under the blonde wig and large sunglasses.

Liz took a seat at the back of the crematorium. It was packed with people, with many having to stand at the back and around the sides of the room. She noticed the large doors had been left open for the people standing outside. The first song started along with a slide show of photographs of Justine as a baby. The song was 'Forever Young'. Although Liz had attended a lot of children's funerals and she felt she was quite resilient to the sadness and the sheer tragedy of losing someone so young, this song hit her most vulnerable spot. She kept her sunglasses on while she, along with many others, sobbed for her own losses. Her children would be forever young. The rest of the funeral was a bit of a blur through tears and memories of her own children's funeral. She heard Led Zeplin's Stairway to Heaven start to play as people started to shuffle and get up and leave. She moved along with the rest of the crown outside.

It was easy to spot the police at the funeral; they were the ones not dressed in brightly coloured clothing. Liz made sure she kept her distance, staying well in the background. There were a few people taking photos, particularly when the butterflies were released. She stayed out of shot, by turning her back while it was happening.

After it was over, Liz walked to the phone box on the corner and phoned Ken. He was there within a few minutes. She gave him the address of the wake. He asked her how the funeral went. She told him it was terribly sad watching a mother saying goodbye to her child. She paid Ken again in cash with another generous tip. She said she wouldn't be very long, just wanted to pay her respects with the family, and asked him if he could possibly come back in an hour to take her back. He agreed to return in an hour and would wait out the front for her.

Cars lined both sides of the street, there must have been at least fifty people gathering at Margaret's small house. Although the house itself was quite small it did have a large back yard, and as it was a sunny day, most of the visitors had chosen to sit outside. Margaret appeared busy serving food and drinks to everyone.

The house looked like it had been built in the seventies, with little if any changes. The front entry door to the house led directly into a small lounge room. Liz's eyes wondered around the room, drawing in the homely ambiance. Two dark brown lounge chairs that looked wonderfully comfortable and were clearly well used dominated the room. A well-worn overstuffed couch appeared to be made from some kind of light brown woollen fabric, with a handmade quilt slung over the back. Liz wondered if it had been a family heirloom. A large flat screen television sat on a modern looking modular unit and seemed out of place in the old-fashioned lounge room. Liz suspected that Justine may have had a hand in those acquisitions.

A lovely ornate wooden table sat in the middle of the dining room covered with plates full of food. The table had been highly polished and sat next to a matching glass cabinet that contained a jumble of drinking glasses, glass bowls, photos and evidently Margaret's precious treasures. A collection of photos in an assortment of frames sat on top of the cabinet. Most of the photos had Justine's smiling face among them. Some Liz had recognized from the slide show at the crematorium.

As she walked into the kitchen, Liz smiled. She felt like she'd walked back in time, right into the very kitchen where her mother had taught her to make scones for the first time. It had the same pinewood cupboards and speckled olive-green Formica bench tops. The floor was a terracotta tile with wide grouting. The pantry door was made from wooden slats, and it even had the same type of squeak when it opened and closed. Her stress levels immediately eased, bolstered by the familiar surroundings, she immediately felt secure. A sense of tranquillity swept over her like she was cocooned in her mother's arms, protected and safe from hurt. This delightful impression was born from a time well before all the pain and suffering had begun.

Liz's pleasant reverie was abruptly broken by the loud burst of laughter coming from outside. Liz noticed through the kitchen window the rather eccentric celebrant was flapping around talking to groups of people who were outside eating and drinking. She seemingly had a lovely knack of helping people express laughter and delight even in the gloomiest of circumstances. Liz loved her positive energy and influence.

She also noticed an abundance of colourful potted plants in little nooks and crannies clustered around the garden. It had made the garden look so charming, like something out of a children's fairy tale. Throughout the house and in the garden hung colourful balloons and brightly multi-coloured cardboard cut-out butterflies.

Liz found herself a drink and something to eat, so she didn't look out of place. She went up and spoke to a few of the young people who were standing around chatting to each other in the lounge room. They all seemed to be from Justine's school and had said they have been given the day off school to attend the funeral. Checking her watch, she still had about forty minutes before her taxi would be out front; plenty of time. After she finished chatting, she walked back to the kitchen and put her plate and glass directly into the sink. It was full of warm soapy water, because Margaret's neighbour June was already on the move and keeping things clean and tidy.

Liz asked June where she might find a toilet. One of the young people she had been chatting with overheard and offered to show her. She took Liz along the passageway to the rear of the house and pointed to a door that was right next to the bathroom. Liz thanked her and went to open the door.

On her way down the passageway, she had noticed there was a large group of girls gathered in one of the bedrooms. They seemed to be chatting with each other while sitting on the bed and the floor. They were picking up stuffed toys and cushions, hugging them and then putting them back in place. The young person who was escorting Liz down the passageway told her it was Justine's bedroom, and Margaret had said that they were welcome to go in and sit around if they wanted.

Liz went to the toilet and then went into the bathroom to wash her hands. The bathroom looked like it hadn't had any renovations since the house was built. The bathroom, like the rest of the house was spotless. The bathtub was a baby blue and sat next to a small white faux marble cabinet with a blue sink. No flick mixer taps in sight in this bathroom, just the old-fashioned metallic taps with their colour coded discs. There was a double mirrored cabinet above the sink. The walls were painted in a warm beige colour, which perfectly (and probably deliberately) matched the set of towels that were folded on the side. The floor tiles were a pattern of tiny light and dark blue squares, about the size of large postage stamps. Liz immediately imagined with fatigue the effort it would take Margaret, on bended hands and knees to scrub the expanse of grout to keep this bathroom floor spick and span.

After looking around the bathroom, Liz quickly locked the door and put on a pair of latex gloves that she had put in her handbag earlier that morning. She had a scout around the bathroom for anything that might look like it was Justine's. There were the usual things, moisturiser, makeup, toothbrushes, but she didn't know what belonged to Justine and what belonged to Margaret. 'Damn it,' she said in a loud whisper to herself. What was she expecting, everything to be labelled 'property of Justine, do not remove?' She opened the cupboards one at a time and again found just the usual stuff, toothpaste, soap, cotton buds.

There was something interesting at the back of the far-left cupboard. It contained a small nail grooming kit with a nail file, a small set of nail clippers and nail scissors. Liz picked it up with gloved hands and looked at it a bit closer. This was the sort of thing she was looking for. Something small and personal. It was very tempting, but Liz couldn't be sure that Justine had used these items recently. What if they were Margarets and not Justines? It was just too problematic.

Feeling a bit disheartened she carefully placed the nail kit back in the cupboard. She opened the mirrored cabinet that sat over the sink and had a scan. It contained things like tampons, medicines, Band-Aids, deodorant, again the stuff you would expect to find in a bathroom, but nothing that specifically looked like it belonged to a young person. She closed the cabinet door with a sigh. She had been in the bathroom for some time now and didn't want to draw attention to herself by someone knocking on the door. She thought she better keep looking elsewhere in the house for something that was obviously Justines.

Liz pulled on her jacket, which had large pockets that she casually slipped her gloved hands into. To the unsuspecting bystander, she could just look awkward. As she came out of the bathroom she walked instinctively into the bedroom where about six or seven girls were gathered and were talking to each other. There was quite a lot of traffic going in and out of the room. Some were just briefly walking in and around and then out of the room, while offering greetings and comments to the others already in the bedroom. It felt like a procession in an art gallery, with people walking around, standing in front of objects, and making comments on what they found interesting. They were all so focused on comforting each other they barely noticed Liz walk in.

Clearly, Justine liked the colour purple. The rug was purple, the curtains were purple and one of the walls had wallpaper with light and dark purple vertical stripes. The other three walls were painted a light creamy colour. The three walls were covered haphazardly with different sized posters. Liz suddenly felt ancient, not recognising a single celebrity or band.

There was a modern looking wardrobe and dressing table on one side of the room. It had been painted a stark shiny white, and the dressing table had a large backing mirror where Justine had clipped photos of her smiling friends. Liz walked over to the dressing table and saw a lot of Justine's things spread out all over it. A hairbrush that looked like it was full of trapped hair, a comb, lipsticks, perfumes, all the sort of things a fifteen-year-old would have used most days. The brush and the comb appeared to be part of a set, each had colourful beads glued over the handles. She was tempted, but they were too big to sneak into her handbag, and besides, someone would probably notice if one of the pair suddenly went missing. A lipstick might be okay, but she couldn't be sure it would have any trace of Justine on it, what if it had been one of her friend's lipsticks she had borrowed? She could see in the mirror that nobody was paying her the slightest bit of attention, they were all too busy gesticulating and talking over the top of each other, then dramatically hugging or squeezing each other. She just lightly brushed her gloved hands over the top of Justine's things, careful not to move anything. She wanted to appear to be to be just admiring Justine's belongings if anyone bothered to observed her.

She noticed a small wooden box toward the front of the dressing table. The box appeared to have leaves, or a flower pattern carved into the lid. Liz wondered if this might be a place where Justine would keep jewellery, or other types of keep sakes. She was praying it was not some sort of music box, which would spring into a rendition of Greensleeves when the lid was opened. It didn't look like a music box to her, and besides, if it did spring into song, she would just have to apologise and make it look like it was an accident. And then leave the room promptly. The box seemed like her best bet to get something small and personal.

Trying to keep her breathing slow and natural, she took out a tissue from her handbag while she hovered over Justine's things and put it in her pocket. She moved to the bookcase and spent a few seconds looking at the magazines and books, not wanting to spend too much time hanging around the dressing table. Three new girls came into the room and began hugging the girls who were already there, causing a bit of a commotion. They were sobbing and weeping and saying things to each other in a distressed voice like 'I can't believe she's gone' and 'School just won't be the same without her.' *Do it now*, she thought to herself, as the noise level would cover any sound that she might clumsily make.

While still keeping half an eye on everyone in the room, she moved back towards the dressing table. She could see everyone's reflection via the mirror. Her hands were trembling, and she could feel sweat starting to appear just above her lips. As quick as a flash she lifted the lid with her forefinger and with her other finger she hooked the first thing she could feel. She then slipped it straight into her jacket pocket, all in one speedy and efficient motion. She then, in a rather deliberate action, removed the tissue from her pocket, feigning the need for a tissue to wipe her eyes, but in reality she needed to wipe the sweat build up just above her top lip, all the while keeping a steady eye on the mirror watching the other girls in the room. Liz had noticed their eyes were locked on each other. They were all still chatting amongst themselves, still weeping, hugging and comforting each other.

Breathing a sigh of relief, Liz was aware she had managed to snag something that felt long and metallic. Maybe a necklace or bracelet. Now with the item securely tucked inside her pocket she hovered in the room for just a split second longer before she nonchalantly walked out. The passageway was clear, so she quickly moved back towards the toilet, closed and locked the door behind her.

Still visibly shaking, Liz sat down on the toilet lid and took a deep breath, feeling faint. She cupped her hands over the mouth, closed her eyes and breathed out long and slow. She must have sat there for a good two minutes, trying to stop her hands and legs from shaking. She kept telling herself, *you did it, you bloody did it. Oh my God you actually did it.* She almost jumped out of her skin when someone tried the toilet door handle and knocked on the toilet door,

'Sorry, I'll be out in a moment.' Liz said apologetically.

Quickly, she pulled out a brand-new plastic sandwich bag she had taken from her kitchen drawer earlier that morning and popped the item inside. She had a hasty look at the item she had taken. It was a silver chain-linked bracelet with purple stones in between that gave it a splash of colour. The fact that it had purple stones gave Liz some hope it might be a favourite, although it looked rather old fashioned for a fifteen-year-old. She prayed she had taken something Justine still wore occasionally. It'll have to do, she told herself, as she was quite certain her nerves couldn't take going through that again. She sealed it tightly in the bag making sure the airtight seal was secured. She removed her latex gloves and put them in her handbag. She then put the scrunched-up tissue in the toilet bowl and flushed the toilet. She put her handbag over her shoulder and unlocked the toilet door.

She apologised to the person waiting just near the door for taking so long and went into the bathroom to wash her hands, this time not bothering to shut and lock the bathroom door. As she washed her hands, she caught sight of her own reflection in the bathroom mirror. She smiled to herself, raising both her eyebrows with a mischievous glint. It was a weird feeling, like looking at someone else on the outside, but the same person on the inside. She wondered if that's what an actor experiences when they see themselves on the screen. It was a real trip to see herself blond and freckle-less.

She checked her watch: ten minutes before her taxi would be out front. She walked slowly back to the living room, where there were even more people now gathered, eating and drinking. She smiled and nodded at several groups but did not stop to talk. She gave them a quick general goodbye wave and then simply walked out of the house as if she'd never been there at all.

It took almost five minutes of deep and calm breaths before the shaking started to subside and her heartbeat was back to normal. She felt a combination of euphoria and apprehension. She traced her steps in her mind. She was sure no one had taken much notice of her. The house was still bursting with guests and there were more still turning up to the house as she walked down the driveway. She stood at the front of the house and waited for her Taxi to pull up. Within five minutes Ken had pulled into the driveway. She got in and asked him to drive her back to the shopping centre where he had picked her up earlier that day.

Ken did most of the talking as he drove her back to her car, but Liz was barely listening. She once again went through what she had done step by step in her mind. She knew after watching so many true crime documentaries, that mistakes were easy to make. One of the girls in the bedroom could easily have seen her but hadn't wanted to make a fuss at the time. They might be talking about her right now to Margaret or worse, to the police. What if the bracelet was Margaret's and not Justine's? What if it was Justine's but she never wore it? What if, what if, what if, was all she was thinking about during the drive back. She had to tell herself over and over to stop; that she'd drive herself crazy.

Liz got out of the Taxi, thanked Ken for taking her to all her stops and again paid him in cash with a handsome tip. She walked into the shopping centre and went straight into the ladies' toilets. She went into a cubicle and shut the door. She took off her oversized sunglasses and put them in her handbag. Then pulled off the blond wig, folded it the best she could and stuffed it into her handbag. What a relief to get it off. She unpinned her hair took out her hairbrush and brushed it out. Still paranoid, she flushed the toilet just in case anyone was in one of the other cubicles. After opening the door, she walked over to the sink. She took out a packet of make-up remover wipes and wiped her face vigorously. It took several attempts, but she was able to remove most of the foundation on her face.

The toilets were a busy place with a constant flow of women and children coming in and out. Music was being pumped into the room, the blowers repetitively being used to dry big and little hands. Conversations between stressed mothers and disobedient children being hurriedly moved on all helped Liz to relax. No one had the time to pay the slightest bit of attention to her. She washed and dried her hands, threw the wipes into the bin and looked at her reflection in the mirror. Looking and feeling like herself, she proceeded to the other side of the shopping centre where her car was parked and got in.

She pulled up into her garage and went straight into her kitchen and checked her phone. A couple of missed calls. One from her mum and one from work, but no messages had been left. She could call them back later. Her mum was probably just checking in to see how the funeral went, and if she was okay. If it was an urgent call from work, they would have left her a message.

She couldn't wait to shower and change her clothes, but she felt compelled to put the piece of jewellery in a safe place first. She hadn't thought about where to hide it. Probably because she didn't honestly believe she would actually go through with it. *Underwear drawer is a bit obvious,* she thought. Then she remembered a concealed pocket on the inside of her raincoat. She had only found it herself by accident one day when she was wearing it, and her watch had snagged the hidden zip. Perfect she thought, not that it was likely anyone would come looking for it, but she knew she would feel more relaxed if it was hidden somewhere discrete. She again had a brief peek at the stolen piece of jewellery before she put it away, still desperately hopeful it belonged to Justine.

Needing to do something routine and calming, she changed into her walking clothes and took Buster to the park. A light breeze had begun to blow the trees and long grass around. The sun was still shining providing a brightness that suggested the day was far from over. Small children were buzzing with energy, riding their bikes or climbing on the play equipment, laughing and bellowing at each other. Liz could hear them calling to their parent's, 'Look at me, Mum! Watch me, Dad!' It reminded her of her own children with energy to burn after being let out of school.

She watched the children for a while, the sense of loss still ran deep. She tried to think of the good times now and not the end, as she desperately wanted to keep the wonderful memories of her children alive. She still wanted to remember their individual faces and personalities, how their hair smelt when they first got out of the bath, how they felt when she cuddled them, how they spoke to her when they were excited, she just didn't want those memories to fade because that was all she had. And it had to be enough to sustain her.

She was jolted back to the present by Buster vigorously pulling at his lead, almost choking himself. He was trying to reach two children that were running towards him. With huge smiles on their faces, they asked if they could pat Buster. He seemed to have a bewitching effect on children, he would draw them in wherever he was. He loved every minute of the attention he received, and never seem to tire of the pats and hugs he was given. To their enjoyment, he responded to the children with whimpers of delight and a wagging tail. They asked the same questions most children ask dog owners: what sort of dog was he? what was his name? how old was he? This was exactly what Liz needed to bolster her strength and resolve, to bring her back to the present, children being children. As she walked back from the park, she was already planning her next move.

Chapter Twenty

Although Margaret was keen to get home, she felt torn. Leaving the crematorium meant leaving behind her baby. She told herself she was not leaving her behind, it was only her body. The Justine she knew and loved would be with her forever. She had memories and experiences she would never forget. The precious recollections of the things they had done together, the ups and downs and everything in-between. She had been warned that grief was a complicated process; she would have good days and bad days. The advice was to enjoy the good days and reach out for help on the bad days.

She knew Joy was planning to go home with Bill in a few days. Margaret totally understood that Joy was missing her husband, and he was missing her. She would be forever grateful to Joy for her love and support throughout the last few weeks, it felt like they had developed a genuine closeness and an unbreakable bond. She doubted she could have made it this far without her sisters' strength and resilience. She looked around for the last time at the vast numbers of people who had attended Justine's funeral. A sense of pride came over her; her daughter was truly loved by so many. Margaret was assisted back into the limousine by Bill and Joy, the expressions of satisfaction on their faces indicated to Margaret they felt the same way. '*Right, one step at a time,*' Margaret said quietly to herself. She just needed to get through the wake.

By the time Margaret had arrived home, June had been busy getting everything organised. She had the hot food in the oven, and the cold food out of the fridge and on the dining room table. She had the kettle boiling for those that might want tea, as well as the glasses laid out for those that preferred a drink. She had organised for a group of young people to walk around and start handing out plates, while others were handing out hot and cold food, glasses of wine, napkins. June was clearly in her element, grateful for her Army nurses training, it had taught her how to get things done with minimal fuss.

Margaret had tried to encourage June to sit down and relax, but she insisted she was happier when she was busy. She told Margaret, 'Go, mingle with people, they are here to talk to you, not me.' Margaret marvelled at June's organisational skills, she was already filling the kitchen sink with hot water and detergent so that people could wash their plates and glasses when they were done.

It was a small house with only three bedrooms, one bathroom and toilet, a kitchen, laundry and a combined lounge and dining room. The room Joy and now Bill were sleeping in had been set up as a study for Justine but was currently being used as the guest room. Margaret had intended to move into that room for the next few days, so Joy and Bill could have her room. The study was very small and only had a single bed. She was expecting some push-back from Joy and Bill, but she would insist. She could of course sleep in Justine's bedroom, but she was not sure if she was ready for that just yet. It was a strange feeling. It's not as if Justine was coming back, but it still felt like it was her daughter's private space none the less.

Justine's school friends had asked Margaret earlier if they could sit in Justine's room and talk together. Margaret had no hesitation in saying yes, as she knew this would have been fine with Justine. Margaret was even okay with her friends touching her things, sitting on her bed, and just doing what they would normally do if Justine were with them. She also had to admit she liked hearing the laughter coming out of Justine's bedroom: it felt comforting and natural.

Ben introduced Margaret to his parents and sister. They expressed their sympathy to Margaret for her loss. Ben's sister looked about the same age as Justine. Although she had only just met the family, she liked them immediately. It wasn't hard for Margaret to imagine Ben's family welcoming Justine with open arms. Maybe marriage and grandbabies would have followed. Not only had Justine been robbed of a future, so had she.

Margaret freed herself from Ben's family, with the excuse she needed to say goodbye to someone who was leaving. She needed some breathing space; she could feel herself starting to fall apart with thoughts of what sort of future lay ahead for her now. Awkwardly, the person who was leaving had said her goodbyes rather swiftly to a group of young people standing in the lounge room and was virtually out of the door, not giving Margaret a chance to make it over to her and thank her for coming. She didn't recognise the person who was leaving, but that was no surprise, she didn't recognise half the people that were here. She wondered privately if she was perhaps a teacher from Justine's school and was in a hurry to get back to work.

Margaret could hear talking and laughter coming out of Justine's bedroom and for a moment it felt to her like the world had stopped spinning and time had stood still, like nothing had changed. She hadn't been surprised that her daughter made friends so easily, always happy go lucky and at ease around people. She did have some of her father in her after all. People used to tell her her husband could sell ice cubes to Eskimo's. She had to admit, he did have the gift of the gab. It was probably what had attracted Margaret to him in the first place. Little did she realise at the time, it was also this trait that also got him into so much strife.

Justine blossomed in social situations, unlike Margaret who often felt ill at ease around people, even today in her own home she felt uncomfortable. She walked up the passageway and into Justine's bedroom. The room fell into a deafening silence as the girls all turned their heads and looked at Margaret. They immediately put down Justine's things and all went to leave.

'Oh, sorry to disturb you girls, please don't leave, I just wanted to check that you were all okay.' Margaret said apologetically.

Like the flip of a switch, the mood in the room had instantly gone from noisy and chirpy to quiet and sombre. Margaret regretted walking in and disturbing the girls from their lively conversations. She wondered how she could quickly retrieve the situation. She told the girls how much Justine loved having her girlfriends over, how much it meant to her they'd gone to the funeral and had come back here to visit. How good it felt to have them sitting in Justine's room like she was still part of the group, and then she left them alone. As she walked back down the passageway, with relief she heard the murmurs of a conversation beginning to take off again. She made a private promise then to Justine, feeling her presence slightly, that she work on her people skills and her awkwardness. 'I'll start right here, today,' she affirmed out loud, feeling bolstered.

With the essence of Justine by her side, and somewhat emboldened, she walked right up to a group of people she had seen earlier at the funeral but whose name's she didn't know and joined their conversation. Although it didn't feel natural, it wasn't as difficult as she had expected. She did more listening than talking, but it was a start. The group happened to be members of Compassionate Friends. They explained to Margaret that they supported anyone who has lost a loved one in any circumstance. They invited her to come along to one of their meetings next month and spoke to her about the walk of remembrance that was coming up soon. Margaret agreed to attend the next meeting, and she really liked the idea of the walk.

It was getting late, and Margaret was still moving around trying to make sure she has spoken to most of the people before they left. There was an army of people inside and out, helping to tidy up and put away the crockery. Every time Margaret tried to help, June would insist that she go and talk to her guests. Francesca floated over to Margaret and told her she was departing. Margaret could not thank her enough for how she had conducted the funeral.

Margaret was not surprised when Francesca told her that most of her colleagues prefer to oversee weddings, but not her, she truly preferred funerals. Although Weddings are a happy and joyous affair, funerals were the most rewarding for her, she informed Margaret. She told Margaret she had done her celebrant training about ten years ago. It was after the sudden and untimely death of her sister. They'd had the whole traditional religious funeral and burial, as that was what her parents' thought was appropriate for her. Francesca recalled it was the most depressing thing she had ever attended. It had not reflected her wondrous and productive life; in fact, it had been quite the opposite, with a melancholy and miserable atmosphere.

After that Francesca had vowed to become a celebrant who specialised in funerals. She wanted to ensure it was a celebration of the person's life no matter what age they were, or what the circumstances of their death had been. She understood that it is an incredibly sad and difficult time for most people and acknowledged that her methods and ways did not always suit everyone's idea of a service. She told Margaret she had performed over a hundred funerals, but a funeral for a child was always the most difficult to accomplish well, because it just seemed so unfair that a young life had been cut so short. Today, she told Margaret, it felt like a genuine tribute to a brief but wonderful life. Although she had never met Justine, she felt a deep connection with her now. Margaret gave Francesca a hug and thanked her again for everything.

The sun was beginning to sink low in the sky. Most people had left to go home. Joy and June were busy inside the house putting away the last of the food and drink. Margaret was out the front saying goodbye to the last of the visitors. Bill was out in the back yard with John from down the road, folding up and taking the borrowed furniture back to the neighbours. After everything was cleared away, June put the kettle on, and they all settled down for a last cup of tea. John had stayed talking to Bill, they both realised they had a keen interest in fishing. John had offered to take Bill and the others out on his boat. When Bill explained that he and Joy were heading home Monday afternoon, they quickly arranged to go out on the boat Sunday morning.

Margaret, as usual, was ready to politely decline the offer, but she surprised herself and agreed to go along. June was unable to make it as she helped out with the Ladies church group every Sunday morning, so it was only going to be the four of them. Margaret had not given John much thought over the years, though he had once asked her out on a date. At the time she had made it abundantly clear that she was not interested, and he had respected her wishes. She looked at him and thought with a smile that he had aged quite well, he had clearly kept himself in good shape. As Margaret sat and drank her tea with the others, she could imagine Justine smiling. And that was the moment she promised to live life for both herself and Justine.

Chapter Twenty-one

It was Saturday morning, and even though Liz felt like a cat on a hot tin roof, she needed to stick to her unhurried and regular weekend routine as much as possible. Even though she'd been totally exhausted after yesterday's mission, she had been unable to fall asleep until the early hours of the morning. It was nothing new, Liz was used to being sleep deprived and would regularly operate on only a few hours' sleep.

She went to her usual coffee shop and ordered her coffee and muffin while she read the newspaper. It was hard to concentrate on anything she was reading. Her mind was racing ahead and plotting out what she needed to do today. On page six there was a small article about Justine's funeral. The newspaper reported that the police didn't have any suspects in custody and were not chasing any new leads. It also reported that a re-enactment of Justine's last known movements was planned for Sunday at 6pm, as this was the same day and time Justine had gone missing. The police were hoping it might jog someone's memory.

Liz continued to read the rest of the newspaper but was not really absorbing anything. After about thirty minutes she left the coffee shop and walked aimlessly around the shopping centre. She went into clothes shops, shoe shops, bookshops, looked at stuff, picked it up, put it down, and walked out. She was not really in the mood for shopping, but she was trying to stay calm and relaxed. Constantly checking her watch, time seemed to be moving very slowly.

After about an hour she decided to go home and try to keep busy there. She put on washing, changed her sheets and towels, cleaned the bathroom, vacuumed carpets, and washed floors, all the time checking her watch. At about two she stopped to have some lunch. She made herself a cup of tea and a sandwich and took a book outside into the garden to sit, eat and read.

Although she felt hungry after all her activity, she barely touched her lunch, in the end she had fed most of it to Buster.

She was momentarily distracted by the phone ringing. She just made it in time before the phone had gone to her answering machine. It was her brother asking if she could babysit her niece and nephew next weekend. He and his wife had been invited to a fiftieth birthday party. Liz had readily agreed, she loved looking after the children, and told him to bring them over early so that she could plan something with them in the afternoon. Maybe they could go to see a movie or the Zoo. He was more than happy to accommodate her request. She went to get her diary to write down the commitment for next weekend. While she had it open, she flipped through the last few weeks, making sure there was nothing noted in her diary for the last few days that would divulge her movements… she wondered absently if she was being a little paranoid.

She checked her watch again for the umpteenth time, only 4pm. She knew the sun was starting to go down at around 6:30pm, so she needed to be ready to go by around 6pm. Two hours to kill. She opened up her laptop and went onto Google earth again to check the surrounds of Nathan's property. Before she closed down her laptop, she cleared her search history, though she'd watched enough true crime documentaries to know any computer technician worth their salt would be able to find her searches in about 30 seconds. But if it had come down to a computer technician trawling through her search history, that would probably be the least of her problems. It would clearly mean she had been arrested and identified as a person of interest to the police.

At 5:30pm Liz changed into her long black exercise pants and a black light weight windcheater. She put on her joggers, tied her hair back and put on a baseball cap. Buster was getting all excited, expecting to go for a walk. 'Sorry can't take you with me this time Buster,' she said while she gave him a belly rub. In one pocket of her windcheater she put two pairs of latex gloves, just to be safe she thought. In the other pocket she put the sealed plastic bag containing the bracelet. She zipped both pockets up so that none of the items could fall out by accident. She took a deep breath and tried to stop her hands from trembling. She left her mobile phone on the kitchen counter and left the TV and lights on in her lounge room and kitchen.

At 6pm Liz got into her car and drove for about twenty minutes. She drove slowly passing Nathan's property. She could see his truck and his old car were both parked in the driveway. There were lights on in the house, so she had to assume he was home. This time instead of parking her car at the children's park down the road, she parked her car about 30 metres past Nathan's property. She had chosen this spot because there was a large tree that partially hid her car from the road, and the tree made it impossible for her car to be seen from Nathan's driveway. The spot was also close enough to the neighbours' home to not look out of place parked there.

She sat in her car and waited for the sun to go completely down. It was a beautiful crisp clear night. It wasn't going to be a full moon tonight, but the half-moon that hung low seemed unnaturally bright in the cloud free sky. She sat in the car trying to psych herself up for the task ahead. It was a Saturday night, yet it was really quiet in this part of the neighbourhood. She'd hoped Nathan would be out. This would have made her job a little easier, but beggars couldn't be choosers.

It was now 7pm and the sun had been down for a while. There were streetlights on, but none close to where she was parked. Though her hands were trembling, she managed to put on one pair of the latex gloves, keeping the second pair in her pocket, just in case. Just in case for what? She wasn't sure, but 'just in case' made her feel better. She took the small LED torch that was attached to her keyring and put it in her pocket. She had been given this little torch at a home safety training workshop. At the workshop she had been advised to put in motion detection lights at the front and back of her home as a deterrent. She was yet to follow this advice.

However, the little torch had been quite handy, instead of using the torch function on her phone to locate her front door lock when she got home for work late, she had used the little torch. She also often used it in the middle of the night as it illuminated just enough light for her to see to get a drink of water or go to the toilet. She had also been strongly advised to purchase plug in or free-standing battery motion sensor lights for inside the home as well. Looking around while she was sitting in her car in the dark, waiting to sneak onto a property, she realised just how vulnerable her home was to intruders. She made a mental note to herself that she would get this done as soon as possible.

Back to her plan, she turned the inside light to off, so when her door opened no lights would come on. She opened her door to check; with relief no lights came on. She quickly shut the door again, she was so nervous, she was not ready yet, she needed to stop her heart from racing and get her breathing back in control before she got light-headed and dizzy. While she was sitting there trying to slow down her breath and telling herself in a confident voice that she can do this, she noticed the taillights of a car as it backed out of Nathan's driveway and onto the road. She could see it was the old car Nathan drove, and it looked like there was only a driver in the car, no passenger. The driver was almost certainly Nathan.

Maybe her luck was changing. Perhaps he was going out for a Saturday night outing after all. She waited for a few minutes, took a deep breath, and blew it out, then told herself *it's now or never Lizzy*. She put on her baseball cap and pulled it as low as she could to cover her face. She got out of the car and crept as silently as she could towards Nathan's property, making sure she kept close to the fence line. It was about twenty meters back from the road and obscured her from any potential passing cars.

As she inched up Nathan's driveway, she noticed the limestone gravel was quite loose, she was leaving footprints where she walked. Keeping low, she crept back down the driveway and pulled a small low hanging branch off a tree, and used this to clear her footprints as she tiptoed up the driveway again. Nathan had left the kitchen light on, and it cast enough light so she could clearly see the truck parked by the shed. She patted her pocket nervously to check that it still contained the bracelet. Although it was not particularly cold, her teeth were chattering.

As she neared the truck, she could see there was a large black spider web pattern painted on the front, and red parallel lines down the side, each line with an arrowhead at the end. The rest of the truck appeared to be mostly white with a metallic trim. From her crouched position she could see the steps that led up to the driver's door. She willed herself to take just a few more steps. She was so close now. All she had to do was climb those steps and open the door and shove the bracelet down the back of the seat.

She looked around, and as silently as she could manage, she climbed the steps and pulled on the door handle. 'Shit' she whispered to herself; the door was locked. She pulled again to check that it wasn't just nerves. *What the hell am I going to do now?* She moved around to the other side, climbed the steps on the passenger side. 'Shit, shit, shit. She admonished herself for not considering this. She quickly climbed down and looked towards the house to where the door stood that led straight into the kitchen.

She stood there for what seemed like an eternity, but in reality, it was just seconds. She put her hands up to her mouth and blew out a long breath.

Before she had even considered her next move she was creeping towards the door, almost like she was in a trance. She put her hand on the door handle and gave it a twist; to her complete surprise the door was unlocked. She stood there contemplating, with her hand still on the doorhandle. Should she? *'This is crazy,'* she told herself. *'I can't just walk into someone's home. I don't even know if there is anyone there.'*

At that critical moment, she got her answer. She could see car headlights coming down the road. She backed away towards the truck and crouched down low behind it, so she couldn't be seen from the driveway. Shit. The car pulled into the driveway and parked in the carport. It was Nathan, he was back. Breathing fast and with her heart thumping out of her chest, she imagined he could hear her. Not wanting to peek in case he saw her, she stayed low. She heard the car door open and then shut. She looked under the truck and could see his feet shuffling towards the back of his car. He made a loud scraping noise with his feet on the limestone gravel as he moved around. She could hear the boot open and then slam shut. By the clinking of bottles, she assumed he had been to the bottle shop. She could just make out his silhouette as he moved towards the kitchen door. He seemed preoccupied as he slowly scuffled towards the house.

Then the worst thing that could possibly have happened, happened. Her mobile phone rang. She froze. She panicked. She did not know whether to run or give herself up. Cry and beg forgiveness or feign that she was lost. Time just appeared to stand still. Crazy scenarios snapped in her brain in what seemed like a nano second. She had to choose. Make a decision. But all her explanations seemed absolutely ridiculous. Then somewhere in her foggy brain came a realisation. She didn't have her mobile phone. She had left it on her kitchen counter at home. She almost fainted with relief when she realised it was Nathan's phone ringing. He juggled the carton of beer as he stopped to answer his phone. She could easily hear his side of the con-versation.

'Nath,' he answered. 'Nope, I got a job tomorrow, startin early, I need'ta be gone by 6… Yep, probably be gone for a few days, maybe longer if I get a load to bring back.'

She could hear his muffled voice, as he walked into the house and closed the door.

She sat there for a few moments with her trembling hands covering her face, the strong odour of latex from her gloved hands making her stomach roll She moved, stealth like, back towards her car, ensuring she had brushed any evidence of her footprints with the tree branch as she moved down the gravelly driveway. She leaped into her car, and immediately locked the doors. Taking in a couple of deep breaths, she felt like she was going to vomit. She violently pulled her gloves off her hands and threw them has hard as she could onto the floor. She began to sob from the sheer relief of being safely back in her car. 'What a total cock-up,' she hissed to herself. 'You stupid, stupid woman, of course his truck would be locked.'

Liz drove home feeling dispirited. She went through every step again in her mind and continued to berate herself throughout the drive back home.

When she got home, she ran a hot bath and got in. As she lay there attempting to soothe herself, she thought about what she had tried to do, and started to lighten up on herself. *You did your best*, she thought, gently. *It's not your fault that you're not some master criminal.* As she put her face under the water, she suddenly remembered something Nathan had said on the phone earlier. She whooshed up into a sitting position, hugged her bent legs and put her chin on her knees, and with eyes wide open she sat there plotting her next moves.

Chapter Twenty-two

The next morning after breakfast, Margaret supposed it was probably about time to start going through Justine's things. She had insisted that Joy and Bill take her car and go off to do something nice together before they headed back home. They had decided to drive down to the coast for lunch. They had both tried terribly hard to convince Margaret to come with them, but she had told them she wanted to spend a bit of quiet time on her own sorting through some things. Joy had reminded her warmly that she would have plenty of quiet time to sort stuff out once she and Bill were gone, but Margaret insisted, she was going with her newfound self-awareness. She told them that today felt like a good day for her to start the process of adjusting to a new way of life.

After she had said goodbye to Bill and Joy, Margaret walked into Justine's room feeling quite strong and upbeat, she sat down on her bed. Suddenly and most unexpectedly she became overwhelmed. Her entire body started trembling, like she had just walked into a blizzard. She laid on the bed and hugged Justine's old teddy and sobbed unabatedly. It seemed like once the floodgates had opened, she could not control the intense feeling of loss. For once she did not battle the tears but allowed herself to accept the total onslaught of pain and grief. The old Margaret would have told herself to get a grip, that this was not acceptable behaviour. The new Margaret had decided she was going to roll with the punches, whatever that meant.

She suddenly woke up and looked at her watch, two hours had gone by, she had clearly cried herself to sleep. She sat up and rubbed her eyes and brushed the hair aside that had glued itself to her face. She recalled she'd had the strangest dream. She had dreamt about her old bike. She was given the bike for her eighth birthday. It was her pride and joy; sparkly pink with

a basket on the front and streamers flowing from the handlebars. In her
dream the bike had lost both its wheels, and she was not able to find them
anywhere. She was crying because she couldn't ride her bike without them.
She told her mother that a bad man had stolen them. The new self-aware
Margaret took that as a sign, that before she could get on with life, she
needed to strengthen her support and build a strong foundation.

She got up off the bed and opened the wardrobe and pulled out some
of Justine's clothes. She had started to make two piles; clothes that could be
donated to a charity shop and those that needed to be disposed of, when
the phone rang. It was the police wanting to discuss the arrangements for
the re-enactment at 6pm tomorrow. They told her it was definitely going
ahead, and they had found a young police officer with similar features to
Justine. She had the same colour hair and a small build. Although reluctant
at first given she was somewhat older than Justine, but without makeup and
with her hair up in a ponytail she'd surprised everyone just how much
younger she had looked.

They wanted Margaret to prepare herself for the shock of seeing someone that not only resembled Justine but would be wearing similar clothes
and acting as her. Ben had also agreed to drive the young police officer to
the drop off point he'd told the police he'd dropped her off. The re-enactment was to be televised on the state-wide seven O'clock news, but there
could be other TV news cameras, newspaper journalists and other paparazzi
there trying to get coverage or a statement from Margaret.

Margaret put the phone down after affirming she would be ready for the
police to collect her at 5pm tomorrow. She went back to sorting clothes
until her stomach informed her by a gigantic rumble that it was time for
lunch. She looked around at the mass of clothes on the floor, on the bed
and hung over a chair. Well, at least she'd made a start. With that, she went
to make herself a cup of tea and a sandwich.

As she put the kettle on, she thought why not see if June would like a
cup of tea. The old Margaret would have lacked the confidence for fear of
rejection, or not wanting to bother someone. But the new Margaret decided
if she was not available to come over, that was perfectly fine. She wouldn't
take it personally, but if she never asked, she would never know. She picked
up the phone and called June. June was delighted to come over and would
be there in a couple of minutes. They sat outside and drank their tea and
chatted about yesterday. June leaned in closer to Margaret, and with a glint

in her eye said she thought John from down the street was rather cute. Margaret immediately blushed, giving herself away, but said with a cheeky grin. 'Hadn't really noticed.'

'Well, I suggested that you take a good long look when you go fishing with him on Sunday morning,' June said with a sassy chuckle that made them both laugh.

They were still there chattering away when Joy and Bill walked into the house from their day out. June had been trying to convince Margaret to get out and join clubs, hinting that she needed to be more social. Margaret knew she was right but seemed to have an excuse for each suggestion. 'Join a book club,' suggested June.

'Oh, I don't read much.'

'Join a gym or yoga group.'

'Oh, I don't really enjoy exercise.'

'What about a craft group?' Suggested June, not yet prepared to give up.

'Oh, I'm not really very crafty, but I do like sewing,' Margaret admitted. 'Maybe a quilting group, if I could find one.'

June was satisfied she had at least gotten one positive response from Margaret and left it at that. Joy and Bill joined them outside and described their day. They had gone to a winery for lunch and enjoyed a glass of local wine. They had purchased a couple of bottles and suggested they open one right now and offered June and Margaret a glass. As they sat outside sipping a glass of wine, Margaret recounted to them the phone call she had received from the police.

'How do you feel about that?' Asked Joy.

Margaret knew the police didn't have any new leads, and it was important to try and jog people's memories for any miniscule detail, no matter how small, that might bring Justine's killer to justice. But she had to admit, she was worried she would get distraught with emotion on seeing Justine's look-a-like.

'Well, that would be perfectly natural,' assured Joy, 'but we'll all be there to hold your hand.'

'What else have the police been doing?' Asked Bill, feeling frustrated that his niece was so easily abducted, raped, and murdered, without any leads.

Margaret only knew what the police had told her. She let Bill know the police had interviewed all known sex offenders in the area. Margaret was shocked at the time that sex offenders actually resided in the area. She had never given it much thought before, but the police had informed her they had interviewed over ten known perpetrators. All lived within range of the lake, but all had solid alibis for the time that Justine had gone missing. She had asked them if they had managed to collect any of the murder's DNA from her body, but they had told Margaret Justine had been in the water too long.

The Police had suggested that Justine's phone had been deliberately smashed and broken into pieces and the pieces were wedged in the bottom of the lake with a large rock on top. As a result, they were unable to obtain any useful information that may have been helpful for their investigation.

What they hadn't told Margaret was that they were yet to locate her jeans and underwear. In their experience killers sometimes take a keepsake as a trophy to remind them of their accomplishments. Because stranger killings were rare, they were so much harder to investigate. Usually, the killer is known to the victim, and that's why they concentrate on family and friends. But in this case, they now strongly believed it was someone unknown to Justine.

When Sunday morning came around, Margaret wasn't sure it was such a good idea to have agreed to go on a fishing trip. She had finally taken a sleeping pill in the early hours of the morning after tossing and turning listlessly, and now she was still feeling the drowsiness that the packet warned about. She made coffee and poured herself a large steaming mug, hoping it would reduce her feeling of sluggishness, and give her a bit more vigour for this morning. Bill was clearly excited about going fishing, Joy told Margaret he had been out of bed at the crack of dawn, searching on the internet about the types of fish he might catch here. Margaret suggested to Joy that maybe the boys should go on their own. Joy suggested it would be good for her to get out and do something to keep her mind off what would be happening this afternoon.

While Joy and Bill were eating breakfast, she went into her bedroom and looked for something to wear. She didn't want to give John the wrong message. The problem was, she wasn't sure herself what message she wanted to give. She certainly didn't want to look like she'd dressed to impress, but at the same time she had to admit she wanted to look nice. In the end she dressed in a pair of knee length shorts, thinking she would likely have to step into the water, a loose-fitting tee shirt and a large warm cardigan, in case it got breezy. Thongs for her feet, and a sun hat to protect her face.

They walked down the road to John's house. Margaret and Joy had packed a picnic basket with sandwiches for lunch, a flask of tea and some other tasty things to share. Bill carried a small esky with a bottle of wine and a couple of beers. John was supplying all the fishing gear.

As they were nearing home, Margaret was glad she had gone on the fishing trip. Not because of the fishing, which hadn't been all that successful, with Bill catching only one small fish and John two, but because it had been a lovely distraction. She hadn't once thought about this afternoon's re-enactment.

While on the fishing trip she had learnt that John was divorced and had two children who both lived with their mother. He had trained as a heavy-duty motor mechanic and had driven trucks for years before taking a job with a large mining company. He had just been promoted to the maintenance supervisor for the large vehicle workshop. He works a fly-in fly-out roster of one week on and one week off, but occasionally on his days off he still drives a truck to help out his old business partner. He'd hoped to give that up now he'd just received a significant pay rise.

He had insisted against Margaret's protests that she take both the fish he'd caught. He told her his freezer was full of fish, and he didn't have any room for anymore. She wasn't sure she believed him, but thought it was a lovely gesture all the same.

John had insisted on filleting the fish first and said he would bring it round later. She reminded him she would be busy with the police later with the re-enactment of Justine going missing. He apologised for being so thoughtless and said if it was okay with Margaret, he would drop by on Monday night instead. She assured him he had nothing to apologise for and she would be very grateful for a visit on Monday. And to her surprise, she took the bold step of saying that she could cook the fish if he wanted to stay for dinner on Monday. He told her he would really like that if it wasn't too much trouble.

The police arrived at 5 O'clock, an hour before the re-enactment was due to start. They wanted to go over the details with Margaret. DS Andrews introduced Margaret to PC Jane Withers, who was dressed in similar clothes to Justine the day she went missing. Although she had a similar build and height and the same colour hair, she had a completely different face. Jane had told Margaret how sorry she was for her loss, and she hoped this would help to bring her killer to justice.

DS Andrews gave Margaret an update on the investigation. They still didn't have any new leads. He told Margaret they had been given more resources and had re-interviewed Justine's friends, door knocked all neighbours, and were still going through CCTV footage that had been expanded to beyond the original area.

They didn't want to give Margaret false hope, but every little piece of information helped them to build up a picture of what happened to Justine and might give them an insight into who may have murdered her. They told her they suspect it may have been a local or someone who knows the area, as you can't see the lake from the truck bay, he'd had to have known it was there, and how to get there. It wasn't much, but they wanted to let Margaret know they weren't giving up.

Ben arrived at 5:30. The police had returned his car and he had agreed to drive it in the re-enactment for authenticity. He would drop off the Justine look-a-like at the same spot he dropped off Justine. He gave Margaret a hug and they both asked each other how they were doing. Ben told Margaret he was finding it difficult to concentrate at Uni and was doing his best just to pass each assignment and exam. Margaret told Ben Joy was leaving on Monday, and she was going to go back to work starting next week, just part time to begin with. She needed to get some routine back in her life. She asked Ben to come and visit her as she wanted to stay connected with him. He agreed to come over for dinner one day next week.

Next to arrive was the news crew. It wasn't actually a crew, just one reporter and a cameraman. They also introduced themselves to Margaret and passed on their heartfelt sorrow for her loss. At around 5:45 Margaret got into the police car, and they drove to the scene. The police had blocked off the road at both ends with barricades and a police car with its red and blue lights flashing, so all the traffic had to be re-directed around the town to go north or south.

A large crowd had gathered to watch. The police had also set up barriers along the side of the road to keep everyone back and out of the way. Joy and Bill had walked down and were amongst the crowd, deciding they wanted to see firsthand the steps Justine had taken that night. A local news journalist was also there and wanted to have a quick word with Margaret. The journalist had just asked Margaret a couple of questions about what

Justine was like, when the police told Margaret it was starting and to come with them.

The police opened the north road barrier to allow Ben to drive his car through with PC Jane Withers in the passenger seat. He stopped at the truck bay and Jane stepped out of the car. Although they were not sure what happened next, Ben had told the PC that Justine had said she was going to walk down the road, cross over to the other side so that she could jump over her back fence, rather than walk all the way to the bottom of the road and turn into her street. So as Ben had suggested, PC Jane Wither as the Justine look-a-like walked south for about one hundred metres, then crossed over to the other side of the road and walked towards the back fence of Margaret's house. The cameraman walked along side getting the footage for tonight's news. Later Margaret noticed the TV news journalist was talking directly into the camera, probably recording the story for the news.

That was it, it was over in a moment. Margaret wondered what could have happened in such a short space of time that would lead to her daughter's murder. It just didn't make sense to her. It dawned on her that Justine had been so close to making it home. If she had been dropped off one minute earlier or one minute later, she may have made it. It was so unfair, that one minute could make all the difference to her daughter being alive or dead. She actually felt anger for the first time, in place of sadness. She was angry that someone had snatched her daughter when she was so close to home. So close to being safe. So close to having a future.

The police started to pack up the barricades and open the roads again to the traffic. People started to go back to their homes. The police offered to drive Margaret back home, but she said she would prefer to walk back with Joy and Bill. The police would be in touch with any updates. Margaret said goodbye to Ben and then walked over to where Bill and Joy were standing.

'How do you feel?' Asked Joy

Margaret told Joy how confused she felt. She looked at Joy, shaking her head while saying with tears streaming down her face: 'She was so close Joy, just a few steps away from home.'

'I know sweetheart.' Joy whispered as she tried to comfort Margaret with a hug.

Joy, Margaret, and Bill walked home in silence, caught up in their own thoughts. The 7 O'clock news was due to start in fifteen minutes, and they were keen to watch the re-enactment. Bill had fileted the fish he had caught earlier that day, there was just enough for a small piece each. Joy was busy in the kitchen crumbing the fish, while Margaret was gathering the ingredients for a salad, when Bill called out, they both dropped what they were doing and immediately went into the lounge room where a large screen television was tuned into the news.

Eyes glued to the television, the story took less than a minute to run, but it did get the message across, thought Margaret. She hoped it would jog someone's memory. They all made positive comments about how well it seemed to go, and how sure they all were that it could make the difference. Joy and Bill told Margaret they were immensely proud of her, and how strong she has been during this time.

They all sat there eyes still towards the television; the next story was something about a major city hospital that was in need of repair. Then Bill broke the ice by saying, 'How's that fish?' Margaret and Joy in unison turned and went back to the kitchen to resume preparing dinner. A bottle of wine had been opened; it would be the last time they all would be sitting down to dinner together for some time. They all commented on how delicious the fish was, and how much they had enjoyed the fishing that morning.

They steered clear of any conversation around Justine. Bill talked about what he needed to do to the house when he got home. Joy talked about how much her garden would have grown in the last few weeks and would be in need of some weeding and maintenance. Margaret didn't say a lot, she preferred to listen, and offer the odd comment or two. After dinner Joy and Bill went to pack their bags ready for tomorrow's departure, and Margaret did the dishes.

The next morning, Margaret had offered to drive Bill and Joy to the airport, but they had insisted on getting a Taxi. They said they preferred to say their goodbyes here and not at the airport. Joy had tried again to talk Margaret in to coming with them, to stay with her for a few weeks. But Margaret wanted to get back to work and get herself in a routine. With one final hug and kisses Joy and Bill left for the airport. Margaret walked back inside her home with mixed feelings of relief, that she no longer had to act like she was tough, along with a dread like a vacuum had just sucked out all the air in her house.

She was alone.

Chapter Twenty-three

Liz set her alarm for 5, what a waste of time that had proved to be. She had woken up at 4 and had kept one eye on the clock ever since. After twenty minutes she couldn't stand it a moment longer and got out of bed. She had been up half the night anyway going through the possibilities, the what ifs, the just in cases, all the while trying to formulate her latest plan in her mind. Could it work? Or would it be a complete waste of time? There was only one way to find out! The one thing that years of physical rehabilitation had taught her was to never give up. Your mind and body are screaming at you to stop, telling you you're not capable of taking one more step, but you do, and then you take another one.

After a shower she put on an old, faded pair of jeans with a plain white tee shirt, and an old pair of joggers. She applied the foundation makeup that completely covered her freckles and pinned her hair closely to her head. She took down the other wig she kept at the top of her wardrobe. This wig had medium length straight brown hair. When she put the wig on and looked at herself in the mirror, she was disappointed with the result. She thought the wig looked fake. It was too coarse and shiny and looked more like horses' hair than human hair. She was concerned it might attract unwanted attention. The wig was of poor quality, she had purchased it many years ago from a market stall. It was clearly not to the same class or standard as her blond wig. She looked through her wardrobe and pulled down a plain blue baseball cap and put it on her head. To her surprise, this made a remarkable difference, it took all the attention away from the wig.

At 5:15 She made herself a coffee to go. She couldn't face eating breakfast, the butterflies in her stomach were swarming at warp speed. She placed her purse, sunglasses, latex gloves, a packet of tissues, a jumper, a water bottle, and the bracelet still in the plastic bag, into a backpack and swung it over her shoulder. She left her mobile phone on the kitchen table and got in her car.

At ten minutes to six she slowly drove past Nathan's property. She could see him moving about in the driveway, preparing to leave in his truck. She turned her car around and drove to the children's park down the street, parked and drank her coffee and waited. After about 5 minutes Nathan's truck rumbled past. She pulled onto the road, hanging back a couple of car lengths. She could afford to hang right back, as there was only one road out to the main road, and then out of town. It was Sunday morning and traffic was light, but she managed to sit two cars behind Nathan's truck. It was proving far easier to follow than she had imagined. His large truck was hard to miss.

She followed the truck for about forty minutes before it pulled off the main road into an industrial area. She slowed right down to give him plenty of room to turn right. Then she drove on for about 50 meters until he was well down the side road. She did a U-turn and continued to follow at a distance. The initial high from an adrenaline rush was long gone. She was now running on fear and dread. She tried to clear her mind of the what if's and concentrate on where Nathan was going.

He pulled his truck up to a fenced off area with a security gate. A security guard stood beside the gate and waved him through, indicating where to pull up his rig. There were other trucks already in the process of hitching up a load. Liz drove her little white Mazda into the driveway of a small industrial cleaning business car park, which sat diagonally opposite the truck depo. From her position she could easily observe what was going on across the way.

She watched Nathan get down from his cab and walk over to talk to someone who was holding a clip board and talking into a handheld radio. Nathan had left his driver's door open as he walked away. Liz looked on with sheer disbelief, his door was wide open, but there were just too many people around. 'God dammit.' she said out loud as she hit her steering wheel with her fist in frustration. The first opportunity was no opportunity at all. There was no way she could get past the security guard without being seen, and she couldn't think of a plausible excuse that would give her access to the area. As she looked around, she could also see several security cameras pointing in all directions. Far too risky. She would just have to be patient.

She watched while a trailer was hitched up to Nathan's cab, all the while he was standing away from his truck and chatting to other drivers. He never once looked over in her direction. After checking the taillights were working, he pulled his truck out of the secured area, waving to the security guard as he left. Liz waited a few moments and then pulled her car out of the parking area and onto the road and followed.

He made his way back to the main road. His truck made a loud hissing sound as he slowed down to turn back out on the highway. The truck, now heavily loaded, moved sluggishly in jerky movements until it picked up speed along the highway. Liz sat back behind a four-wheel drive. It helped to obscure her small car from Nathan's rear view mirrors.

She began to worry she could be following Nathan for hours. She had a full tank of fuel, so wasn't worried about running out of petrol, but at some point, she would need to decide how long to follow him before aborting her plan. There would be no way she could follow him all the way up north, which would take days and be far too obvious. Besides, she had a full day of work tomorrow and she desperately needed to get some sleep tonight. She resolved she could afford to spend half the day following him before she would make the decision to turn back for home.

Ten minutes after Nathan had picked up his load, she noticed a large green sign on the side of the road that listed the next four towns in distance order. What immediately caught Liz's attention was the very next town was Lake Swan. What luck! She'd hoped Lake Swan was on his route, but until now she couldn't have been absolutely confident. This knowledge made her even more determined to complete her plan.

Entering the town, she passed a large welcome sign. The sign identified Lake Swan as a historic town, first established in 1834, though there had clearly been some recent developments. A newfangled flashy looking train station stood out like an epithet to the historic railroad that had once been the lifeline of the town. Though Lake Swan still held a certain quaintness about it. The hardware store was locally owned, and the grocery store was not part of the gigantic conglomerate of supermarket chains that seemed to be taking over the country one rural town at a time.

Liz continued to follow Nathan directly down the main highway that split the town in half. It was obviously a low socioeconomic town, notable by the number of houses that looked tired and shabby and in need of some urgent TLC. After they had passed through the town the highway seemed to open up onto some very picturesque farming properties. Liz could almost imagine she was on a pleasant day out driving in the country, if it wasn't for the dreadful feeling in the pit of her stomach. The fact that she was in the process of following Nathan until she had an opportunity to plant evidence to link him to a terrible and heinous crime, was not lost on her. Did the means justify the ends? She had to hope so.

With relief, after about an hour Nathan's right indicator flashed on. It looked like he was turning into a petrol station, just outside a town called Roana. It was a large state-of-the-art looking petrol station, with several dedicated bowsers around the side purposely built to refill large trucks. Clearly this was a popular truck stop, as there were several trucks already in the process of filling their tanks.

Liz was well aware that most petrol stations had security cameras pointed in the direction of the driveway to catch motorists who absconded without paying. Just about every true crime documentary she had watched, a suspect's whereabouts had been confirmed by being caught on video refuelling at petrol station. The cameras often had an expansive range of views from all directions and were frequently instrumental in bringing down criminals. Aware of this as a possibility, Liz pulled her car off to the side of the road well before the petrol station and watched as Nathan pulled up alongside a diesel bowser. Again, with exasperation she watched as Nathan did not shut his driver's door but left it ajar as he jumped down and filled his tank.

After paying for the fuel, Nathan jumped back into his cab, and started his engine and pulled away. Liz watched while shaking her head and rolling her eyes. She began to question herself, maybe this was not the best laid plan after all.

As Liz continued to watched Nathan, she noticed that he didn't pull back onto the highway right away, but instead cruised his truck through the petrol station and onto an unsealed track that lead to what looked like a well-used truck stop café. The café was situated around the corner and about two hundred meters past the petrol station. She watched him as he parked up in front of the café and got out of his cab and proceeded towards the front entrance of the café. Her heart started to race. She was almost certain he had not locked his door. She had not noticed any physical movement towards locking the door, or any blinking lights to indicate that a locking device had been activated. No question, this had to be her chance. She needed to make it work.

As she pulled back onto the highway, she noticed a small side street to the right, just past the truck stop cafe. She turned into the side street, drove down it for a few hundred meters and did a U-turn, so that she could park her car on the side of the road, just behind and out of site of the entrance to the café. Although she parked her little car facing the highway, she was confident it was far enough back to be out of shot of any dash cams. Was she being paranoid? Probably, but she liked to phrase it as cautious. It didn't sound as manic.

Checking herself in the mirror, she put on the blue baseball cap and sunglasses. She assumed the truck stop would have security cameras both inside and outside the facility. It used to be just banks that relied on security cameras to deter criminal activity, but now it was the norm for all businesses. She left her car and walked toward the café. There was only one other vehicle in the carpark. It was a white four-wheel-drive caked in red dust.

Keen to get a better look at what Nathan was doing, Liz walked into the café, hoping her disguise made her look like a garden-variety backpacker. She had kept her baseball cap pulled down and her sunglasses on. The girl behind the counter hardly looked up when she approached her.

She ordered a regular take-away cappuccino and tried to sound like she had a foreign accent and using the German word 'bitte' instead of please.

Liz being Liz was well prepared with a back story in case the waitress opted to start a conversation with her. She had Googled cities in Germany and decided she liked the look of a city named Leipzig. She liked the way it sounded when she said it out loud. And, she guessed, it was a large enough city that a lot of people had probably heard of it. The one fact that she thought might sound good to offer if asked was that it was the birthplace of Wagner. Her name, she decided if she was asked, was Claudia, she had been practicing saying it to herself in the car so that it sounded spontaneous and natural.

The waitress behind the counter informed her the cost of the coffee was five dollars and asked for a name. Liz reached into her backpack for her purse, and habitually went to grab her credit card, fortunately catching herself before handing it over. Obviously, the name on her credit card would not have been Claudia, the name she had just given the waitress. The bigger issue would have been leaving an electronic record that could be traced back to her. The waitress had not taken any notice anyway, busily writing Liz's order onto the lid of a take-a-way cup. Liz found a five dollar note and handed the cash over, then promptly walked away from the counter not wanting to engage in a conversation.

While she waited for her coffee, she saw another waitress bring Nathan a large breakfast with a big mug of steaming hot black coffee. He had grabbed a newspaper and was vigorously turning the pages, swiftly checking the headlines on each page, until one particular article appeared to attract his attention. He then seemed to concentrate on that particular article while eating his breakfast and drinking his coffee. From her vantage point, Liz could see he had parked his truck in full view of his window seat, obviously so he could keep an eye on his load.

The waitress behind the counter called out to Claudia that her coffee was ready. She had placed it on the counter and had gone back to whatever she had been doing previously. Liz grabbed a napkin out of a dispenser sitting on the counter and placed it around the coffee cup. She smiled inwardly, she felt like she was stuck in some sort of B grade spy movie.

She pretended to take a sip of coffee, and then walked outside. The other couple that had been in the café were now getting into their car and driving off to their next destination. Liz walked over to an old decrepit looking wooden table and bench that stood in a grassed area out the front of the café. It was shaded by a large gum tree and afforded a good view inside the café's dining area. She sat down and continued to feign at slowly sipping her coffee.

The aroma of the hot coffee smelt so good. She so badly wanted to take a big gulp. But why go to all the trouble to disguise herself and change her accent, only to then leave her DNA behind for someone to find. Again, she wondered if she was being paranoid. Probably, but she was determined to try to stay rational and not let her emotions rule her.

She rested her backpack on the table in front of her. The table looked like it had not been cleaned this century. It was covered in muck and dried bird poo. She could see where people had gouged their names in the rotted dry wood on the bench and table. She traced her eyes over 'Charlie woz here' and 'Linda luvs Paul' before she recovered her attention to the job at hand.

While Liz sat their faking sipping her coffee, she casually looked around for security cameras. She had noticed one inside the café, which seemed to be pointed directly at the cash register. And one other that was pointed in the direction of the emergency exit door. To her relief she couldn't see any cameras outside the front of the café. She opened her backpack and took out the plastic bag that contained the bracelet and put it in the back pocket of her jeans, all the while keeping an eye on the breakfast-eating Nathan.

His truck was only about twenty meters from where she was sitting. Nathan had parked the truck longways on the edge of the carpark and adjacent to the road. That meant the driver's door was facing the road and not the café. Even so, she could easily tell she would not be able to climb up to the cab and open the driver door without him seeing her through the café window. He had placed himself in the perfect position to watch his truck. Luckily, a row of densely leaved trees lined the carpark and obscured the truck from the road. The one positive was that passing motorists would not be able to observe her if she attempted to enter the truck from the driver's side.

Liz considered the possibility that she could walk behind the truck and wait for a moment when he was not looking. But this would place her in a position where she would not be able to observe him, so that was not going to work. She needed a distraction, she thought. Something that would take him away from his seat. She could start a small fire in the bin. Maybe set off an alarm. She knew instinctively this was possibly the best opportunity she was going to get today. However, she needed to stay calm and not panic. She could ill afford to take any ludicrous risks.

Feeling anxious and a bit twitchy from the pressure of waiting for an opportunity, she decided she needed to do something calculating to feel like she was getting prepared. She took out the pair of latex gloves from her backpack and put them on. She took in a large breath and felt better. It was one more step forward in the strategy. A planned and deliberate action was what she needed, to ease some of the tension she was feeling.

For her own sanity she needed to keep moving forward with her plan. Next she took the plastic bag from her back pocket and opened the seal, and just rolled the bag up into her hands, so she could quickly and easily retrieve the bracelet when and if she needed to. If she got an opportunity, she was ready.

Although the café was close to a major highway, it was deathly quiet in the carpark except for a scraping sound. Liz realised it was her. Her legs were shaking so hard the wooden bench was moving and making a scrapping sound. She shifted her legs and crossed them to stop the movement. 'Oh god I can't take much more of this' she whispered to herself.

While she sat there drowning in anticipation, Nathan finally made the move to get going. He folded the newspaper he had been pouring over, and put it back on the shelf, and lumbered towards the counter. Liz assumed he was going to the counter to pay for his food and coffee. A thousand urgent options simultaneously seemed to go through her mind:. *it has to be now. Not enough time. You may not get another opportunity. Do it now. I Can't. Yes, you can.* While her mind was zipping a mile a minute, she noticed he was not paying his bill, but walking toward the toilets at the back of the cafe.

It had to be now.

Upending her cup into the bin, she swung her backpack over her right shoulder and flew towards the truck. Her legs were stiff and sore from sitting in the shade, but that couldn't matter right now. Without giving herself time to re-evaluate the situation for fear she would be immobilized with panic, she half hobbled half ran toward the truck and tore up the truck's steps in an ungainly manner. She was now eye height to the cab. By this point she wasn't even considering the potential of being seen, she didn't care, she was just so desperate to get this over and done with. She pulled on the door handle, and to her elation the door opened. She was hit with an overwhelming smell of disinfectant.

Momentarily distracted by the strong odour, she quickly regained her senses and in one swift motion she slipped the bracelet out of the bag into her gloved hand and tossed it under the driver's seat as far toward the back as she could manage. Not even looking back to see if she had been spotted. It would be too late at this point anyway. She slammed the door so quickly that the momentum hurled her forward. She momentarily lost her balance and had to jump down awkwardly by holding onto the side handle and swinging her legs towards the steps. Unfortunately, she missed the first step but managed to get a toe hold onto the second step, and sort of slipped and skidded down the last two steps.

The muscles in her arms and legs were working fiercely to keep her strong and balanced. 'Shit,' she hissed under her breath, she had hit her arm forcefully and painfully on the handle of the door. Unsteadily, she almost lost her footing on the gravel. Her feet felt like they were on an ice rink. Her legs were reeling and staggering, going in different directions. She almost fell backwards. Slipping clumsily towards the ground. Somehow, she managed to regain her balance. It felt like it took ages to recover her stability, but in reality, it was probably just a split second. She took in a short sharp breath. Not looking back and trying to appear inconspicuous, she fast walked painfully and awkwardly towards her car.

'Oh my god, oh my god, oh my god. You did it. You did it. You did it.' Rang through her head as she leapt back into her car. Scrunching down, but keeping her eyes directly on Nathan's truck, she could see him walking nonchalantly toward the left side of the truck. She held her breath. He didn't look around or appear to be concerned about anything. Then with total relief, she heard the moaning and groaning of the engine, and could see the truck trembling as it thundered back to life. The truck moved slowly towards the exit and pulled back onto the highway. She watched with relief as it drove past, knowing it was on its way to its next destination carrying the bracelet tucked safely beneath the driver's seat.

Liz had a weird feeling in the pit of her stomach, like an internal dread, like something bad was going to happened to her, because she had done something bad. But she concluded, something bad had already happen to her, and nothing was going to change that. Therefore, surely, she was entitled to some credit for effecting a bad deed, if in fact it was a bad deed. Her intentions were good, she was trying to save a child from abuse. And besides from her experience, good things happen to bad people and bad things happen to good people all the time. She was just going to have to live with what she has done and somehow justify it to herself.

She ripped off her latex gloves and threw them on the seat next to her. It felt so good to get them off. She looked around to see if anyone was paying her any attention. Not a person in sight. The trucks and cars oblivious to her actions continued to thunder past on the highway in a blur of movement between the trees.

Liz threw the baseball cap into the back seat and slipped off the wig. She unpinned her hair and gave her head a good shake, raking her hands through her unruly red hair. She turned the rear-view mirror towards her, so she could look at her face and hair. That would have to do for now; the makeup would have to stay until she got home.

She slowly inhaled and blew out a long and deliberate breath. With her hands still trembling she started her car. She could've really used that wasted cappuccino right now. Driving cautiously down the highway in the opposite direction to Nathan, she looked for somewhere to stop and buy herself a well-deserved caffeine hit. She spotted a small shopping complex and parked her car. She dropped the latex gloves and the plastic bag that had contained the bracelet into a bin on the outskirts of the shopping complex on her way in to grab a very strong hot coffee.

Chapter Twenty-four

Liz checked her mobile phone as soon as she walked through the door. Two missed calls, one from her brother about thirty minutes ago, and one from a work colleague Kate, just over an hour ago. She then checked her landline; her brother had left a message. She called him back first and explained that she had been in the shower. She felt a pang of guilt lying to him, but what concerned her more was how easily the lie rolled off her tongue He had just wanted to see if she could change family night to Tuesday, as Monday night was parent - teacher night at the children's school. She told him it was not a problem and would see him on Tuesday at their parents' house.

Liz then phoned her work colleague back. Kate sounded dreadful; Liz could hardly understand a word she was saying, she was so nasally. She had just wanted to give Liz the heads-up that she may not be well enough to attend work on Monday and was concerned about the full day of clients she had booked, starting at 9am. Liz told her to look after herself and not to come in on Monday. Her clients would either be rescheduled to next week, or someone else will fit them in if it was urgent, so not to concern herself and take some time to restore her wellbeing. Counsellors were not often great role models for looking after themselves. Kate agreed to call Liz Monday afternoon to advise her how she was feeling, and whether she would need more time off. Liz emphasised light-heartedly, that she could keep her germs to herself, she could hear the relief in Kate's laugh.

Buster was at the laundry door whimpering and scratching for her attention. She let him in, and he immediately started sniffing her feet and legs. 'Yes, I'm sure the table I sat at earlier had lots of interesting muck on it,' she said to Buster while giving him a belly rub. She told him she would take him for a walk later, but right now she desperately wanted to remove the caked-on make-up and take a long hot shower.

After taking a shower and dressing in her walking clothes, she noticed a large and unsightly bruise beginning to develop on her left forearm. It made her reflect, ironically with gratitude, that she hadn't had a bruise as large as that for a good many years, but it used to be the norm. Still, she would need to think of a cover story like she had done so habitually in her past.

She put the wigs, the backpack, some old shoes along with some used clothes into a couple of plastic shopping bags. She decided she would drop them off at a charity collection bin on her way to work in the morning. As she moved the bags to the front door, she took another look and had second thoughts about the blond wig. It was too good for dress-ups. Maybe she would look for a hospital or cancer charity.

She was just about to pull the blond wig out of the bag when there was a loud banging on the front door. Liz almost jumped out of her skin. 'Oh God…' she thought, 'try to act calm, how could they have nabbed me so soon?' She took in a deep breath and opened the door with trembling hands.

Her entire body slumped with relief as she recognised her neighbour.

'Hope I'm not disturbing you? I've just picked these beans and tomatoes from my garden, it's too much for me,' her neighbour explained, as she pushed a bag towards Liz. 'Thought you might like some fresh vegies with your dinner tonight.'

'Oh, perfect thank you so much, yes how wonderful.' Liz stuttered nervously trying to cover her anxiety at the sudden knock at her door.

'Are you feeling Okay Liz? You look a little pale.'

'I'm fine really. I've just been busy cleaning, and now I'm just about to take Buster out for a walk, he's been harassing me all morning.'

Liz adored her neighbour, Mrs Finchley, but she could be a little nosy, and sometimes wanted to gossip about the other people in the street. Liz often wondered what she told the others about her. She had noticed sometimes the sad and sorry looks she got from some of her neighbours. Mrs Finchley looked at the two shopping bags Liz had left by the front door.

'Just having a bit of clean out.' Liz said with a smile. Not wanting to engage Mrs Finchley in further conversation she made a big fuss of Buster telling him that she would take him out for a walk soon.

'Oh, well I won't keep you then,' said Mrs Finchley.

Liz thanked her again for the vegies, and promised to bring over some lettuce and cucumbers from her own garden when they were ready. As she shut the door, Liz almost passed out with relief. How was she ever going to get through this, she wondered.

Determined to keep her mind busy, she decided to bake some blueberry muffins to take to work on Monday and then take Buster out for a walk. She could smell the muffins before she took them out of the oven. They smelt so good, her stomach rumbled and reminded her she hadn't eaten anything today. Although still quite hot, she wrapped one of the muffins in a paper towel to take with her on the walk. 'I'm sure no one would deprive us of one muffin,' she said to Buster with a cheeky grin. She put her runners on and strolled out the door with Buster on a lead in one hand, the blueberry muffin in the other.

She took in deep breaths to stay calm and relaxed during her walk, rehearsing over and over in her head the final step in the plan. She knew what she needed to do, and where she was going to do it from, she just needed to be clear on what she was going to say.

It had been an exhausting day, which had started incredibly early with little sleep the night before. The highly gruelling undertaking had started to take its toll on her weakened body. She felt drained both physically and emotionally. She was hoping the extra long walk with Buster would free her mind of the pent-up guilt she felt. What choice did she have? A defenceless little girl the same age as her beautiful Molly was in need of her protection, and she wasn't going to fail this time.

After dinner, Liz collapsed onto the couch with mind and body exhaustion. She turned on the seven O'clock news. The first story was about a domestic violence murder, the reporter announced it has been the tenth domestic violence homicide in the state this year, bringing the national total to over one hundred. She watched with sadness as they went through the long history of abuse and breaches of violence restraining orders. She yelled in frustration at the Police Commissioner, who the news reporter was interviewing, that nothing will change until the law allows us to micro-chip repeat offenders. The next story was some celebrated footballer who had been dropped from the senior team, and then gotten mixed up with methamphetamines. They showed footage of the footballer in his heyday, juxtaposed with recent footage of him being busted. He was half naked and making obscene gestures to the police. Just another one sadly, with so much talent and a bright future, ruined by drugs. She was just about to get up and make a cup of tea when the next story caught her attention.

A news reporter was broadcasting the footage of a young girl dressed in skinny Jeans and a sleeveless checked shirt walking down a deserted road. The reporter was saying that at around 6pm on Sunday the 12th a young fifteen-year-old girl was abducted, raped, and murdered from Lake Swan. If anyone saw anything suspicious around that time to please call crime-stoppers, and the number flashed on the screen. '*Anything no matter how small could be important, and I urge you to make the call,* repeated the reporter.

Liz's plan was to make the call from a public phone box, just around the corner from her parent's house on Monday night. It was one of a select few of public phone boxes that were still around, and last time she noticed was in working order. It was on the side of the road, in a quite secluded spot, just off an access road to the beach. And she had a legitimate reason to be in the neighbourhood on Monday night, just in case someone observed her in the vicinity.

It just occurred to her that family night had been changed to Tuesday. She just wanted to get this thing over with and go back to her boring life. She definitely did not want to make the call from near her home, or near her place of work. There would be public phones at shopping centres, bus, and train stations, but would they have security cameras monitoring the areas.

Suddenly, an image entered her mind. What about the public phone box she had used to summons the taxi driver after the funeral in Lake Swan? It would be perfect and much more plausible coming from a local call in Lake Swan. Now the only question was when? She resolved to stick to her original plan and call Monday in the early evening before it got too dark.

Liz went to retrieve her little black notebook from her handbag and started to construct what she wanted to say. A few scribbles later she was happy with the wording. She put Buster in the laundry for the night and went to bed. She opened her book and started reading, hoping it would send her off to sleep.

Thankfully, she had managed to get some reasonable bouts of sleep. Freshly showered and dressed, she said goodbye to Buster and drove to the charity bins to drop off her bags, and then to the office. Her first task upon getting to the office was to reschedule clients for her absent counsellor. Luckily, Kate's clients felt okay and were rescheduled for the same time and day the following week. She then checked her own diary and was thankful she had a full and busy day. No time to dwell on what she has planned later that evening.

With a clinical staff of eight, and a non-clinical staff of three, some part-time, some full-time, Liz had to be amenable with her schedule. It was important to support her staff on a need's basis, as well as provide structured supervision. The clinical team needed individual supervision sessions once a fortnight and a group supervision session monthly. It never seemed to feel like a month had passed before sitting down to the next staff meetings or the clinical team meetings. Liz also had to schedule her own external supervision sessions monthly to ensure she met the obligations of the funding conditions.

Like most small agencies there were also many other administration duties the manager needed to perform. Liz knew one of her weaknesses was her inability to delegate. She had been trying to work on this failing by giving some of her duties to her senior counsellors, but she still had a long way to go. It wasn't that she did not trust them to do a good job, it was more that she knew how busy they all were and didn't want to burden them with administration tasks.

The board of management met on the first Thursday of the month at 6pm. Liz was required to present a report to the board members on their financials as well as the day-to-day happenings of the agency. Liz had attended management training when she was promoted to the manager, and the number one take-away for Liz was to never go to a board meeting ill prepared. Don't go asking for decisions, go with recommendations, she'd been advised. And Liz had lived and breathed that advice.

She had put together a five-year plan and presented it to the board. She had wanted to take the agency into the 21st century with the introduction of an on-line component to the agency, as well as systems that allowed for inter-agency collaboration. Unfortunately, things didn't move as quickly in a not-for-profit agency as she would have liked, but they were moving forward, and that gave her a lot of energy and enthusiasm to take it even further.

The one downside for Liz was that with so many meetings to be scheduled in her day, she had little time to schedule client sessions. She was thankful for her small client list, as it offered her the chance to keep up her clinical skills and practice. She often only saw a few clients a week, but in this line of work even a few sessions a week kept you on your toes. After completing a couple of individual supervision sessions in the morning, Liz had one of her long-term clients booked in that afternoon.

She was halfway through the session when things seemed to turn in a different direction. Liz had been listening to her client Helen describing an event in the past, when all of a sudden, she took off her glasses and handed them to Liz saying in a childlike voice.

'I not lowed t'wear Helen's glasses.'

Liz smiled at her, realising that one of her 'littlies' had appeared. It was gratifying for Liz when one of Helen's child-like personalities revealed themselves in a session. It suggested they have a good deal of faith in her, as they were very shy and didn't trust many people, especially adults. She told the Littlun, who identified as Pippy and was only five years old, that maybe she would slip the glasses in her top pocket and keep them safe for when Helen needed them again.

The last twenty minutes of the session were spent with Liz and Pippy drawing pictures with coloured pencils. Pippy didn't talk much while she drew a picture of a toy dog.

'That's a lovely dog, does it have a name?'

'Yes, its name is Doggy.'

'What a lovely name. Has Doggy been around for a long time?'

'Uh hu, Doggy's always been here and he members everfing.'

When Liz asked what Doggy had seen, she just kept colouring in and shrugged her shoulders, and without looking up she just said, 'Lots 'a-bad stuff.' Then she looked at Liz and told her that Doggy was scared. They spent the rest of the session colouring in and talking about why Doggy was frightened, and why Doggy didn't need to be frightened anymore.

As the session came to a close, Liz had not managed to reconnect with Helen, so Pippy was still fronting. Liz booked another appointment and popped the appointment card in her client's top pocket along with the glasses for Helen. Still a little concerned that Helen had not reappeared, Liz walked Pippy out of the office. Pippy had told Liz she was being picked up in the car park. When Liz asked her what type of car she needed to look out for, she said, 'A blue car.' Liz smiled and walked Pippy out towards the carpark. As Liz was walking Pippy out she grabbed her hand. They walked hand in hand out to the car park, where thankfully Helen's partner was waiting, in a blue car. Liz had met Helen's partner before and recognised her as she stepped out of the car. She walked over to Liz and noticed the hand holding and said with a grin to Liz. 'Mmm, looks like we are going for ice cream.'

The rest of the afternoon seemed to wiz past. Liz could hear people saying goodnight, see you tomorrow. She checked her watch, it was 4:30 already, where had the rest of the day gone? She packed up her things and locked her files away. She had a quick look at her diary for the next couple of days. Tomorrow looked quite hectic. Liz and Karen had a group therapy session for the entire morning. Liz had a new client booked in the afternoon. It had been a long time since she had been able to take someone off the waiting list. She had finished up with one of her long-term clients last week and wanted to fill the regular spot with a new client. Wednesday and Thursday had been blocked out with prep time and interviews. She flicked over to both days quickly and noticed she had five interviews spread over the two days. 'Oh that's right,' she muttered to herself, she had forgotten they were interviewing for a new counsellor.

Liz got into her car; her day had been so frantic she'd had little time to worry about what she was about to do. Up until now, she could stop and there would be little consequence for what she had done. But after tonight there would be no going back. She had to ask herself, do the ends justify the means? Could she be saving one child, but risking others? If her plan worked, she would have to live with consequences. That a murderer could roam free, to do it again.

Chances are, she told herself, it would only delay the investigation. It would just throw the police a bit of a curve ball, shine some light on Nathan as a possible suspect. At best, she told herself, it would keep him busy and pre-occupied, not wanting to do anything that might bring more attention to himself. That was the ultimate goal, Liz told herself. Yes, there would always been questions about how the bracelet got into Nathan's truck, but once they clear him, she reassured herself, the police would just get on with their investigation and find the real murderer. It would just buy them a bit more time to keep Lilly safe, while continuing to work on her protective behaviours. She was convinced that Nathan would need to be on his best behaviour with both Lilly and her brother while the police were breathing down his neck. He wouldn't want Sally turning up to the police station again with more accusations of abuse.

These questions and answers were going around and around in her head as she drove out to Lake Swan, so much so, she had arrived and couldn't recall the drive. The sun had just started to go down when she pulled into the crematorium carpark. There were a couple of other cars parked here and there, so her car didn't look out of place. She assumed the cars belong to either people working at the crematorium, or they belong to visitors, who were probably visiting the beautiful grounds where the ashes of their loved ones had been placed in Rose Gardens or the likes.

She took out her black notebook and turned to her scribbles from last night and read and practiced what she was going to say. She said it out loud in several different accents. She gave a nervous giggle, then admonished herself: this was serious. But it did help her to relax somewhat. She practiced again, keeping her voice a couple of tones lower than normal. When she was happy with how it sounded, she put the notebook back into her hand-bag and stepped out of her car, and quickly walked across the road to the public phone box.

She went into the booth and turned so her back was facing the road. She took the notebook out of her handbag and opened it to the page with her scribbles and the phone number she needed to call. She wasn't sure if there would be a person manning the number or if it would just be a recording. She took a deep shaky breath. By now her heart was racing, her breathing was rapid, and her hands were trembling so much, she wondered if she could keep the notebook still enough to read the words she had written.

She took a deep breath, removed a tissue from her handbag to cover her fingertips while dialling the toll-free number. To Liz's horror, it was an-swered right away, by a real person and not a recording. This just made her panic. Her first thought was to put the phone down, and that was exactly what she did. 'Shit, you bloody idiot,' she admonished herself.

She took a deep breath, trying to calm herself. At least she now knew it was going to be answered by a real person. She blew out a long breath. 'Okay take two.' This time without feeling panicky, she wrapped her fingers in the tissue and dialled the number. When it was answered, instead of hang-ing up in a panic, she read out what she had written in a calm and emotionless manner, trying to keep her voice an octave or two lower than normal.

'I don't want to give my name, but after watching the re-enactment last night on the 7 O'clock news it reminded me that on the night that young girl went missing in Lake Swan, I saw a large truck parked in the truck bay. The cab was mostly white, with two red stripes down the side and a black spider's web type pattern painted across the front.'

She hung up before anyone could ask questions. Surprisingly feeling rather calm, she casually walked towards her car and got in. She went to put the notebook back in her handbag but had a better idea. Opening the book, she tore out the all the pages that contained any information about Nathan, his address, the description of his truck. Getting out of her car once more she crossed the carpark towards a large rubbish bin and tore the pages into tiny pieces and dropped them in and coolly walked back to her car. She wondered if it would all hit her later, but at the moment she had a weird feeling like she was a superhero and she had just saved the world from a disaster. No, it's more personal than that, she thought, I don't feel so powerless anymore.

Although she was feeling quite fearless, she drove home conservatively, not wanting to attract any attention by receiving a speeding fine or being pulled over for a random breath test. Liz had been pulled over a few weeks ago for a random breath test while driving home from work. She had not had anything to drink, so had nothing to fear, but had still felt extremely nervous. It was probably the way she had been brought up, to do as you're told and not to question authority, as somebody else always knew better than you.

That was probably why on some level she couldn't believe what she had done. She was not a risk taker, but she guessed there are some things that just push your limits to the edge and give you the courage you never thought you had. Or was it stupidity? She could be arrested and charged with perverting the course of justice. Probably even go to prison. She could justify it to herself alright, but how many others would see it her way? After all the law is the law.

As she parked her car in the garage and turned off the engine, a feeling of relief washed over her. She was home, back to her sanctuary, her safe place. The feelings of exhilaration had long gone. She made herself an omelette for dinner. She sat on the couch with Buster at her feet while she tried to concentrate on the television show playing. She gave up after an hour and went to bed with her book.

Chapter Twenty-five

Later that morning DS Andrews called Margaret to tell her he thought she had done really well during yesterday's re-enactment. It couldn't have been easy for her he'd said, but thought it had been well worth it, as there had been over thirty-five calls to Crime stoppers so far, and he expected more to come in over the next few days. He told Margaret his team would be reviewing all the calls this week, and if they had any new leads he would let her know as soon as he could. He also wanted to let her know that they had approval to offer a reward for information leading to the arrest and charges for Justine's murder. He told her there would be posters with Justine's picture placed around the area where she had gone missing, with a phone number to call with information. He hoped seeing her picture around wouldn't upset Margaret too much. He promised her sincerely that Justine's murder would not be put on the backburner, in fact it was quite the opposite, his Superintendent was asking for more resources to assist in this case. Margaret thanked the DS for his call and the update.

After Margaret had stripped the beds and put all sheets and towels in the washing machine, she took a break to have lunch. John would be there for dinner in about five hours, and she was already feeling uneasy. It had been fine when Joy and Bill were here, as she wasn't under pressure to keep the conversation going. But now it would be Margaret alone with John, and she was worried she wouldn't be able to sustain her side of the conversation all night.

At 5:30pm Margaret heard a knock on her front door. She nervously smoothed down her hair. She usually tied it back in a ponytail but had decided to leave it untied for a change. Was that a mistake? Oh God, she told herself *stop second guessing every decision you make.* She had a quick look in the mirror as she walked past; to reassure herself her hair was fine the way it was. She glanced at what she was wearing and thought with a grin, Justine would have shaken her head in disgust at her outfit. Justine had always referred to her dress style as looking like she was wearing a tent. She had to admit her dresses were shapeless and loose fitting. She had always felt and probably acted older than her years. Maybe having Justine when she was young had done that to her. There was no such thing as a yummy mummy back in her day. Anyway, she always enjoyed spending most of her pitiful allowance on clothes for her baby.

Margaret had never had the money to keep up with what was trendy, luckily, she had never really given a lot of thought to what was in fashion. She recalled feeling very self-conscious in anything that revealed her curves. As long as what she wore was comfortable, she was happy. She wondered where exactly that had come from? Her childhood? Her marriage? When looking back at photos of herself it was clear that right from her early twenties, she had dressed like she was middle aged. There weren't any photos of her in tight little shorts, miniskirts, or body-hugging knitted tops. All her outfits seemed to be sensible, unappealing, and dull. Alex used to comment that she looked like a slut if she wore make-up or dressed in anything other than her unflattering clothes out in public. He was constantly on her back, asking who she was trying to impress. In the end she guessed it was just easier to dress like a granny than argue with him all the time. And this had just became a habit. She reminded herself she was thirty-seven, and yes maybe Justine was right, it was time she dressed like she was still young and attractive.

She answered the door. John looked nice, dressed in a plain button-down shirt, jeans and loafers. In one hand he had a bottle of white wine and a bunch of flowers. In the other hand he had the filleted fish and some sort of gooey substance in a plastic container. It turned out the gooey substance was a beer batter John had made. Margaret accepted the flowers appreciatively and looked for a vase. John looked around the room; it was still filled with flowers from the wake and funeral.

'Sorry, you probably don't want any more flowers.' John said sheepishly.

'Oh, no I love flowers, please don't apologise for a lovely gesture, they're beautiful.'

Margaret managed to find an empty vase and put the flowers on the table. She took the fish and the batter into the kitchen and handed John two wine glasses so he could pour them both a drink. Margaret had already made a salad and had smashed potatoes baking in the oven. She floured the fish and then dunked them into the batter ready for frying. Feeling a bit awkward Margaret took a large sip of her wine. John broke the ice by asking her where she went to school, because he didn't think it was likely she'd been local. It was a great question to break the ice. Margaret told him about her early days in school and that she had wanted to be a vet, until she realised all the years she would need to study. Her mother had suggested maybe vet nursing would suit her better, and that was it, Margaret laughed, she had decided at eight years old what she would do for a career. But things changed, she told John soberly, boyfriends and a baby came along, and that was the end of her dream.

John talked about his early days. He was not a good student. His parents told him he could leave school if he got a job, so he went out and got himself an apprenticeship as a heavy-duty diesel mechanic. He loved it as soon as he started. He enjoyed fixing engines, maintaining, and servicing vehicles. He even got to drive the odd big rig now and again he said with a grin.

By the second glass of wine, Margaret was feeling more relaxed and a lot less self-conscious than she had been. Margaret was surprised how easy the conversation was with John. After they had eaten, he helped Margaret with the dishes, all the while talking about life in general, steering clear of topics like children, death, and divorce.

'Ya know Maggie,' he said. Margaret had told him to call her Maggie. 'It's not too late for your dream.'

Margaret looked at him strangely. 'What dream?' She asked a little confused.

'A career change, vet nursing. You could study part-time at the local technical college while you work.' John suggested with a smile.

Margaret launched into a thousand and one reasons why she couldn't possibly do that, but she sounded unconvincing, even to herself. What was stopping her? She looked at John and said in barely more than a whisper. 'I've always played it safe. I'm not like you. I'm not a risk taker. I don't know how.'

John just gave Margaret a knowing smile and laughed at her assessment of him as a risk taker. He reassured her he didn't exactly live on the edge. He didn't take unnecessary risks, he made calculated decisions. He had learnt how to evaluate the situation and hope for the best, while planning for the worst. He didn't always get it right, but that was okay. What he really wanted to tell Margaret was that he had made plenty of mistakes, but as long as you learn from your mistakes it was okay. However, given the recent events he didn't want to go there. He just left it at that. It was time to go, he told Margaret, as he got out of the chair he was sitting in. He asked Margaret to think about what he had said about study. She said she would give it some thought. They both seemed to have enjoyed each other's company. John said they should do it again, but next time he would cook.

'I'll looked forward to that.' Margaret said with a cheeky grin.

They both said their goodnights. It was 9:30, they'd been talking for four hours, Margaret couldn't believe how easy the conversation had flowed. She didn't feel like going to bed just yet, she wasn't feeling particularly sleepy, but she didn't feel like watching TV either. As she wondered past the study, she looked at the computer sitting there, and sat down and turned it on. I'll just have a quick look at what I would need to do to study vet nursing she told herself. Just in case sometime in the future I get brave enough to try.

Margaret woke up the next day feeling low. She had been warned she would have good days and bad days, and that it was all part of loss and grief. Some days it felt like the reason to get up out of bed each day had gone, while other days it felt like she was turning a corner and felt a need to do something so that Justine's short life mattered. Today was a bad day. The phone had rung several times, but she just didn't want to talk to anyone, feeling on the verge of tears and knowing anything small was likely to tip her over the edge. She wasn't sure how to get herself out of this mind set. Maybe talking to someone might be the pathway out of this deep dark hole she feared she was slipping into.

In the end she decided to call her neighbour June, but unfortunately the call had gone unanswered. She didn't want to call Joy, as she knew she would be at work. She decided to call DS Andrews to see if there was anything new. He seemed to have a way to lift her spirits, just by his positivity and his down to earth way of taking to her.

DS Andrews always had time for Margaret, no matter how busy he was. He told her that although there was nothing new, calls were still coming in from crime stoppers. Margaret felt a little better after speaking with him, she knew he was doing everything he could to find Justine's killer. Although it wouldn't bring Justine back, what she wanted more than justice was to understand why. Was it just a random act, or was it personal? Did the killer know Justine and deliberately hurt her? Or was it a stranger murder, she was just in the wrong place at the wrong time?

Margaret knew justice mattered to DS Andrews and he wasn't going to give up any time soon. Margaret wandered absently through the house. As she passed Justine's room, she thought there is still so much to do, but not today, she didn't have the energy. She was going back to work part-time starting tomorrow, so today she decided might be a good day to take herself shopping. Maybe a bit of retail therapy would do the trick.

DS Andrews had just put down the phone from Margaret's call, when DC McDonald called him over to listen to one of the crime-stopper calls. They both listened to Liz's call.

'This is about the tenth call we've had that describes a truck parked in the truck bay at about the time Justine disappeared.' Implored DC McDonald to his DS. 'But this call is different,' he said. 'It gives us a more detailed description. How many trucks would have a black spiders-web painted across the front?' He said excitedly.

'Okay put the information on the board, under the unknown assailant tab, and then check with any contacts we have in the transport business, and see if anyone knows this truck, or who might drive it.' Replied DS Andrews

The first call made by DC McDonald was to a weighbridge inspector he had worked with when still in uniform. It was an investigation into some unsafe transport practices in the scrap metal trucking industry. He operated a heavy vehicle safety station on one of the major highways that stopped and inspected heavy duty trucks to ensure they were meeting safety and roadworthiness standards. Unfortunately, he didn't recall seeing any trucks that fitted the description. He said he could put the word out and see if any of his other colleagues or driver friends knew of the truck. DC McDonald wanted to be cautious, he did not want to spook the driver. He was concerned if he thought the police were asking about him, and he was involved in the murder he may destroy evidence. With that in mind, DC McDonald asked him to keep it to himself at this stage, and he would contact him again if he needed him to follow up with a wider group.

The next two phone calls were also disappointing, maybe this was going to be harder than he thought. Not discouraged, he phoned a Heavy-Duty haulage company, which operated in the transportation of agricultural products. He introduced himself, and then told the supervisor they were just looking for the driver, as he could have been a witness to an accident. 'Bingo' yes the supervisor was familiar with the truck, and knew the driver's name. He explained he was an owner operator they sometimes used to transport farm equipment or produce out to the regions. The supervisor said the drivers name was Nathan Black, he didn't have an address, but he did have a mobile phone number. DC McDonald thanked the supervisor for his help and hung up the phone.

'We have a name.' Whooped DC McDonald to his DS with a large grin. He wrote the name Nathan Black in big back capital letters on a yellow sticky note and walked over to the investigation board and stuck it up on the board under the tab for the unknown assailant. At this point he wasn't sure if Nathan was a witness or a suspect, but it didn't matter, what mattered was they had a break and they needed to speak to him as soon as possible. The address would be easy to find. DS McDonald got onto it straight away.

DC McDonald called for a patrol car to do a drive by past Nathan's home address to see if his truck was parked up there, and if it was he wanted a brief description. While they were waiting for the description and confirmation that Nathan was either at home or on the road DS Andrews wanted to get all his ducks in a row.

'Let's just have another look at those crime scene photos,' said DS Andrews.

DC McDonald spread the photos out onto the desk and pulled out the photos of the tyre tracks that had been photographed on the dirt road out to the lake. Unfortunately, the truck tyre tracks were just one of many tyre tracks that had been photographed on the dirt road, as it was a popular haunt for teenagers to party out of sight of their parents. The other issue for the officers was that it had rained several times over the ten days that Justine had been in the water. However, there were a few small patches of tyre tracks that were still visible.

They were able to check the truck tyre tracks with a data base, that a young police officer had put together last year, just for this very purpose. It had saved them so much time, as prior to the data base it would have involved a lot of leg work to tyre dealers, viewing and checking each brand. The data base suggested the type was a pretty common tyre used by over one hundred thousand trucks on the road. So, if this tyre matched the tyre tread on Nathan's truck, it would not necessarily prove he was there, but more importantly it didn't disprove or eliminate him from being at the scene.

The other crime scene photo they wanted to check were the boot prints that had been discovered at the edge of the lake. Similarly to the tyre tracks, several boot and shoeprints had been photographed at the scene. However, there was one distinct boot print that was found near one of the truck tyre tread prints, and a partial print again closer to the edge of the lake. Like the tyre tracks, if the boot print is found to match the size and type of boots Nathan wore, it doesn't prove he was there, but it sure as hell keeps building up a jigsaw puzzle, piece by piece to an image that was starting to reveal the full picture. The DC compared the boot print crime scene photo to a data base of boot and shoeprints that the same young police officer had put together last year. It suggested the boot print was a Hard Yakka steel capped safety boot. Unfortunately, that boot is about as common as weeds in a neglected garden, thought DC McDonald.

First, they needed to check out Nathans tyre brand and secondly his boot brand and size. With the description of the truck from the crime stoppers call, it might just be enough evidence to get a search warrant for his truck, hoped DC McDonald. But first they needed to speak to Nathan as a witness and ask him if she saw anything that night.

The call came from the patrol car that Nathan's truck was parked at home. The description supplied matched the crime stoppers call. DC McDonald thanked the officers and he and DS Andrews drove out to talk to Nathan. Unfortunately, when the detectives arrived at Nathan's property and knocked on his door, there was no one home. It was hard to believe they were only minutes from suburbia. It was so quiet, the only sound they could hear was the crunch of their boots on the gravel driveway, and a few birds squawking in some nearby trees. The truck was still there but it seemed Nathan had gone out. While they were there, they took photographs of the truck, the tyres on the truck, and the tyre prints that were on Nathan's gravel driveway. They also found some boot prints on the driveway and photographed them as well.

'Well not a totally fruitless journey,' said DS Andrews. He stepped back into his car and called Nathan's mobile number.

'Yeah, Nath speakin.'

'Nathan Black?' Asked DS Andrews

'Speaking?'

'This is DS Andrews of the South Metropolitan Police.'

There was silence on the phone for a good ten seconds, then Nathan quietly said, 'Okay.'

DS Andrews didn't want to spook Nathan. What he wanted was cooperation, so he explained to Nathan a truck had been seen parked in a truck bay on the main road in Lake Swan on the 11th at about the time they believe a crime had taken place. The truck's description matches Nathan's truck. And he was wondering if Nathan would mind calling into the police station so they could ask him some questions about what he might have seen, if anything.

'Lake Swan, Lake Swan.' Repeated Nathan like he was trying to recall something. 'On the eleventh? No, man, I don't think that was me. My truck looks like a million other trucks,' he said as casually as he could.

The detective then asked Nathan the type of question he loved, one where he already knew the answer.

'Would your truck happen to have a spider's web painted on the front, and two red stripes down the sides of the doors?'

Nathan confirmed it sounded a lot like his truck. Then miraculously he remembered he may have had a job that took him that way, but he would need to check his work schedule. He explained to the detectives trying to sound as laidback as he could, even though his mind was spinning out of control, that he does a lot of driving and sometimes he doesn't even know what day it is, let alone where and when he was at places, but he had it all recorded in his schedule.

'The 11th ya said, right?' Nathan knew exactly where he was on the 11th, but he was not going to let on to the police. 'Am I in some sort of trouble?' He asked cautiously.

'No not at all Nathan, we're just interviewing anyone that might have been in Lake Swan travelling on the main highway in the early evening of the 11th and may have seen something.' It was DS Andrews turn to try and sound casual.

Nathan asked the DS if he could just talk to him on the phone later, as he didn't like police stations. The DS explained to Nathan they would really appreciate a face-to-face meeting with him. Especially if he saw anything, he would need to make a statement and sign it to be of any use to them. He agreed reluctantly but explained he'd need to check his schedule first. Then he could come into the station at about 2pm for a quick chat. DS Andrews told Nathan that would be most helpful, and he appreciated his cooperation. After the DS hung up the phone, Nathan stared at the phone in his hand and spat out the words: 'That bitch, this is all her fucking fault.'

Chapter Twenty-six

At 2pm as promised, Nathan walked into the police station and asked for DS Andrews. DS Andrews thanked Nathan for coming in, and again told him that he really appreciated his cooperation. They were merely here to ask him some questions about what he may have seen on the 11th. In DS Andrews experience the best way to get someone to reveal something they did not intend to, or catch them in a lie, was to treat them like they weren't under any suspicion. Like their best buddy, just asking them to help solve his case. Give them plenty of rope and let them hang themselves.

Nathan was led into an interview room and instructed politely to sit down opposite DC McDonald and DS Andrews.

'Do I need a lawyer?' Nathan said with a smirk on his face The little voice in his head whispered. *Don't be stupid only guilty people need lawyers.*

DS Andrews reiterated to Nathan that he was not in any trouble, he was here as a witness, though they would be taping the conversation as per the correct procedure. DS Andrews asked Nathan for his name and address for the tape. Nathan rolled his eyes and then complied.

The detectives asked Nathan if he had heard about the recent rape and murder of a young girl in Lake Swan. Nathan very nonchalantly said that yes, he had read something in the newspapers about a girl going missing, but he did not realise it was in Lake Swan.

'Unbelievable,' said Nathan as he shook his head. 'Kids aren't safe in their own backyard.' The detectives looked at each other. Did he just reveal that he knew Justine was so close to her home it was practically opposite her backyard or was he just spouting a common phrase? They'd save that for later.

Trying to sound relaxed, Nathan told the detectives that he'd checked his work schedule and yes, he did do a run that took him through Lake Swan on the 11th, and that he did recall pulling off into a truck bay for a quick nap, but was unsure of exactly where that was, but yes it could have been on the main road that goes through the town of Lake Swan. The detectives asked Nathan approximately what time he took a nap. He thought it was around 5pm but he couldn't be sure. But he remembers using his phone as an alarm so that he only slept for an hour. No, he did not see anything unusual, or anyone hanging around the truck bay. He didn't see a fifteen-year-old girl there, or anyone else. As soon as he woke up, he headed home. The detectives asked Nathan if it was usual for him to take a nap when he was so close to home?

'It's what, about 40 minutes from Lake Swan to your home?' Asked the DS.

Nathan, in a rather conceited manner explained that yes, it was unusual, but he is a very responsible truck driver, he was feeling sleepy, and he knows that most accidents occur when you're close to your home. You think that you can make it, and that's often the problem. So, yes, although he was only about 40 minutes from home he decided to do the safe thing and take a nap.

'Fair enough,' said DS Andrews holding up his hands in a show of surrender. 'Do you live alone Nathan? Can anyone verify what time you got home?'

Nathans mood seemed to change almost on a knife's edge. He went into a rampage, raising his voice he shrieked 'What the fuck, yeah I live alone, I got home when I got home, I don't go round checkin' me watch every five minutes do I?'

'*Stay cool, remember, you've done nothing wrong so just chill,*' whispered the voice.

Nathan quickly caught himself and apologised to the detectives. He explained his outburst was due to being under a lot of pressure to deliver goods on time, with large penalties if he was late. He's an owner driver, and it is tough to keep going by himself, competing against large haulage companies. He had recently separated from his wife and wasn't sleeping well. He reminded the detectives that he didn't like police stations and if that was all he would like to go.

The detectives walked Nathan to the door of the police station, shook his hand and thanked him for coming in. They told him to contact them if he remembers anything no matter how small, and that they may be in touch again. Nathan walked to his car, got in and drove home. After he left the two detectives looked at each other with a look of shock on their face.

'What' ya think?' Said DC Mc Donald.

'Oh, he's definitely on something,' said DS Andrews.

'Interesting that he said he didn't see a fifteen-year-old girl. I mean he could've read it in the papers, but we didn't tell him that she was fifteen. And that comment about kids not being safe in their own backyard… again it just sounded off,' suggested DC McDonald

'Oh, he's hiding something, it might just be drugs, but he definitely has something to hide for sure,' confirmed the DS.

Both detectives agreed that Nathan was not telling them everything and they needed to do a bit more digging before they talk to him again. They need to get the team to check CCTV from a wider range. That means the team has to hit the road and check for any cameras that can put Nathan in the vicinity, now they know what they are looking for.

After acting as the look-a-like in the re-enactment, Constable Jane Withers had asked her Sergeant if it would be possible to join the team investigating the murder of Justine, she had received approval this morning and was now part of the team heading down the road checking for video footage, before and after Lake Swan in a hundred-kilometre radius. She and the other members of the team headed out to collect any footage recorded on the 11th from petrol stations, shops, council buildings and grounds, Government buildings, private houses and any other properties that had the main highway in its line of sight. Unfortunately, a number of the camera's recorded on a rotation time limit. This meant that it taped over the previous footage. This was disappointing and not helpful to the investigation. Luckily, for the team they found some businesses that didn't record over the previous days but used and stored individual tapes for months.

Well into the early hours of the night, several exhausted members of the dedicated team were still laboriously looking through hours of footage for any sightings of Nathan's truck, while others had gone home for a few hours' sleep so they could come in early and take over, allowing those members to go home. The team also had traffic light camera footage as well as any speed camera's that were in the area. They had called for any dashcam footage from motorist's travelling on the highway but were yet to receive any.

By early the next morning, they had found several sightings of Nathan's truck and could put together a basic timeline that suggested it was more likely than not that Nathan was in Lake Swan around 6pm on the 11th. They had found two traffic light camera sightings, one approximately seventy-five kilometres from Lake Swan and one about twenty-five kilometres from Lake Swan. They had a good estimate of the speed he was travelling between the cameras. He was captured at approximately 5:15pm on the first traffic camera, and then just 25 kilometres from Lake Swan was captured again at approximately 5:45pm. Conservatively it gave him ample time to get to the truck bay in Lake Swan by around 6:00pm.

After reviewing previous statements, the DS called and arranged for them to meet Ben early the next morning at his home. Ben was still incredibly angry and upset that they had suspected him of raping and murdering his girlfriend. He'd been devastated by her brutal murder, and wondered how he would ever get over it. He'd told the DS over the phone for the umpteenth time that he had nothing to do with her murder, he loved her and would never hurt her. The DS assured Ben he didn't need a lawyer and swore to Ben he was no longer a suspect. He wanted to talk to him as a witness.

Ben still felt uneasy as he answered the door to the detectives, not completely believing he was no longer under suspicion, but he was prepared to give them the benefit of the doubt. DS Andrews explained to Ben that after re-reading his statement he noticed that Ben had mentioned a large truck had passed him on the road, just after he dropped of Justine. Yes, Ben definitely remembered the truck, it was huge and had a large metal Bull Bar on the front. He was sure about the truck because the truck had started to slow down and had moved to the middle of the road as if it was turning right, and he'd manoeuvred his car to the left for fear of running into it. In actual fact, the main reason he had to swerve was because he had drifted into the middle of the road, while looking in his rear-view mirror and waving at Justine, but he didn't want to confess this to the detectives Did Ben notice anything else about the truck, any patterns, or markings that he could remember? Ben thought about this for a moment.

'Yes, actually' he told the DS while still contemplating what he could recall from that night. 'It had something on the door and the side of the truck as I went past it, stripes I think. And I'm pretty sure they were red,' he said sounding unconvincing.

'Anything else Ben, any other markings you can recall? It would be really helpful,' said the DS.

Ben took a moment and tried to picture the truck in his mind, 'There might've been something on the front, like a net maybe? Honestly I kind of only half looked.'

'In your opinion, could that net pattern you saw be a spiders web?' asked the DC.

The DS looked at DC McDonald with raised eyebrows and shook his head, as if to say, be careful you do not want to be accused of putting words into Ben's mouth.

Ben thought about that for a moment and scratched his head and shrugged his shoulders 'Yeah, I guess, it could've been a spider's web now that I think about it.'

The DS wrote all this down, and thanked Ben for his time, and that they may need him to repeat this in a signed statement later. As they walked to the car the DS suggested to DC McDonald they needed to get something more concrete. It would be risky to rely solely on Ben's statement given the 'helpful suggestion' by him as to the pattern being a spider's web. Any lawyer worth their salt would have it thrown out of court. The DC reluctantly agreed and apologised to his DS. He knew he'd taken a risk when he led Ben to the conclusion, but he was more interested in what his answer would be than not. He just had to hope they would find further evidence to collaborate Ben's speculations.

DS Andrews and DC McDonald knocked on the glass door of their DI's Office. They could see she was sitting at her desk eating what looked like a bacon and egg muffin. The DI looked up with a shameful expression on her face, knowing she'd been sprung once again eating an unhealthy breakfast. Darn, she had been looking forward to enjoying the guilty pleasure of it while it was hot and tasty. The desire had now disappeared. Thank goodness it was only the DS and DC and not her husband.

The DI waved them into her office, with a challenging look that screamed. *Don't you dare mention my breakfast.* Trying to ignore the heavenly smell of bacon and eggs, the DS and the DC laid out what they had so far. They showed her the crime scene photos of the tyre and boot prints. They explained that both prints matched Nathans boot type and size, and the tyre impressions were a match for his truck tyres. Although, they had to admit that the work boots and truck tyres were both fairly common brands. But it meant that they couldn't rule Nathan out.

They continued to explain they had also found CCTV footage that puts Nathan on the main road heading towards Lake Swan, suggesting an arrival at about the time Justine was last seen. They also had Nathan on record saying he'd pull over into a truck bay in Lake Swan for a nap. They also had the crime stoppers call and Ben's description of the unique markings on Nathan's truck. At this point it was all circumstantial evidence both conceded, but believed it was enough to request a search warrant to examine the inside of Nathan's truck and house and bring him in for further questioning, this time as a suspect.

The DI congratulated them on all their hard work. She agreed with them, but suggested they apply for a search warrant and have it as a backup if Nathan is uncooperative. She recommended firstly to ask for Nathan's permission to search his truck and house to test his attitude, see how he responded. If he has nothing to hide, then he won't object. You catch more flies with honey than vinegar, she reminded them. Then, if he was reluctant to assist them, slap him with the warrants. Ask him nicely to come in for further questioning, but if he refuses then arrest him. The DS didn't like playing these sorts of games. He liked to play it straight, but on the other hand, he'd experienced, that when caught off guard some suspects had slipped up and given more information than they had intended to.

The DS had his warrants within the hour, he checked his watch, still early. He was eager to get going. If he was going to make an arrest, he preferred to make it in the morning, giving him the rest of the day to gather more evidence while the clock started ticking. He was mindful that although the law states he can keep a suspect in custody for a reasonable amount of time, it was generally only six hours before he had to apply for more. Once arrested he would be required to either charge him or let him go, so the more daylight hours he had to amass evidence the better. He was well aware of the tricks that some of the more experienced and astute criminals play, by hiding out and then handing themselves in at midnight, knowing full well the clock starts ticking as soon as they're in custody. And it was difficult to gather evidence in the wee hours of the morning.

The DS and the DC excitedly jumped into an unmarked vehicle and headed straight out to Nathan's property. They were closely followed by two other officers including PC Jane Withers in a patrol car. They arrived at Nathan's and noticed his truck was parked at the end of the driveway, and his old car was parked in the carport. The officers in the patrol car stayed in their vehicle, while the DS and the DC got out of their car and walked up the driveway to the house. They banged on the door and waited for a response. Nathan came to the door rubbing his face and looking very dishevelled, wearing only boxer shorts and a tee shirt, he looked like he had just woken up. When he saw who was knocking, his expression changed to one of anger.

'What now? I told'ya everything I know.'

The detectives asked if they could come in and talk to Nathan. He explained his house was a mess and he would prefer to talk to them outside. Trying to keep it civil, they all stepped outside to talk. The detectives explained to Nathan they'd had further information that put his truck at the same truck bay, and at about the same time that Justine had gone missing. Nathan shrugged his shoulders and said, 'I already told'ya I pulled off and had a snooze, so what?'

The detectives asked if they could search his truck. Nathan looked straight at the DS and rubbed his hands over his face, while he thought about the request. He then held up his hands in submission and said with a cocky resignation 'Ya know what, if it'll get youse off me back, then go ahead, I got nothin to hide.'

The detectives hoped they wouldn't find nothing, but didn't say anything to Nathan, they had been surprised that Nathan had agreed to the search. They were even more surprised by his confident attitude, it seemed to them he was almost goading them. Nathan went into the house to get the keys, while the detectives put on latex gloves and put their phones in camera mode. As they got closer to the truck the detectives noticed the truck looked extremely clean, like it had just had a full wax and polish.

'Jeez you keep your truck nice and clean Nathan,' said the DS with a surprised look on his face. It didn't match the state of the house or the garden. The house and garden looked so neglected it could have been mistaken for an abandoned property. Also, Nathan's other vehicle looked like it hadn't had a wash in years, with cobwebs all over the side mirrors, and a windscreen that you would have trouble seeing through.

'Yer well that's my livelihood aint it, gotta look after it don't I.' Nathan said sounding unconvincing.

Nathan unlocked the truck for the two detectives. The first thing they noticed when they opened the door was the smell of a cleaning substance. It smelt like someone had been splashing bleach around like a madman. The inside was immaculate, no dirt on the floors and the seats were spotless. They noticed a small bed behind the front seats, which had been neatly made with what looked like freshly laundered or new sheets, and a blanket snuggly tucked in; the set up would put a few hotels to shame. Still, it just didn't feel right. Clearly he had gone to a lot of trouble to clean the inside of his cab.

Feeling dejected, they were obviously too late. Undoubtedly any evidence would be long gone. Regardless, they continued to search the inside of the cab, opening the glove box, the console compartments and tipping out the contents, finding nothing out of the ordinary. They unmade the bed and pulled it apart; it didn't look like anyone had slept in it recently. Much to their frustration they found nothing. There were no obvious strands of hair or fibres, but of course they were not forensics. The DS looked under the seat and scratched around with his hand as far as he could reach. He felt something move, something small and metallic. He managed to get his finger close enough to pull the thing out from under the seat. He looked at it while it hung from his gloved finger. It appeared to be a silver bracelet with purple stones. The DS nudged the DC and showed him what he had pulled out from under the driver's seat. He placed it back on the floor and took photos with his phone, then placed the bracelet in a plastic evidence bag. They climbed down from the cab, and showed the bracelet to Nathan, asking if it was his or had he had seen it before?

'No way, that was not in there before, na, na, tha, tha, was not in there,' stuttered Nathan, while shaking his head vigorously. 'You must'a put that in there.'

'Are you accusing me of planting evidence?' Asked DS Andrews. 'Because that's a very serious allegation.'

Nathan, now with his hands completely covering his eyes, and shaking his head, totally confused, whispered. 'I don't know, all I know is that it wasn't there, someone musta put it there coz I cleaned out that cab last week, took everything out and gave it a real good scrub.'

'Any reason you had to clean it to within an inch of its life?' Asked Detective Andrews suspiciously.

'Some hitch-hitcher I picked up the other week had been drinking and puked up all over the cab, the smell was disgustin.' Replied Nathan hesitantly.

'Was the hitch-hiker male or female?' Asked DC McDonald, going along with Nathans explanation.

'Um female, I guess it could be hers. Na, but I can't believe that I woulda missed it.' Nathan said, almost to himself, sounding like he was trying to analyse the situation.

The detectives asked Nathan if he had had any other females in his cab lately, his wife or daughter perhaps? Nathan just shook his head, still feeling a bit muddled about the discovery. The DC almost felt sorry for him, his cockiness now long gone. He had a blank expression on his face, like he was a child trying to solve a difficult maths problem and just didn't understand how to formulate the answer. The detectives informed Nathan they were now going to search his house and property. This seemed to snap Nathan back to reality. With a bitter expression, he protested and told them that he would not agree to the search of his house.

'Sorry mate got a search warrant here that allows us to search your house and surrounding property,' said the DS in not a very sorry voice at all.

The DS called the two patrol officers over and asked them to start searching the house. The DS then asked Nathan if he would accompany him to the police station for further questioning.

'Jesus no, I've had enough of this., I'm not goin anywhere while you lot are ransacking my house,' said a defiant Nathan.

'Well, you give me no choice then,' said the DS to the bewildered Nathan. The DS told him he was under arrest for the abduction, rape, and murder of Justine Harris. While the DS read him his rights, Nathan kept vigorously protesting his innocence. He was almost incoherent, swearing and cursing, refusing to go quietly. The DS told him to save it for the interview.

'Well can I at least put some clothes on?' Spat Nathan in an angry tone.

The detective nodded his head in the direction of the house and followed Nathan to his bedroom and watched and waited while he got dressed. He noticed Nathan's mobile phone next to his bed and picked it up and put it in an evidence bag. He then asked the DC to cuff him and put him in the back of their unmarked police car. They drove in silence back to the station.

Chapter Twenty-seven

Liz had one of those rare nights where she actually slept from the time her head hit the pillow until her alarm clock had abruptly woken her at 6am. And not because she had taken a magic pill to fog her brain. She flicked off the alarm and onto the news, so she could listen to what had happened in the world overnight, before stepping out of bed. She usually tried to give Buster a quick walk in the mornings, and then a much longer walk in the afternoon. So, trying to stick to her normal routine as much as possible, she put on her tracksuit and joggers and walked Buster around the block. After a quick breakfast she showered and dressed for the day. She was amazed at how calm she felt, or perhaps it was just exhaustion. She had tried to stop punishing herself with the 'what ifs', but it was a losing battle. Maybe nothing would come of her phone call last night. Maybe crime stoppers wouldn't even pass it on to the police investigating the case. Afterall, her call was quite vague. *You need to stop obsessing about it,* she warned herself. Trying to put last night out of her mind, she drove to work. Just another day at the office, she told herself.

The one thing about Liz's current job was she needed to be one hundred percent present when she was with a client. There was no opportunity to drift off and daydream or fixate on the other things going on in her life. It would not only be unprofessional but unfair. She'd had previous jobs where during meetings her mind would wonder off to what she was cooking for dinner, or what she needed to pick up from the shops on the way home. But not this one; she needed to keep her mind focused on the job. She visualised putting all her activities from the last few days into a box, locking it, and then throwing away the key.

Liz and Karen were co-facilitating an eight-week group therapy program this morning. Only twelve of the expected thirteen participants had shown up. After a quick phone call to the missing participant by Karen, she informed Liz the client had so little self-worth she had assumed no one would miss her or even notice she was not there. When it was pointed out to her that not only was she missed, but the other participants were asking about her, and were in fact worried about her, she was in disbelief, saying she had not expected anyone to care if she was there or not. Liz and Karen were very pleased, it was a good sign, the group had already formed compassionate and supportive bonds with each other. And they knew it was a valuable message for this client. When others care about you, it makes it easier to care about yourself.

The client said she was on her way and would be there in five minutes. The group elected to wait for her to arrive before they started. While Liz waited for the client to arrive, she recalled with amusement that when she first started at the agency, they ran groups called The Depression Group, and wondered why nobody used to turn up each week. The group they were running today they had named, 'Hearts and Minds'. It was an eight-week program with weekly sessions inviting participants to open up and heal past experiences together. It was week six, and the previous five sessions had been a graduated build up to this session. Week six's session was named 'mindful breathing' and it was the most intense session of the program. It started with a graduated relaxation process, followed by a process of rhythmic breathing to music, building in intensity until a crescendo where they were breathing as deeply as they allowed themselves, into places and feelings that had been buried and suppressed for a long time. It was often an extremely emotional session, with participants feeling exposed and vulnerable. It was important to take it very slowly with plenty of time at the end for the participants to debrief and discuss how they were feeling.

While waiting to start, some of the participants were arranging to meet up for a coffee later in the week - another good sign that the group was bonding. This group had had a difficult start. The team had only been running 'Hearts and Minds' for about a year and were still learning themselves about the dynamics of group work.

The agencies clients were predominantly female who had experienced abuse from largely male perpetrators. However, male clients who experience family and sexual abuse were starting to become more customary. For the first time since Liz had started group therapy sessions, one of their male clients had been referred to the group. Liz completely trusted her counsellor

Kate's recommendation that her male client was suitable and ready for group therapy. However, they'd made the decision to call each participant prior to starting the group therapy process to advise them there would be a male participant in the group. It was done in the hope of avoiding surprises that could possibly disrupt and unsettle the start. The male client had also been advised of this and was incredibly understanding and had said upfront that he would not attend if the female participants were not comfortable with his presence. All but one were fine with his attendance, and most had expressed the view that not all men were perpetrators, and they would be pleased to have him join them. However, one female participant was upset and said that she could not possibly attend.

Liz had convinced her to give it a go before pulling out. If she still felt the same way after the first session they would review the decision. Liz was observing her now while she was speaking happily to the male participant. To Liz's surprise she had become his number one supporter, often electing to partner-up with him during exercises. He was a very gentle and polite man and it had proved to be a huge turning point for the reluctant participant. He had shown her that not all males were violent and angry. He had demonstrated to her that males could in fact be soft and compassionate.

Once the latecomer had arrived the group got on its way. Although they hadn't needed to be, Liz and Karen had been nervous about how session six would pan out. They never knew what to expect, but the experience of running the group for just over a year had taught them that they could deal with almost anything that came up. There were always lots of tears – some of joy, some of sadness, sometimes even laughter. The atmosphere was nearly always supportive and nurturing. It always felt quite magical to Liz.

After a debrief with Karen about the group session today, Liz was eager to learn how she was tracking with Sally. Karen told Liz that Sally had described Nathan's recent behaviour as erratic. He was still demanding to see Lilly, shouting and swearing at her down the phone, but then not following up with any times or days. She was completely confused, but extremely wary of him still. She had confided in Karen the reason she had left Nathan originally was due to his drug use. She understood he was under pressure to stay on the road, but she didn't want her children being exposed to his drug taking. She said she is just trying to steer clear of him at the moment, and it had been made a little easier as he seemed to be doing a lot of jobs that were taking him away for days on the road. She was still prepared to run with the kids if she had to, but at the moment she is keen for Lilly to keep attending the protective behaviours sessions with Julie.

After a quick lunch break, Liz had a first appointment scheduled with a new client. She didn't know much about him, except that he was a victim of child sexual abuse while residing in a boy's home. After listening to her new client's story, usually her first question is why now? Why not last year or perhaps next month? What has happened recently for you to seek counselling now. The trigger to contact the agency was quite a familiar one. He had two boys; one had reached the age he was when the abuse started. He had told Liz he was so ashamed of his past and lived in utter terror someone would find out about him. He dreads that if parents learn about his history, they might stop him from coaching the boys' basketball team, because everyone knows all victims of abuse turn into perpetrators themselves. That, she told him, on the list of one hundred myths about sexual abuse, was the easiest to rebuke. She was able to show him the research evidence proving the opposite, that the overwhelming majority of survivors do not become abusers.

He went on to tell Liz that when his kids were little his wife would often ask him to shower the boys while he was taking a shower himself. He broke down in tears as he described to Liz how he had showered with his boys with his underpants on, because he was so afraid he would turn into a perpetrator. Liz spoke to him gently about how exhausting it must be for him to carry around the burden of guilt and shame that unquestionably did not belong to him. To finish the session, Liz took him through a guided meditation, where he packed all the guilt and shame into a backpack, dumping it at the squeaky gate on entering a magnificent meadow, where he could roam free and easy, and on his way out he walked back through the same squeaky gate, and ignored the backpack. She booked him an appointment for next week and set homework that revolved around putting the guilt and shame where it belongs, onto the shoulders of his perpetrator.

Liz found it more difficult later in the afternoon to keep her mind on the present task. She was preparing for interviews for tomorrow and Thursday. The agency had applied and received some new funding from the state government for a youth counsellor. They were so excited as they had received enough funding for a counselling position for three days per week. None of the current counsellors had the capacity to cover the three days, so they needed to look for a new counsellor. After advertising, the agency had received over fifty applications for the new position. After shortlisting and ranking the top twelve applications, Liz had decided to interview the top six. Three on Wednesday and Three on Thursday. And if there was little success with the top six, then she would arrange to interview the last six on the short list the following week.

The interview panel included herself, Karen, her most senior counsellor and Terri, who was the chairperson on their board of Management. All positions on the board were voluntary. They had been extremely fortunate to attract a very experienced and passionate board of local professionals to oversee the agencies management and future direction. Some of the members had been there from the start, while others had been convinced to join along the way.

Liz had sent the list of questions to the panel last week for feedback. Liz preferred to ask behavioural type questions in interviews as this gave her an insight into the experience the person has had, and what they actually did in situations when they came up. Questions like can you give me an example of a time when this happened, and what did you do about it and what was the outcome? But the feedback from the Chairperson was that the agency traditionally only used scenario type questions. Questions that asked the applicant what would you do in this situation? Liz argued that anyone with a good theoretical knowledge could answer the question, but whether they would actually do what they said was another thing. Acknowledging the chairperson of the board was very experienced in these matters, Liz decided she would compromise and included both types of questions. She had sent the updated interview questions back to the Chairperson, and after checking her emails this afternoon she had received the feedback that the questions were good to go. Liz then spent the rest of the afternoon printing out resumes and interview questions in preparation for tomorrow.

It was family night tonight. Liz wanted to make sure she had time to go home and walk Buster, before leaving for her parents' home. Liz arrived at her parents' home just as Paul, her younger brother was telling her parents about Parent-teacher night. As a result of his autism, he was often intense and serious, but at the moment he appeared to be having a light-hearted conversation with his mum and dad.

'Lizzy, come here and listen to this,' said her mum as she waved her through the door. Liz gave them all a peck on the cheek in greeting. She always included Paul even though he often went rigid when she touched him. Paul was telling them that at the Parent-Teacher night, the parents had been asked to bring along a piece of artwork to display along with their children's class art. He told them some of the pieces of art were amazing. There were paintings, quilts, pottery, jewellery just to name a few, clearly he'd suggested some of the parents were very talented. Paul explained to his children's teacher that he had not brought anything in, as he lacked any sort of talent and would only have embarrassed his children. The teacher just smiled at Paul and told him his gift was producing such wonderful children. They all had a giggle and Liz told Paul the teacher sure got that right.

After dinner, the conversation moved to Liz's health. She thought she had done a better job of covering her rigid and painful movements, but both parents had pointed out how stiffly she was moving. The extra stress that Liz was putting herself under seemed to be playing out in her noticeably worse body movements. When she was tired or under extra stress, she seemed to lose control of her muscles. They seemed to have a mind of their own. If Liz were her own counsellor, she would be saying to herself, 'Your body doesn't lie, it tells you the truth, and you need to listen to it.' At the moment Liz's body wasn't talking to her, it was screaming at her. She knew she needed to do more meditations and relaxation exercises.

Her mother was saying to her that before the accident you were so fit and healthy, you were frequently at the gym or running. Liz had noticed her mother had started referring to her injuries as an accident. She wanted to say to her it was no accident, it was a deliberate act, but she knew this would only upset her. Unmistakably, her mother didn't want to talk about the darker side of human behaviour.

Instead of challenging her mother, Liz just changed the subject to her work. She told them the agency had received some extra funding and she would be interviewing for a new counsellor over the next couple of days. She was thrilled because they had received some excellent applications, and she was highly optimistic they would find the right person from the pool of shortlisted candidates. Liz was mindful she always felt totally exhausted after interviews, maybe it was the concentration, or maybe it was the responsibility. It was only a small team, and the wrong person could make work a nightmare. She did take heed of her mother's concerns, she really did need to spend some time on her own rest and relaxation, or she would pay the hefty price of long-term damage to her body.

Chapter Twenty-eight

While DS Andrews and DC McDonald strategized about their next move, Nathan was processed by the custody sergeant. He was photographed, DNA swabbed and fingerprinted. He had been advised that he could make a couple of phone calls once the police were satisfied the search of his property had been completed. Nathan's mobile phone had been seized. DC McDonald asked Nathan for the pin number to unlock it. Nathan's response had been predictable. Apparently he was in so much turmoil and confusion right now, he was unable to remember his PIN number. Yeah right, the DC thought., but was not too concerned, he knew the Digital Forensic Lab Team had the latest software to unlock the phone and extract all the data they needed, even if Nathan had attempted to delete it. It would just take a little more time.

While Nathan sat in a police cell feeling sorry for himself, the detectives drove out to Margaret's. They had phoned her earlier to make sure she would be home and up for a visit. The last thing they wanted to do was to distress her further by turning up unannounced. Margaret watched with interest from her window as the two detectives pull up in her driveway. As they exited the car, they both put on their suit jackets, re-tucked the back of their shirt tails into their pants, and then in perfect unison, smoothed down their ties. She wondered with amusement if they learnt the moves in detective school.

The detectives had not told Margaret much on the phone, in case it turned out to be a fizzer, but they were hopeful Margaret might be able to identify the bracelet. After some polite enquiries about how Margaret was coping, the DS took the plastic evidence bag that contained the bracelet out of his jacket pocket and showed it to her. With a disturbed look on her face,

Margaret put her hand over her mouth and drew in a large breath. She immediately recognised it as Justine's. This particular bracelet was the one she'd given to Justine just last year.

The bracelet had been Margaret's mothers and was the only personal possession she had been given after her mother passed away. As she led the detectives into Justine's bedroom, she told them Justine loved that bracelet, it was one of her favourites, though she had not worn it lately as the catch was loose. Feeling a little embarrassed at the mess, she quickly tried to clear a bit of space for the detectives to stand in. There were clothes strewn all over the bed and floor. Some had been placed into bags or boxes, ready to donate to charity shops, while others were chucked into piles taking up most of the floor space. Margaret had just shut the door on the mess after she had run out of steam to finish the job. She now wished she had at least tidied up a bit.

Margaret went over to Justine's dressing table and found the wooden box she had kept her jewellery in. It was mostly full of junk jewellery, but there were a few earrings Justine had received as presents that were of some value. Another thing that needed Margaret's attention she thought. She looked through the drawers in the dresser and in other places Justine may have put her things but could not locate the bracelet.

Shrugging her shoulders and with her hands on her hips, Margaret said with resignation 'Well it doesn't appear to be here anywhere that I can find.' Indicating to the plastic bag the DS is holding. 'So, I'm guessing that's Justine's bracelet in the bag. Where'd you find it?' she asked as an afterthought.

The detective explained that he didn't want to go into too much detail, but what he could tell her was that they had someone in custody helping them with their inquiries.

'Do you recall if Justine was wearing the bracelet the day she went missing?' The DS asked Margaret.

Margaret shook her head, while she was trying to recall. 'I really don't know,' she said with apprehension. 'Sorry, I didn't take much notice, but as I said it was a favourite.' Margaret closed her eyes trying to picture the last time she saw Justine. 'She could've been wearing it, but the catch needed fixing, so she wasn't wearing it as often. Oh, I'm sorry I'm not much help, am I? I just can't be certain.'

The detectives reassured Margaret she had been extremely helpful. All they really needed to know was if she recognised it as Justine's. Margaret confirmed she definitely believed it was Justine's because she had given it to her on her 14ᵗʰ Birthday. She knew Justine's favourite colour was purple, and the bracelet contained natural amethysts. Although the style was old fashioned, to Margaret's delight, Justine loved it. She told the detectives Justine had almost lost it a few months ago, when it fell off in the car, so she stopped wearing it until it could be fixed. The detectives thanked Margaret for her help. They were in a hurry to get the bracelet off for forensic analysis.

By the time they had returned to the station, PC Jane Withers had phoned to give the DS an update. Unfortunately, they hadn't found anything in Nathan's house to link him to Justine as yet. However, they did find a stash of drugs. She had bagged up what she thought was Marijuana, pills that looked like speed, and another product she believed to be Meth. They would be booked in and analysed as soon as possible. Nathan's truck had been picked up by the forensic team and taken back for further analysis, and two other members of the forensic team were now going over Nathan's house and property in a lot more detail. She had also retrieved Nathan's work boots from his house and would bring them back to the station to compare the tread against the photos taken at the scene.

It had been a couple of hours since Nathan had been arrested. They had let him stew for long enough, now it was time to talk to him. He had been re-read and asked if he understood his rights by the booking officer. He was, but he was yet to demand a lawyer. To the detectives surprise he had not made any phone calls. Maybe the poor sod didn't have anyone who cared, thought the DS. It was now time to talk to Nathan, tell him what they had, and see if he had any more information he wanted to share with them.

The two detectives had discussed their plan of action, and what questions they were going to ask. They wanted to give Nathan enough rope to hang himself. Just let him talk, they'd decided. The more lies they could catch him in the better. So, the plan was not to give him all the circumstantial evidence they have just yet.

Nathan was already seated at the table in the interview room with a cup of coffee in hand. The two detectives made a bit of a show of walking into the room, removing their jackets and hanging them over the back of the chairs opposite to where Nathan was sitting. Nathan wasn't handcuffed, and as he lifted the cup to take a sip of coffee, the detectives could see his hand shaking. *Good*, the DS thought. If he hadn't been showing signs of nervousness he would have been worried. They stared at each other for what seemed like minutes, but in reality, was only a few seconds. They asked Nathan to confirm his name and address and reminded him the interview was being video recorded.

Nathan was asked to tell them about his movements on the 11th. He stuck to his story that he was on his way home from a long-haul job up north. Although he was only about forty minutes from home, he suddenly felt tired, so he pulled over into a truck bay in Lake Swan and took a nap. He thought it was around 5pm. He set his phone alarm for thirty minutes. When it woke him up, he drove home. When he got home, he went to bed. No, he didn't drop off the empty trailer until the next morning because he needed to sleep. End of story. No, he didn't see anyone at the truck bay. No, he didn't pick up any hitchhikers that day. He couldn't explain the bracelet found in his truck, except to say that someone had put it there on purpose to get him into trouble. The questioning had gone on for over two hours, Nathan's story hadn't changed. Each time he was asked about the bracelet, he insisted it had been planted. When asked by who and why, he told the detectives if it wasn't them, then it had to be his wife who had planted the bracelet. They were in a bitter custody dispute, and she would do anything to get him into trouble.

The detectives had read the statement Nathan's wife had made earlier about her suspicions around the abuse of their daughter. They were well aware of the acrimonious custody battle that was on going. Although they believed it was a long shot that Nathan's wife had planted the bracelet, he was so adamant, they thought just to be sure, maybe they should check it out.

Nathan was put back into his holding cell while the DC and the DS went to organise a meeting with Sally, Nathan's estranged wife. The detectives had called ahead to arrange a time to meet with Sally, telling her they had some questions they'd like to ask her about Nathan. Sally had assumed it was regarding the complaint she had made earlier, and the detectives said nothing to dispel her assumption, hoping to catch her off guard. Sally explained she needed to pick her son up from school at 2:45 in the afternoon but would be home by 3 O'clock onwards and would be more than happy to speak with them then.

Just after 3 O'clock the DS and the DC were knocking on Sally's door. She wasn't what they were expecting. The way Nathan had described her they were expecting someone who resembled a card-carrying witch. In their eyes, Nathan had erroneously described her as being covered in hideous tattoos, with long scraggly hair she'd home dyed in ludicrous colours. What they found was a softly spoken, attractive women in her early thirties who had politely asked them to come in. If the DS had been asked to describe her hair, he would have said it was long and wavy with a small amount of pink in the front. Yes, he would concede the dye job didn't look like it had been done by a professional, but it didn't look bad, it actually suited her. She was wearing a pretty floral print summer dress that exposed her arms, but as far as hideous tattoos go, she had a couple of tattoos on both her arms and legs, but they were clearly professionally done, and were quite decorative, thought the DS.

The children had been set up in front of the television with snacks, and what looked like a Disney movie to watch. She told the detectives it would keep them occupied for a while. She deliberately took the detectives into the kitchen, so the children couldn't overhear what was being spoken about. It looked like she had been preparing for the meeting, as the kitchen table had a file with some documents inside. A notebook that appeared to have dates recorded, and some photographs. She was all ready to open the file when the DS handed her his phone with a photograph of a bracelet and asked her if she had seen it before.

Sally looked puzzled as she viewed the photo. She shook her head while her eyes were locked on the phone in her hand. 'No, I don't recognise it. What's this all about, I thought you were here to asked me questions about Nathan. You know, about what he has been doing to Lilly,' she whispered, as she spread her arms in disbelief.

'Yes, we are here to ask you questions about Nathan, but in regard to another matter,' said Detective Andrews matter-of-factly.

Totally confused, Sally asked the detectives what other matter. Not wanting to give too much away at such an early stage, the DS did not want to elaborate much more. He explained to Sally they had discovered the bracelet in Nathan's truck. They believe the bracelet belongs to a victim of a serious crime, and Nathan was unable to explain how it got there, except to say it had been planted by someone, and that someone may have been her.

'I don't understand, why the hell would he say that? What's this got to do with me?' She asked.

DC McDonald re-assured Sally she wasn't in any trouble, but they were obliged to check the allegation out. He told her that Nathan could be in serious trouble if it turned out the bracelet belonged to the victim. He explained to Sally that Nathan had suggested it would be in her interest if he was in a lot of trouble.

'I still don't know what you're talking about, but I've never seen that bracelet before, and I've not been near Nathan or his truck for weeks,' Sally responded. 'You know it's probably the drugs talking. It's the reason I left him in the first place. All his drug taking. It was like an emotional roller-coaster ride with him. I know the truck business is pretty cutthroat, but he was on drugs to wake up, drugs to chill out. He was becoming aggressive and paranoid, thinking that everyone was out to get him. I tried to get him to stop taking the drugs, I told him I'd leave him if he didn't, but he doesn't like being told no and he especially doesn't like being told what to do by a woman. I just didn't want me or the kids to be around that sort of thing. You know what I mean?' Sally explained.

Both the detectives nodded their heads in understanding. Looking at the door to the room where the children were still watching television and double checking it was still shut, Sally whispered. 'Then the other stuff started happening, you know.' She pointed to the file she had on the table. The detectives explained they were not here for that today, but on another matter. Her previous complaint would be in the hands of the child exploitation team. Regrettably that complaint was not within their jurisdiction. Sally was just about to go into a tirade about police ineptitude when the DS shut her down by raising his arms in a surrender motion. Wanting to keep her focused on the investigation at hand he said.

'Just one more question. How often does Nathan clean the inside of his truck?'

'Nathan? Clean his truck?' Sally said with a surprised chuckle. 'He never cleans his truck, he's a pig. The only person that ever cleaned the inside of that truck was me. It was usually covered in take-a-way containers and the floor was a mess with sand or dirt because he never wiped his boots. It was disgusting, and it always smelt of sweat. He never changes the sheets on that bed that he uses,' she protested.

'So, in your opinion, it would be out of character for him to have a spotlessly clean truck cab?' Asked DS Andrews

Before she could answer the door flew opened. It was Lilly looking for a mummy hug. Sally just nodded to the detective in confirmation. Seeing they were about to be disturbed, the detectives thanked Sally for her time and let themselves out.

The detectives discussed what they had discovered on the car ride back to the station. They both felt that Sally had a genuine motive for wanting Nathan out of the way. Just to be sure, they decided they would check something out with Margaret.

'Back so soon detectives?' Said Margaret as she opened the door.

The detectives apologised for disturbing her again. Just a few more questions the DS told her. Has she had any strangers in her home recently? Or anything unusual happen? Has anyone touched Justine's personal things? Margaret almost laughed at the questions. She explained that half the town had turned out to Justine's funeral, and most came back to her house for the wake. Ninety percent of whom she did not know. She explained she'd had people everywhere, inside and outside her home. She did recall that several of Justine's friends had been in her bedroom, and yes probably touched her personal things, but nothing unusual to her memory had occurred.

The detectives asked Margaret if she had seen this person, as they held out a blown-up driver's licence photo of Sally. They also described how she had coloured the front of her hair bright pink and had very distinct and colourful climbing rose tattoos on her arms and legs. Margaret told them she did not recognise her or recall anyone by that description attending either the funeral or the wake, but she had a lot of photos on her computer from the day, and they were welcome to have a look. The detective spent the next hour reviewing all the photos from Justine's funeral and wake. It had amazed them just how many lives Justine must have made an impression on, as there were so many people in attendance, but none that resembled Sally. A quick phone call to Sally by the DS about her whereabouts on Friday afternoon would be easy to verify.

It was getting late in the day; the detectives went back to the station to talk to their DI. They explained to her that they could charge Nathan with drug offences and let him go. But their preference was to keep him in custody overnight while they followed up on some further leads tomorrow. They accepted they didn't have enough evidence to charge Nathan for Justine's murder at the moment, but they were waiting for DNA evidence from the bracelet that had been found in his truck, and anything the forensic team may discover inside his truck.

'Okay let him sweat overnight, but I'll need to see some hard evidence to approve any more extensions,' conceded the Detective Inspector.

Chapter Twenty-nine

Wednesday's interviews had been a total disappointment, none of the candidates had made the grade. The first interview was cut short, as it became evident after the first couple of questions the candidate didn't have the experience they were looking for. Clearly there had been some exaggeration and embellishment on their resume. The panel members had pre-arranged a signal to indicate if one of them wanted to wind up the interview early. The signal was to take off their watch and place it faceup on the table. Once the signal was given, if the others agreed, they would move to the last question and end the interview. If they did not agree, the panel member would just go to the next scheduled question on the list. Shortly after candidate one had started answering question three, Liz removed her watch and placed it on the table in front of her. It was Karen's turn to ask the next question. Karen gave Liz a surreptitious smile, clearly agreeing with her assessment and moved to the last question on the interview guide and wrapped up the interview early.

The second candidate was closer to what they were looking for experience wise, but there were some concerns with the responses to questions about working in a team. The answers and examples given indicated this person seemed to prefer to work alone. The third and last interview for the day started well. The candidate seemed warm and friendly. When she was asked about why she had applied for the role, she spoke about her respect for survivors of abuse, and her desire and passion to work in this area. So far, so good, thought Liz. But then she went on to talk about her own experience of abuse and how it had affected her life. The chairperson, Terri, was very experienced in interviewing for new staff and had tried to cut her off politely, with a further question about her clinical experience. She was obviously trying to bring her back on topic, but the candidate just kept talking about her own issues. Unfortunately, this triggered another early end to an interview, and an early end to the workday.

Liz was hopeful that today's applicants would be more in line with what they were looking for. They had another three candidates to interview. The first interview had gone well, and the panel were very impressed with his experience and attitude; they thought they had probably found the person they were looking for. This was until they interviewed the second candidate. Even better, they had all agreed. 'What a difference a day makes,' remarked Liz, feeling extremely positive. They were just about to interview the final candidate when Claire the receptionist knocked on the door.

'So sorry to interrupt,' she said as she stuck her head around the door. 'But there are two police detectives here.'

Before another word could be uttered by Claire, Liz's face turned porcelain white. She thought she might faint. Suddenly she couldn't breathe. Her heart was racing, and her whole body began to shake. *I am going to be in so much trouble, how could I have been so irresponsible and so stupid* she admonished herself. *How on earth did they find me so quickly?* It was all she could do to stop herself from bursting in to tears. She wanted to throw herself at their mercy, say she was sorry and explain it was a moment of madness brought on by an idealistic need to protect a child from harm. As Liz started to get up her legs were like jelly, she didn't know if they would hold her up.

'I'll speak to them.' Liz said in a soft but shaky voice, trying to swallow the lump in her throat.

'Actually, it's Karen they want to speak to,' said Claire in a matter-of-fact response.

'Oh right,' said Karen with an amused expression as she got up out of her chair. 'I wonder what this is all about.'

Liz tried to breathe slowly as she sat back down in her chair. Her mind was racing a mile a minute. Terri was talking to her, but she couldn't catch what she was saying through the haze in her mind. Liz couldn't understand why they would want to speak to Karen first, were they checking with her to see if Liz had confessed her crimes? She was sure the police were going to burst back into the office any moment and arrest her and humiliatingly march her out in handcuffs.

'Are you okay Liz? You look like you've seen a ghost,' said Terri for the second time, with a genuine concerned look on her face.

Liz looked at Terri in horror and apologised for her lack of reply. She needed to get out of there quickly before she went into hyperventilation. She took off at speed and ran for the ladies and threw up in the toilet. Now, trembling uncontrollably and with tears cascading down her face, she didn't know if she felt relieved to have been caught, or righteous for what she had attempted to do. It didn't matter, because whatever happened now at least it would be over. She would take her punishment. She flushed the toilet and walked towards the sink. She looked in the mirror, her mascara had run down her face, she looked almost ghoulish. She did her best to wipe it off with a wet paper towel. Then she splashed her face with cold water and blew her nose.

'Get a grip,' she said out loud to herself, while she gave herself a slap on the thigh. 'Have some dignity.'

Walking back to the office, Liz could see their last candidate sitting on a chair in the waiting area looking anxious. Liz tried to smile at her reassuringly and gave her a signal that they might need a few extra minutes. The candidate gave her a nod in understanding. Karen, Claire and Terri were all standing there in the office with extremely worried look on their faces. The police were nowhere to be seen.

They had been discussing Liz's abrupt and emotional reaction to the police visit. They had concluded the police visit must have brought back the memories of her children's violent murders. That was the only explanation they could come up with to rationalize her performance.

Karen gave Liz a hug. 'It's alright Lizzy, the police just wanted to ask me about one of my clients,' she said in a gentle and soothing voice. 'I'm so sorry the visit upset you so much.'

'I – I' she stuttered. Nothing further would come out of her mouth. She breathed in long and hard, covering her mouth with trembling hands.

'It's okay Lizzy, you don't need to explain. We're all aware of what happened to you. I'm sure any police visit would take you right back to that place.' Karen said, trying to comfort Liz.

Karen sat Liz down in a chair and gave her a drink of water. As she sipped the water her hands were still visibly shaking. Karen explained the police wanted to know if Sally was in a counselling session last Friday at 11:30. Apparently Sally had given Karen as her alibi for that time and day. Karen went on to say it was something to do with Sally's husband Nathan. He'd accused her of doing something to him, and the police thought that

the most likely time was around mid-day on Friday, so they were just confirming her alibi.

'The police wouldn't tell me anymore. I just confirmed Sally had an appointment, and she had turned up and stayed for the whole hour. That's all
the cops wanted to know. Then they left. Maybe he's retaliated because of
the complaint she made to the police.' Karen offered as an explanation.
'Anyway, she has an appointment booked for next Friday, perhaps she can
tell me what's going on then,' suggested Karen.

Liz was feeling bewildered, while trying to process what Karen was telling her. She was aware that last Friday was the day of Justine's funeral and
wake. Did this mean the police had found the bracelet in Nathan's truck?
Maybe he had accused Sally of planting the bracelet and the police obviously
had assumed her best opportunity to get hold of the bracelet would be at
the wake on Friday, Liz speculated. But fortunately for Sally, she was here
on Friday attending her regular appointment, so she had a solid alibi. It was
the only explanation that made any sense to Liz.

Karen and Terri asked Liz if she wanted to go home, they were genuinely
concerned about her because she still looked like death warmed up. They
told her they could handle the last interview and if it turned out she was the
best candidate, then Liz could arrange to meet up with her for a chat later.
Liz took a deep breath, trying to ease herself.

'No, I'd prefer to stay, it'll take my mind off things,' she croaked.

'Okay if you're sure, let's get to it,' said Terri.

Liz tried to clear her mind and focus on the task; it was no easy feat. She
found herself slipping back to thoughts about the police visit, and what that
may have meant.

Liz was glad she stayed for the final interview, as the candidate was the
best of all three today, and outstanding compared to yesterday's interviews.
In the discussions after all the interviews had been completed, they'd agreed
the three candidates today would all be suitable but ranked them in order
of preference. They had all been there before, pinning their hopes on one
particular candidate only to be devastated when they declined the offer. The
more experienced Liz became in recruiting, the more she understood the
need to have backup candidates.

The decision was to progress with the last two candidates. Psychometric
testing would need to be arranged for both candidates. Although the testing
was an expensive exercise, it had proven to be worth the investment on

several occasions when the testing had revealed characteristics that had not been drawn out in the interview but would have been a disaster for the agency. After the testing had been reviewed the next step would be to reference check both candidates, before making their final decision. It could be a long process from start to finish, but in such a small team it was necessary to be as sure as you could be that you have selected the right person.

The worst part for Liz was calling the unsuccessful candidates and advising them they didn't get the job. She always made sure she had some positive and constructive feedback to deliver to soften the blow. Although from her experience most people seemed to take the news quite well, she just hated being the bearer of bad news or disappointing anyone. She had been on the other end of the phone call herself many times when she first started looking for work and knew just how deflating it could be.

The phone calls were a bit like ripping a band aid off, best done quickly and without delay. But those calls would have to wait for another day. She just didn't have the energy right now. Still feeling the aftermath of her emotional outburst, Liz decided to go home early and try to calm her nerves. After taking Buster for a walk, she ran herself a bubble bath. Conscious of water wastage, it was a luxury she seldom allowed herself. She tried to keep the earlier conversation she'd had with Karen out of her head but was failing miserably. Her conscience was getting the better of her. *What have you done?* She kept asking herself. She had no doubt that this man was despicable for what he was doing to both Lilly and Sally, but he was now a suspect for murder, because of her. What's ten times worse is the real killer is still out there somewhere, probably plotting to kill again for all she knew. *How can you think of yourself as a protector of children, when you may have just placed another child into danger?* She reprimanded herself. *Did you really think this through?* She wondered. *Look, at this stage he's just a suspect* she reassured herself. *Surely with DNA and other forensic science the police will find the real killer. This is just a delay tactic. But what if the real murderer kills again?*

The conversation in Liz's head was not helpful. It was just going around and around in circles making her feel sick to the stomach. She knew focusing on the 'what ifs' wasn't helpful, that she needed to concentrate on the 'what is'. Sally and Lilly were safe for now. She needed to think of something else, anything to take her mind off what she had done. She tried to read a book but couldn't concentrate. She tried to watch a movie but couldn't focus. She wondered how people who commit crimes live with themselves.

In the end Liz decided to follow her own advice. Meditate and try to clear her mind and find some inner peace. Liz found the CD she had been looking for - it was a guided mediation that she had almost worn out when she first came home from hospital. She lit some candles, put some soft cushions on the floor and laid down and absorbed the words and background music. She was amazed when she woke up two hours later. The candles had burnt out and it was dark and cold, but her mind was quiet. Feeling hungry she tried to get up, but her muscles had gone stiff. In a great deal of pain, she got up and started some gentle stretching. After about ten minutes of her regular stretching exercises, she went into the kitchen to find something comforting to eat.

Chapter Thirty

The detectives convened a meeting with the team. Each team member gave an update on where they were at with the investigation. The forensic team had not found any other fingerprints or traces of DNA in Nathan's truck other than his own. It was as clean as a whistle, they'd reported. Someone had done an excellent job of cleaning the inside of that cab. DS Andrews enquired if they had found any evidence that someone may have vomited in the cab. The forensic team acknowledged just how hard it would have been to remove all traces of vomit from all the nooks and crannies in a truck cab. They had pulled out the radio, checked all the grooves in all the switches and knobs, all the furrows and ruts in the dashboard, nothing had come up on the swabs. Obviously they could not rule it out, but they had doubts that anyone had vomited in the cab.

DS Andrews knew from personal experience just how hard it was to clean all traces of vomit from a car. He recalled the time when one of his children had thrown up on their way to the in-laws. Initially he'd cleaned it thoroughly himself, and thought he'd done a good job until a warm day hit and the stench crept out. He then had it professionally cleaned, but every time the car baked out in the hot sun, he could still smell that god-awful odour. In the end his solution was to trade his car in for a new one.

The rest of the team were gradually putting together the witness statements and all the circumstantial evidence they'd had so far. The team walked the detectives through the mounting circumstantial and physical evidence that had been gathered. It was good, but it still wasn't enough to charge Nathan. But, thought the DS, if he confronted Nathan with what they had and painted a picture that made it look like it was far more damming than it was, they might just be able to coax him into revealing something more concrete. They were not allowed to outright lie to the suspect, but they were allowed to embellish things a little to put a bit of pressure on the accused, particularly if they believed it might bring about a confession. However, they needed to be careful about how much pressure they initiated. Nathan was well within his rights to request legal representation, and that would severely slow down the DS's strategy.

The challenge would be to keep a good balance between accusations and questions, with just the right amount of pressure to encourage Nathan to keep talking. In his experience some suspects like nothing more than to talk about themselves. They were often the arrogant ones. The type who thought they were too smart to be caught. From experience, the DS knew the more he can keep a suspect talking, the more lies they often catch themselves in. However, if Nathan started to feel too intimidated he would more than likely ask for legal representation, and the result of that in the DS's experience, often shut down any further progress.

While the detectives were waiting for the DNA results on the bracelet to come in, they decided to check out Sally's alibi for the day of Justine's funeral and wake. They wanted to be able to push back with some confidence when Nathan suggested the bracelet had been planted by his wife. They also wanted to show Nathan that they were listening to him and taking his side of events seriously.

DS Andrews and DC McDonald parked their unmarked car and walked into a building that had been purposely built to house a number of not-for-profit agencies. They found the directions for the agency they were looking for and followed the signs through a labyrinth of corridors. Outside the door was a small waiting area with a nervous looking young woman sitting on the edge of her chair reading some handwritten notes. The detectives walked through the office door and introduced themselves to the receptionist. The DS asked if it would be possible to speak with one of the counsellors for a quick chat. The counsellor's name was Karen they informed the receptionist, and the matter was rather urgent. Claire the receptionist apologised and informed him that Karen was just finishing up interviewing for a new staff position and if they could wait just a few minutes she would interrupt her before she went into the final interview for the morning.

'If that's okay Detective?' Asked Caire in a hesitant manner.

DS Andrews told Claire he was okay to wait a few minutes. She escorted both detectives to a small waiting area just outside the agency's door. While the detectives were standing in the waiting area, the door to the office swung open and a young woman dressed in black pants and a white blouse was exiting through the door. She somewhat awkwardly tried to put on her jacket, while juggling a handbag and some documents. When she looked up and saw the two detectives standing there, she almost dropped all her papers over the floor. Somehow, she managed to grab the papers and shove them under her arm while making her get-a-way. It was clear she had been the interviewee, as both detectives knew that depleted look. They could also hear, 'Thank you, we will be in touch.' The young women in the waiting area took a large swallow and an anxious intake of breath, looking like she was about to be led to the gallows.

As the two detectives walked into the reception area, there seemed to be some confusion in an office just off the reception area. The door was wide open and as the DS looked towards the commotion, he could see a petite red-haired woman who looked like she was about to faint. Then he heard the receptionist say 'No, It's Karen they want to speak to' as a painfully thin, well dressed fifty-something woman was walking towards them smiling and holding out her hand.

'I'm Karen, can I help you detective?' Said Karen looking a bit bewildered at DS Andrews. She motioned the two detectives to walk with her into another small office, which was off to the left of the reception area. She switched on the light and shut the door. They could still hear some disturbance going on outside of the office door.

'Is she alright, the red-headed woman in the other office?' Asked DC McDonald.

Karen was surprised by Liz's over-reaction to the police presence but suggested that it may have been linked to a very painful incident in her past. She told them the sudden unexplained appearance by police detectives may have stirred up some distressing memories from when her husband murdered their children about fifteen years ago. The DS apologised for the visit and explained why he was here. Karen at first was reluctant to divulge the information he requested saying that it was confidential. However, the DS made it clear that Sally had already told them of the visit, he was just trying to confirm her attendance. Sally then corroborated the time and day of Sally's attendance. The detectives thanked Karen for her assistance and left the office.

When the detectives got back to the station, there was a definite buzz in the air. PC Jane Withers couldn't wait to advise the DS that there had been a call from the forensic lab. Before the DS had a chance to take off his jacket, she impatiently informed him the bracelet was unquestionably Justine's as traces of her DNA had been found in between the links, and on the fastener. Unfortunately, they had not discovered any traces of Nathan's touch DNA on the bracelet. She had said it so fast and all in one breath that it had come out a bit jumbled. The DS asked her to take a breath and repeat it but slower this time. It was unfortunate there were no traces of Nathan on the bracelet to completely wipe out his 'someone had planted it' response, but it was another piece of the puzzle helping to build the picture.

The Digital forensics team had some more good news for the DS. They told him Nathan's mobile phone had sent a goodbye signal at 6:02pm when he powered it off on the Sunday night Justine had gone missing. And guess what? They had said with glee. They had located the tower it had been relayed through and could place the whereabouts of Nathan's phone close to the truck bay in Lake Swan at 6:02pm

'You guys are terrific,' the DS said with excitement.

'Oh, that's not all we found,' said one of the tech guys with a cheeky grin.

'Oh please, tell me more,' responded the DS with raised eyebrows.

The Digital forensic tech guys sat down across from the DS and the DC and put a plastic evidence bag that contained a mobile phone on the table in front of the detectives. It was obvious they enjoyed their work by the enthusiastic way they spoke about what they had discovered. They didn't look particularly geeky, or as young as the DS had imagined they would be, but clearly, they knew their stuff. They were so keen to tell the detectives what they had uncovered that they often spoke over each other in the excitement.

'Okay let me see if I've got this straight,' said the DS. 'Nathan switched off his phone at 6:02pm and that sent a signal that puts him in the area of the truck bay at Lake Swan?'

'Correct,' said both of the tech guys simultaneously, while nodding their heads.

'When he switched his phone off, he still had plenty of battery life, eighty four percent, you said, so his phone didn't just die, he deliberately switches if off?'

'Correct,' said the older of the two tech guys.

'Then thirty minutes later he switches it back on, a hello signal is sent that still puts him in the same area. He then puts it into aeroplane mode and uses the torch app for about forty minutes?'

'Yup,' said the younger of the two tech guys.

'Did you find any evidence that he used the clock alarm on his phone during that time?' Asked DC McDonald

'Nope, the alarm was not activated at any time during that day,' said the older tech guy.

The Digital Forensic tech guys went on to tell the detectives they had also looked at Nathan's google search history on his phone and his home computer. He had googled a number of interesting questions like, how long do fingerprints last on clothes, how long before a dead body decomposes, and how long does semen last underwater? He also had visited a number of dubious websites like, 'Raped and abused'.

The tech guys had also found a few questionable images stored on his phone, probably not illegal but violent pornographic pictures that were quite disturbing. It was hard to tell, but some of the images looked like the victims were rather young, so they were sending it to the child abuse team to verify. Nathan had also been googling police reports on missing girls over the last few weeks. Again, not illegal, but his interest was curious.

'You guys are amazing,' said the DS. 'What you can discover from someone's phone is just astounding.'

'All part of the service,' said the older guy feigning a bow. 'People just don't realise how much data is left on their phone, even if they've attempted to delete it.'

'Okay,' said the DS to his DC. 'I think it is time we spoke to Nathan again.' He asked PC Jane Withers to escort Nathan to interview room one and wait with him until they were ready. The DC followed the DS into his office for a quick strategy meeting.

'How do you want to handle it?' Asked the DC

'I don't wanna go in too hard too fast, he hasn't asked for a Lawyer yet, but if we push him too hard, he might lawyer up and then we get nothing,' said the DS.

'I agree,' said the DC nodding his head.

'After what the tech guys found on his phone, I have little doubt he's guilty,' said the DS with a grimace. 'But we don't have enough evidence to charge him yet, we need him to tell us something that we can verify, a confession would be brilliant, but unlikely. But if we try to give him a reason for what he's done, try to make out like it was an accident, like it was her fault, maybe he might talk.'

'Okay, so we present him with pieces of the evidence we have, and then build a story for him that suggests he did not mean to do what he did.' Proposed the DC

'Exactly, let's try to make him feel that we understand. That we're on his side.' Added the DS, as he grinned and raised his eyebrows to the DC.

'Understood,' said the DC returning his grin.

Nathan was looking haggard. He was strung out from the amount of drugs he'd been using lately. He hadn't showered or changed his clothes in a while. His hair looked as though it could use a comb. He had bitten his fingernails so short and had been picking at the skin around them to the point they looked red and swollen. PC Jane Withers could clearly see evidence of his nervous habit, by the amount of dry blood pooled around his fingernails where he had been biting and gouging. She sat motionlessly across the table looking directly at him. Nathan sat with his head down looking at his hands.

As the door to the interview room opened, PC Jane Withers stood up and nodded to DS Andrews and DC McDonald as they walked in. She left the interview room and closed the door behind her. The detectives slowly took off their jackets and put them on the back of their chairs. The DS rolled up his sleeves and straightened his tie, while the DC with folded arms glared at Nathan. Nathan hadn't bothered to look up, he just kept staring at his hands.

The DS blew out a long slow breath. They had all been here before, and all were feeling weary.

'You're still under caution Nathan,' said the DS.

Nathan still did not look up, just nodded his head in acceptance.

'For the tape please Nathan,' said the DC.

Nathan looked up and glared at both detectives and very deliberately and slowly said, 'Yes.' Then looked down at his hands again.

'You were asked before if you wanted legal representation and you said you did not,' the DS reminded Nathan. 'Is that still the case?'

Without looking up Nathan said, 'I don't need a lawyer, I've done nothin wrong.'

'Okay Nathan let's go back to the Sunday when you drove your truck through Lake Swan and parked at the truck bay,' said the DS.

'I already told you bout that. I just parked up. Had a nap. Then went home. Nothin, else, happened.' Explained Nathan in a staccato voice.

The DS placed some crime scene photos on the table in front of Nathan and pointed to each one.

'Well explain to us how your tyre tracks and your boot prints were found close to the lake,' said the DS.

Nathan, clearly thinking that he was the smartest person in the room, looked up and smirked at the DS, 'You guys are unbelievable. How d'ya know they're mine? My tyres are like a thousand other truck tyres, and me boots, well about a million other guys wear the same type of work boots,' he said as he shook his head.

The DS placed Nathan's phone on the table. It was still in a clear plastic evidence bag. 'Tell us again about your phone,' he said.

Nathan looked confused. 'What do ya wanna know?'

The DC made a loud sigh, dramatically flipped through some paperwork on the table and then read out Nathan's previous words.

'You told us that you used your phone as an alarm, so you only slept for about thirty minutes, are you still sticking to your story?' Said the DC goading Nathan.

'Yer… maybe… I think so, it was like weeks ago,' Nathan said wearily. 'That's what I usually do,' he said shrugging his shoulders.

'Mmm, interesting,' said the DS slowly as he pursed his lips and nodded his head. 'Well, our tech guys have had a look at your phone Nathan, and guess what?'

Nathan said nothing, just stared at the DS and raised his eyebrows in question.

'Our tech guys didn't find any alarm being set for that day,' the DS said knowingly to Nathan.

Nathan just shrugged his shoulder and said, 'So what, so I didn't set me alarm, big deal, that don't mean I didn't have a kip in me truck does it?'

'Nope, it doesn't, but it means you lied to us, so what else are you lying about Nathan?' The DS responded.

'I didn't do nothing,' said Nathan emphatically. 'I just pulled over and had a sleep and went home, that's it.'

The detectives raised their eyebrows and smiled at each other. How many times had they heard that comment from suspects? If Nathan as he said, did not do nothing, it meant that he did something, but they did not want to point out to him his erroneous use of the English language, they had more important information to present to him.

'Okay so while we're talking about your phone,' said the DS as he picked it up and placed it back down on the table. 'Our tech guys found some other interesting stuff.'

Nathan continued to look down at his hands, but his legs began to move up and down in a shaking motion. Was this a sign he was nervous, or was he just strung out?

'Seems that you switched your phone off just after 6pm. We can locate you because your phone sent a 'goodbye message' to a tower that puts you in the same area that Justine was last seen, right about the time she was last seen,' said the DS smugly.

'So, I never said I weren't there, I just wasn't sure about the time.' Nathan said shrugging his shoulders and still looking down at his hands. He started to pick at the skin around his fingernails that were still bloody and swollen from previous attacks.

'Can you explain to us why you switched your phone off so soon after you arrived for about half an hour, then switched it back on and put it on aeroplane mode, then used your torch app for over forty minutes. Seems like strange behaviour to me,' said the DS in a confronting tone.

Nathan looked up and started biting at the skin around his fingernails, while he thought about what the DS had just told him. 'I told you I switched if off cos I went to sleep,' he said indignantly.

'Then why put it in aeroplane mode? Why try to hide your location.' Asked the DC. 'Why didn't you want anyone to know where you were, if as you say you were doing nothing wrong?'

Nathan rubbed his hands over his face and shook his head. The voice in his head kept telling him to stay cool, these guys have got nothing. He explained he wasn't trying to hide his location, he probably just switched it to aeroplane mode so he didn't get any calls. He told them he had been having some issues with his ex-wife in regard to access visits with his daughter and didn't feel like fighting with her while he was driving home after a long-haul job.

'Okay, but why was the torch app on for so long?' Asked the DC.

Nathan looked up to the ceiling and closed his eyes for a moment. He then pursed his lips and shrugged his shoulders and ran his fingers through his ramshackle hair. 'Must've been an accident.' He then motioned his arms in a throwing movement. 'Maybe when I chucked it on the seat I accidently swiped the screen, and you know, something on the seat hit the torch app, sumthin like that musta happened, is all I can think of.'

'I've been a detective for over twenty years, and I've developed a pretty good bullshit detector Nathan, and it's going off right now,' said the DS.

Wanting to keep the momentum going, the DS also told Nathan they had discovered his recent Google searches and asked him why he would have been searching for answers to how long fingerprints last, how long it takes for a body to decompose, how long does semen last underwater?

'You also seemed very interested in keeping up to date with any police reports on Justine after she went missing.'

Nathan just shrugged his shoulders trying to act nonchalant, but his body language said otherwise. He again looked down at his hands that were now tightly squeezed together on his lap, his legs were trembling vigorously, and his breathing was getting faster. It was getting much harder for Nathan to stay cool. Although the DS had some further evidence up his sleeve to present to Nathan, he chose to save that for later. The DS decided that now was the time to give Nathan a story that he could hang onto. One where he wasn't a villain. He hated doing this, but he needed to make out that it was Justine's fault. Try to side with Nathan and get him to confess. Even if he confesses it was an accident, it is a start the DS could work with.

'Here's what I think happened Nathan,' said the DS. 'Justine was there, looking for a good time. You smoked a bit of weed together, you know, a private party just for the two of you. You've been under a lot of pressure lately, ex-wife and custody issues, pressure to get jobs done in quick time. Been using a lot of drugs to keep you alert, keep you on top of things. Can't be easy Nathan.' The DS moved a bit closer to Nathan. Nathan looked up and nods his head to the DS. Now that the DS had Nathan's full attention he looked right into his eyes. 'We're just here to get to the truth. I know how it is Nathan. You're having a good time, she's been teasing you, laughing at all your jokes, then all of a sudden she says NO.' The DS stops talking for a moment and keeps eye contract with Nathan trying to fake an understanding between two blokes. Nathan doesn't move, but he is clearly listening. The DS carries on. 'All those drugs in your system, all your pent-up frustration, you just lose it for a moment. You can't stop. You've just gone too far. The bitch is just playing with you. You didn't mean it to happen, it was out of your control.' The DS could see that Nathan was wavering, he appeared to be thinking about what was being said to him. He could see the beginnings of tears start to well in Nathan's eyes.

Nathan doesn't utter a word, he looks down at his hands again, the shaking is increasing, his shoulders are slumped like he has the weight of the world on them. He looks exhausted. He appeared to be thinking about what the DS had been saying. The voices in his head were telling him to listen to the DS.

He continues. 'It was an accident, we understand that, we can tell it wasn't planned by the way her body was hurriedly disposed of in the lake,' the DS said attempting to convey some compassion in his voice. The DC then leans closer to Nathan. 'Get it off your chest, you'll feel so much better mate,' the DC said moving in a little closer and patting Nathan on the shoulder. Nathan looked up at the DC, then appeared to stare at the wall straight ahead. 'Yes, you'll have to do a bit of time, but be a man. Stand up and take some responsibility for your actions.'

Nathan began to chew on his fingernails again, well what was left of them anyway, as he continued to stare at nothing. The voices in his head had gone quiet. The detective was sure he was still listening to him and contemplating what to do next, he just had to keep up the pressure.

'You know Nathan, I've talked to a lot of…' The DS hesitated, he did not want to label Nathan as a murderer, not yet anyway. He could feel he was so close to getting to Nathan. 'Offenders,' he continued. 'They told me that looking over their shoulders for twenty years was worse than doing the time. They told me it was torture waiting for the tap on the shoulder. For the police to turn up and arrest them. You can't sleep, you can eat, you're always on edge.'

Nathan made eye contact with the DS briefly and then looked away. This encouraged the DS to continue along this line. He felt like he was definitely getting to him. 'We eventually get them anyway, coz we never give up Nathan, not on a murder. We're like a dog with a bone. You take responsibility and let us worry about the accountability.'

Again, Nathan made fleeting eye contact with the detective, and then drifted away somewhere. Nathan started to rock back and forth in his chair. The voices in his head were back saying, *'Don't be a fool Nathan.'* He wasn't sure what that meant. The detectives looked at each other, convinced that Nathan was contemplating what they were saying, so they kept pressing him.

'It's no life, constantly looking over your shoulder, afraid every time you see a police officer, that they're coming for you. And eventually they do, and then you do the time anyway.' Continued the DS. 'Clear your conscience Nathan, you will feel so much better once you do.'

Nathan covered his face with his hands and continued to rock back and forth. The detectives had seen this movement many times before: they were close to a confession, they could feel it.

'Look Nathan, forensics are all over your truck, they find just one hair, a scrap of fingernail - you tell us now in your own words before this goes any further. We know you didn't mean it, just tell us your side,' the DC continued not letting up. The DS put another photo on the table and pointed to it. 'The bracelet was hers. Her DNA was all over it. What else will forensics find Nathan?'

Nathan pulled his hands slowly down his face scraping over his unshaven chin, leaving his hands covering his mouth. Still looking confused and staring at nothingness, he shook his head back and forth and garbled 'I don't ged'it. I don't know how I missed that.'

The detectives look at each other with a quick nod: this is what they had been waiting for, what they had been working towards. 'Can you repeat that Nathan,' said the DC trying not to sound too excited.

Nathan suddenly looks up and makes eye contact with the DS. His eyes look like a rabbit caught in headlights. He looks emotionally drained, and on the verge of tears. This time the voices in his head say *'You're such an idiot Nathan. Don't be fooled Nathan.'* He removes his hands from his mouth and says. 'I think I want a lawyer.'

The detectives tried not to show their feelings of frustration. They had him. They were so close they could taste it. They couldn't believe what they'd just heard. What went wrong? 'Could you just repeat what you said before Nathan please for the tape,' said the DC knowing that he was pushing his luck a bit.

'I'm not saying nothin more. I want to speak to a Lawyer.' Nathan said stoically.

'Okay, okay,' the DS said as he raised his hands in surrender. He suspended the interview and walked out of the room. The DS asked PC Jane

Withers to escort Nathan back to his holding cell, while they make the arrangements.

Disappointed, the detectives met with their Inspector and gave her an update on where things were at. 'We almost had him, we were so close,' the DS said with conviction. 'I don't' know what happened, it was like he suddenly woke-up from a dream. We'll get nothing more now; it will be no comments from now on.'

'Do you think we have enough to charge him,' asked DI Sutton.

'The bracelet is a strong piece of evidence,' said the DS. 'But I have to admit, it is a bit weird, that he missed it. I mean he had undoubtedly cleaned his cab thoroughly. It was sparkling clean, not a speck of dirt, and then we find the bracelet tucked under the seat. His wife has an airtight alibi while the wake was happening, but playing devil's advocate, that doesn't mean she couldn't have arranged for someone to attend the wake and grab a piece of jewellery I guess. If I was his lawyer that's what I'd be suggesting anyway.'

'Of course, it's possible, it could've got snagged on something initially, I suppose, and Nathan didn't see it,' said the DC as he shrugged his shoulders. 'And then with the movement and vibrations of the truck on bumpy roads it kind of unsnagged itself and fell on the floor under the seat so it was out of sight.'

'That's possible,' agreed DI Sutton.

'The rest of the evidence is pretty weak, he could easily explain most of it away. Any half decent Lawyer will see to that,' said the DS. 'I mean we still have the drug charges pending for now, and possible illegal porn. We can use that as a bargaining tool, but I want him for the murder, I know he did it.'

'Maybe forensics will come up with something more from the cab,' said DI Sutton hopefully.

'Maybe,' said the DS. All of a sudden, he felt exhaustion overtake him. The last thing he felt like doing was going a couple of rounds with a solicitor. He needed coffee, black and strong.

'I'll approve a further six hours custody,' said the DI. 'But I really need more to extend any further.'

Chapter Thirty-one

DS Andrews had been advised that Nathan's solicitor was on her way. He met with DC McDonald to decide what evidence they would provide to Nathan's solicitor when she arrived. Their normal process in serious cases like this one was to drip feed the evidence to a solicitor as they were under no obligation to disclose everything they had all at once. Although time was beginning to be an issue for them. They couldn't keep Nathan locked up without charging him just because they believed he was guilty. However, in this instance, they both felt the right strategy was to keep the pressure on Nathan.

Although the burden of proof as to guilty or not guilty was for the courts to decide and theirs was to investigate, arrest and charge, they were determined to provide the system with the strongest indication of guilt they could find, even if that meant holding back some of the evidence they had for later. An experienced solicitor would be aware of this strategy, but it was worth a try. It was always a balancing act. They needed to provide enough evidence to the suspect to layout a compelling picture of their culpability. But they also wanted to hold certain aspects back, to either allow the suspect to become tangled in a web of lies that they could then challenge or confirm their own guilt by its disclosure.

The detectives were well prepared by the time Nathan's solicitor, a Ms. Howard arrived. DS Andrews knew most of the solicitors in town, but he was yet to meet Ms. Howard, she must have been new. She did appear to be a little nervous thought the DS as he introduced himself and DC McDonald. She didn't look like your stereotypical solicitor often portrayed on TV dramas. She didn't wear a severe colour lipstick, she wasn't dressed in a power suit, or walk in uncomfortable looking high heels. Quite the opposite, she looked as though she had dressed for comfort in a pair of loose-fitting pants paired with a baggy jumper. She was wearing comfy flat shoes, and her wavy hair was kind of tossed up on top of her head in a chaotic fashion. Her most striking fashion accessory were the bright red reading glasses that sat on her nose. They served to enhance an intense pair of stunning turquoise blue eyes behind them. She had a very gentle manner when she spoke.

The detectives met briefly with her before she had had a chance to speak with Nathan. They outlined the reasons Nathan had been arrested and provided her with copies of most of the evidence they had gathered so far. She was nobody's fool and had asked the detectives if this was all the evidence they had that related to her client. The DS had told her it was everything they were prepared to show her at the moment. Nathan was brought out of his cell and placed into a meeting room for a confidential discussion with his solicitor before his next interview with the detectives.

The detectives were well aware that under the law in Western Australia they were allowed 'reasonable time' to hold a suspect for a serious crime as they continue to collect evidence to charge them. They had also sought the correct approvals every six hours to continue Nathan's captivity. However, Nathan had been in custody for nearly twenty-four hours, and they knew that the solicitor would argue time was now up. She would insist that they either charge Nathan or release him. The property and phone searches had been completed, and forensics could continue to search the cab of Nathan's truck without the need for him to remain in custody. They were the ones now feeling the pressure.

Sometimes the best strategy was to let them go. Let them think that they are in the clear and put the suspect under surveillance to see what they do and where they go when they think no one is watching. Unfortunately, the search of Nathan's property had not turned up Justine's missing clothes.

'If we let him go, we could follow him, see if he leads us to any other evidence,' suggested the DC reluctantly.

'Unfortunately, we may have to. I really thought we had him there. I saw it in his face, he was ready to tell us everything. I would've bet my pension on it,' said DC Andrews.

While the DS and the DC were discussing the events that had occurred earlier, Nathan was meeting with his solicitor. She had introduced herself and asked Nathan to call her Kate. She asked Nathan to go over what he had disclosed to the police to this point and showed him the evidence the detectives had provided to her. Her advice to Nathan was to exercise his right to silence from now on, and to answer any further questions from the police with no comment. She explained to him that this did not make him look guilty of anything. He wasn't there as a witness; he didn't need to assist the police.

'You must help yourself,' she'd insisted. Nathan didn't seem to be listening to her, he seemed to be in a daydream. She had to repeat everything she was saying to him several times before he even acknowledged she was talking. She wondered if he was taking anything in.

Kate was becoming concerned. Was Nathan fit to be questioned? There appeared to be something wrong. His affect and the way he stared into space worried her.

'Nathan you asked for some legal advice, and I am giving that to you. Do you understand?' Kate said slowly and purposefully.

The voices in Nathan's head were telling him to trust no one, especially her. Nathan took in a deep breath like he was contemplating something. He looked at Kate with distain and nodded his head.

'Yeah. I need your help wiv somethin, that's why I asked for a Lawyer.' Nathan said egotistically.

'Okay good, that's my job. I'm here to help you.' she responded with a smile.

Kate was not happy with what Nathan wanted help with. She had advised him that she didn't think it was the right approach, but she could not talk him out of it. She had asked him several times if he was sure he knew what he was doing. He was adamant he understood the consequences. He had told her she was his lawyer, and he was instructing her to do this. After it was done, Kate felt uneasy, but Nathan had insisted it was his decision.

Kate popped her head out of the door and asked PC Jane Withers, who had been standing outside the meeting room, if she could advise DS Andrews and DC McDonald that Nathan was ready to be interviewed. As the detectives entered the interview room and sat down opposite Kate and Nathan, Kate gave the DS the following prepared statement in writing.

'Against my advice, my client has asked me to prepare this written statement for you.' Kate said reluctantly as she looked directly at Nathan.

Nathan gave a quick nod of approval, and then closed his eyes. He looked like he had aged ten years over the last few hours. But over the last few minutes there was a hint of recovery in his look, like a weight had been lifted of his shoulders. The DS read the statement out loud so that the DC could hear, and it would be recorded. He could hardly believe what he had in his hands.

I Nathan Black wish to make the following statement. I deny the allegations of abduction, rape and murder that I have been arrested for. I would like to give the following account of what happened on Sunday 11th May this year. I drove into the truck bay at Lake Swan intending to have a short nap before I drove home. While there I was approached by a young person who I believed to be about eighteen who introduced herself as Justine. We started talking and because it was cold, she got into my cab of her own volition. We smoked a marijuana joint together, started kissing and then she consented to sex. While in the process of consensual sex she started to struggle, she at no time said no. I was holding her shirt up and it must have gotten hooked around her throat constricting her breathing. I was unaware of what was happening until it was too late, and she was no longer breathing. When I realised what had happened, I panicked and made a very bad choice to put her lifeless body in the lake. I did not have any intension of killing her it was an accident. I wish to make no further comments.

The DS and the DC asked to be excused so that they could discuss this together in private.

'We got him, he's confessed,' said the DS with a jubilant smile. 'It's all complete bullocks though.'

'Mmm, consensual my arse,

'Look it's great that we have his confession, but as you know confessions have been retracted before. He could say he was strung out and didn't know what he was saying. He's been in custody for just over twenty-four hours and was sleep deprived or felt pressured to confess. You know what they're like. Without the statement we don't have much. I want more. I want him to lead us to where he put her jeans and underwear.' Clarified the DS to his partner.

The detectives walked into the DI's office to provide her with an update and to discuss their next move. They were confident with the newly acquired confession that they would get approval to charge Nathan. However, the DS had another plan in mind. He wanted to tie this case up with a bow. He suggested to the DI that they appear to accept Nathan's explanation about what happened. He was sure that his solicitor wouldn't buy it, but he would like to try. Convince Nathan they believe him about it being an accident, just like he described. Then ask him for one more piece of evidence, just so they can corroborate his story.

'If he tells us where the jeans and undies are, we have him lock, stock and barrel,' said the DS confidently.

'If he doesn't,' said the DC to the DI, we charge him anyway. We have nothing to lose.'

DI Sutton had been in the job for a long time, and she was tired of suspects, with the help of a good lawyer, wriggling out of convictions. It was disheartening for the team, as well as the new recruits to see a lot of their blood, sweat and tears go unrewarded. She agreed with the detectives and told them to carry on with their plan.

The DS checked his watch: it was getting late, he really wanted to wrap this up today. The DS and the DC walked back into the interview room and sat down across from Nathan and his Solicitor.

'Thank you, Nathan, for telling us what happened,' said the DS trying to sound like his best mate. 'I'm sure you feel so much better getting that off your chest.'

'I do.' Acknowledged Nathan. As he spoke his solicitor swung her head around and looked directly at him and raised her eyebrows. She was attempting to remind him that he did not need to say anything. They had discussed his answers from now on to any further questions would be 'no comment'. Nathan just looked down at his hands, ignoring her stares.

'We know you're tired and would really like to get this over and done with, so you can get a good night's sleep and you'll sleep so much better when you've got nothing left to hide,' the DS said to Nathan ignoring the stern look from Kate. 'But could we ask you for just one more thing?'

'Did you read my clients statement? He said that he did not want to make any further comments.' Kate said indignantly.

Ignoring her comments, Nathan looked up at the DS and took a deep breath and said in a weary tone. 'What is it you want now?'

Kate whispered something to Nathan, but he just ignored her and kept looking at the DS with an inquisitive look on his face and continued to speak. 'What's in it for me?'

On the outside, Kate looked calm, but she was furious. What was the point of her even being here? Clearly, Nathan was not taking any notice of her advice. She wondered if it had been a man sitting in her seat, would he have listened and taken notice of the advice? She was a professional and that meant she would provide her client with the best advice she could, no matter what he had confessed to.

Under her skilled façade, she hated representing clients like Nathan. She hated what he had done, his attitude to women and the way he just disregarded her, but she still had a job to do. She continued, even though he refused to listen, to remind Nathan that he did not have to answer any questions.

'Can't make any promises,' said the DS. 'But your cooperation would be noted, and it would be the right thing to do Nathan. You could put this to bed once and for all today. If you could just tell us where her missing jeans and underwear is located, that would really be helpful.'

'We know it was an accident Nathan, and you're obviously remorseful for what happened. Your help would really assist us to wrap this up, isn't that what you want?' Added the DC.

Nathan shrugged his shoulders. 'Don't see why not, but I'll ave to show you where they're buried. It's a bit tricky to describe it to ya. But It's near the lake.'

'Nathan, look I don't think…' before Kate could finish what she was saying, Nathan turned his head and looked at her with revulsion. The voices in his head sniggered, telling him *you know who your mates are, and she is not one of them.*

'Jus shud'up will ya. I've heard wha you said, okay?' Nathan spat. 'I'm not stupid. I don't need ya advice, I don't want ya advice, you're useless you are. Jus go will ya.'

'Fine,' Kate said as she packed up her things ready to leave. 'I assume that you no longer require my services?' She wanted to tell him that if he thought the detectives believed his ludicrous story, he was mistaken. She wanted to tell him a lot more, like he was just a misogynist pig, but that would have been unprofessional. Nathan just dismissed her with a wave of his hand as she walked out the door.

'Right mate are ya ready to show us where those things are buried?' Said the DS with a burst of new energy.

'Look Nathan, we're gonna have to handcuff you. Sorry, but it's protocol,' said the DC while slapping him on the back and trying to appear on friendly terms with him. It made the DC cringe to have to talk to Nathan in this manner, but once he had led them to the buried clothing, he could stop the pretence. He knew it was all part of the job, but he did not enjoy pandering to suspects like this. He just had to keep thinking about the end game.

The detectives put Nathan into the back of their unmarked police car. PC Jane Withers and another officer followed in a squad car. It was getting dark, so they needed to get this done quickly. They all carried torches but were hoping there would be no need to use them as long as Nathan wasn't leading them on a wild goose chase.

Nathan seemed to be a lot more relaxed now that he had confessed. He was asking the detectives about when he was likely to get his truck back. The DS wondered if Nathan was on the same planet as they were. He just kept it vague and friendly and told Nathan that he could not make any promises, it could be a few days.

Nathan directed the detectives towards the entrance of the gravel track to Lake Swan. Nathan liked being in control. He enjoyed telling the detectives which way to turn and where to go. DS Andrews was on edge. He was concerned that Nathan was enjoying this too much and wouldn't have been surprised if Nathan got them to drive him around for a while and then changed his mind and asked to go back to the police station. The detectives were uneasy; it was a very strange ride.

Nathan was quite chatty in the back of the car, almost like he was on an adventure. It appeared his confession had opened the floodgates. He was telling them about how dark it had been on that night and how angry he had been because he had to get into the water. He told them it was freezing cold, and he had gotten his boots and clothes all wet. He continued to tell them, like the two detectives were his mates, that he was unable to put Justine's jeans back on her, because they were the stupid skinny leg type and too hard to manoeuvre.

'I don't know how the girls get them on in the first place,' he had told the detectives with a chuckle. Even the detectives were willing him to shut up. They reminded him he was still under caution, but it made little difference. DS looked over at DC McDonald and pulled a face that said *this guy is unbelievable.*

'Pull over there,' said Nathan as he pointed with his head.

The DC parked the car where Nathan had suggested and got out. They went to the back door and assisted Nathan out of the car. Although the sun was almost down, there was still enough light to see where they were going, but the detectives took their torches with them just in case. The DC took a shovel out of the boot of the car. Nathan directed them to an area where there was a pile of twigs and brush. He told them to dig about a foot under the brush. PC Jane Withers and another uniformed officer stood with Nathan and kept him back from the crime scene. DC McDonald put on a pair of latex gloves and started digging where Nathan had pointed. After a minute or two he found what looked like a pillowcase. The DS put on a pair of latex gloves, reached in, grabbed the pillowcase and shook the dirt off of it, while the DC took photos on his phone. He peered into the pillowcase and could see a pair of jeans and a small pair of lady's underwear. He nodded to the DC for more photos. He strung crime scene tape around the closest trees to mark the spot and took the pillowcase with its contents back to the car and placed it in a large evidence bag ready for the forensic lab to do their job.

'We appreciate your cooperation Nathan,' said the DS as he helped Nathan back into the unmarked police car. The light had completely gone now, with only a quarter moon shining through a cloudy sky. They drove back to the station in eerily silence, both detectives contemplating the enormity of what they had just found.

The DS could feel the disruption in the station as the night shift team were starting to come in for work, while the day shift were packing up ready to go home. It was hard to swallow the elation they felt at the discovery of the hidden clothes. But they needed to keep a calm impression, this had to be business as usual, they still had work to do. Nathan was escorted back to a holding cell. The DS requested a hot drink and something to eat for him.

The detectives went to speak with their DI, they felt confident to present the case to the DPP to charge Nathan even without any forensic evidence on the clothing. The DI congratulated them on the good work they had done but was not so quick to support presenting the case to the DPP just yet. She acknowledged they must be exhausted with the long hours they had put in and the lack of sleep, but she felt that they just needed to dot the I's and cross the T's.

DI Sutton told the DS that she would arrange to have the evidence couriered to the forensic lab tonight and call them to have it fast tracked for DNA and fingerprint analysis. But even fast tracked they would not get any results until tomorrow. She told the DS to call by Margaret's house on his way home and show her a photograph of the clothing for her to identify. Then she told him that he was to go home and have dinner with his family and get some sleep. She turned to DC McDonald and instructed him to begin the paperwork for the DPP, then he was to go home and get some rest. She would see them both bright and early in the morning.

DS Andrews phoned Margaret to let her know he would like to call by in about thirty minutes to show her something. He told her that he didn't want to go into it on the phone but clearly it was to do with Justine's murder. Margaret had been nervously pacing the room checking her watch every few minutes when the DS finally arrived, it was only 30 minutes, but it had seemed like hours to Margaret. She could tell that this was something seriously significant by the tone of DS Andrews voice on the phone earlier.

He looked tired Margaret thought, when she invited the DS into her lounge room. She'd had to dress quickly, with no one else in the house, as she had gotten into the habit lately of changing into her pyjamas soon after dinner. Margaret had put the kettle on for tea. The DS felt bad for not being more social, but he really wanted to get home. He told her that it was just a quick visit this time as he gave Margaret an update, with a promise to come back tomorrow with further news. Margaret was now back at work part time and would be working tomorrow afternoon. The DS informed her he was confident that the information he was waiting for would be available before lunch time tomorrow, and he would be able to go into more details then.

He explained to her they had arrested someone, but that he had not been charged yet, as they were still gathering evidence. Although the DS was quietly confident that charges would be laid, he did not want to pre-empt the DPP, and then have to turn around and disappoint Margaret. Better not to give her an expectation that he may not deliver. The DS apologised up front for any distress he may cause and asked Margaret to sit down. He warned her that what he is about to show her is deeply personal and may upset her. He pulled out the photographs of the jeans and underwear and handed it over to Margaret asking her if she could identify the items in the photo. Margaret's hand when straight to her mouth as she drew in a shaky breath. She looked at the photo and then up at DS Andrews and nodded her head, as a tear ran down her face.

'Yes. I recognise the underwear. I bought her those last Christmas,' she whispered, as she pointed to the dainty pair of flowery knickers in the photo she was holding. 'Where did you find them?'

The DS felt uneasy. On the one hand he wanted to tell Margaret their suspect had confessed and led them directly to where he had buried the articles. But on the other hand, how could he expect Margaret to keep this information to herself. He knew if it were his daughter who had been murdered, and someone had confessed he would be on the phone to relatives and friends in a heartbeat. So, he didn't lie to her… he just didn't tell her the whole truth. He told her that someone had led them to the articles, but they preferred to wait for DNA and fingerprint results before they could move forward with this evidence. But Margaret wouldn't leave it at that, and he didn't blame her. She kept asking him questions about where they were found. Who led them to the discovery. Who was the person that had been arrested. Was it his DNA and fingerprints he hoped to find on the clothing? The DS did his best to answer her questions without giving her any false hope.

Margaret finally stopped asking questions when the DS repeated to her that the information should be available tomorrow and he would call her as soon as he knew anything more. She apologised for grilling him. He totally understood and told her she had nothing to apologise for. Margaret knew she would get little sleep tonight. As she walked him towards the door, she reminded him she would be at work tomorrow by 2pm, but she would keep her phone with her. He checked his watch, the children would have been bathed, fed and in bed by now. His wife would have put his dinner in the oven for him.

He would eat alone again.

He hoped this case would be over soon so he could make it up to his wife and children. As he drove home, he decided he would take some time off work and take them on a holiday as soon as he could.

His wife would complain she had heard that promise before.

Chapter Thirty-two

Early the next morning DS Andrews and DC McDonald met in the DI's office to discuss the case. Nathan had been in custody for well over thirty-six hours already, so they needed to make a decision to either charge him or let him go and continue gathering evidence. The DI had bought them both a hot steamy coffee and a donut from a drive through coffee van on her way into work. DS Andrews confirmed that Margaret had identified the garments as Justine's the night before. The question was, did they have sufficient evidence to convince the DPP to lay charges? Or do they need to wait for DNA and fingerprint evidence first?

Would the case pass the DPP's two-test rule, was the DI's question. Was there enough evidence to establish a reasonable prospect of a conviction and was it in the public interest to prosecute. There was a big fat tick for in the public interest. The public definitely needed to be protected from the likes of Nathan. So, the only question now was the evidence. Prior to the bracelet, they'd only had flimsy circumstantial evidence to rely on, but the confession and Nathan's ability to lead them to the buried clothes changed all that. With the confirmation the clothing was Justine's the DS felt they could refer it to the DPP right now. Even if Nathan retracted his confession, citing bullying or sleep deprivation the DS was confident to press ahead and present it to the DPP.

The DI was a bit more cautious. She told Andrews and McDonald what a brilliant job they had done so far. She reiterated they'd had a strong case, but she would prefer to approve a further six hours of custody if it meant they could present a more robust case. One that was so tight a Judge would rely on the polices recommendation to deny Nathan bail. She told the detectives she would like to call the Lab and see what time they could expect to get the results on the fingerprints and DNA, as that would make it a slam dunk in her opinion. She told DC McDonald to continue to prepare the paperwork for the DPP and leave a space for the results. If they were likely to be in this morning they would include them, if not then they would send it off regardless, as it was still a strong case.

The DI checked her watch, it was still early but she phoned the forensic lab anyway. The technician answered on the second ring. She explained that everything had been set in motion the night before, and she would expect the fingerprint information would be to hand shortly, they were just waiting for their expert on fingerprint identification to confirm the results. She was confident the result would be in by around 8:30 that morning. The DNA testing should also be completed that morning, she estimated around 9:30ish. The DI thanked her for her help and hung up the phone and went to find DS Andrews.

DI Sutton found the detectives deep in conversation while putting together the information for the DPP. She told them that the DNA and fingerprints were likely to be in soon, and to hang off sending it in for a few hours. She would phone the DPP and advise them what was coming through and request a quick response. They all looked towards the clock on the wall, tick tock, tick tock, two excruciating hours to wait.

The detectives had plenty to get on with for the next two hours, they had felt like they had neglected their other cases. They had been working on a hit and run causing death before this case had come in, and there were lots of statements to review to try to piece together the incident. DC Jane Withers had been doing most of the leg work, talking to the local smash repairers for any vehicles needing panel beating that matched the description. She was just giving them an update when the forensic lab called. The DS took the call. DC McDonald and PC Withers had crossed their fingers while listening to the DS saying, 'Yep, I see, OK, beautiful, thanks.' He looked across to the DC and PC with a huge smile on his face and nodded his head.

As he put the phone down he yelled, 'We got him.' Everyone in the room turned to look at the DS and raised their hands in a sort of hurrah and whooped and hooted. 'His fingerprints and DNA are all over the pillowcase and his fingerprints are on the fabric and the button of her jeans. And as expected her DNA is all over the jeans and underwear,' the DS told DC McDonald and PC Withers with elation.

The DS updated his DI and then the paperwork for the DPP. He was hoping for a speedy review of the evidence and confirmation of the charges, of abduction, rape, and murder. He had to play another waiting game. This was how it was, the waiting, the moment of satisfaction, then starting again on the next case with the realisation that it never ever stops. He didn't have to wait long: the phone call from the DPP was swift and short.

Nathan was escorted from his holding cell by PC Withers. *Finally,* he thought. He was exhausted and just wanted to get home so that he could shower and change his clothes. It took him a moment to react when the charges were read out to him.

'Ya charging me for rape and murder? I don't understand. I told you it was an accident.' Nathan said with bewilderment.

No longer needing to act like he was Nathan's confidante, DS Andrews just sneered at Nathan. 'Oh we understand alright. It's not our job to determine your guilt Nathan, that's the courts job. But you'd better get yourself a good lawyer.'

Nathan was then advised, because of the serious nature of the charges, he would likely be held in remand. The police would be strongly recommending no bail.

'I don't understand. What about my business? I need to get back on the road, I can't afford not to work, they'll take my Truck for sure,' Nathan protested, starting to realise what was happening. The voices in his head were saying, *You're such a loser, you're such an idiot.*

His protests were ignored as he was escorted out of the station. The DS gathered the team and thanked them for all their hard work. He still had one job to do, and that was to advise Margaret. He checked his watch; still time to talk to her face to face. He drove out to her home and knocked on her door. Margaret could tell by his demeanour that for once he was bringing her some good news.

'We got him Margaret, we charged him this morning with the abduction, rape and murder of your daughter. We will be opposing bail and hopefully he will get life and won't be out for a very long time,' said the DS with some satisfaction.

'Thank you, Detective, for coming out to tell me in person.' Margaret said with a sad voice. 'I'm glad you got him, I'm very grateful to you and the others for all your hard work.'

The DS gave Margaret the full update. He thanked her for being so solid and ready to help in a time that would have been emotionally tough for her. He truly believed it was the result of the reconstruction that offered the breakthrough they had so badly needed to solve the case. Without the crime-stopper call he doubted that Nathan would have been on their radar.

After the detective left, she called Joy with the good news, followed by her neighbour June, not wanting either of them to hear it on the news. Margaret then called John. They had gotten quite close since Justine's funeral. He came straight over. As he walked through the door, she moved swiftly into his arms.

'It's over,' he had said, 'hopefully you will be able to move forward with your life now.'

'I miss her so much John,' Margaret said tearfully. 'I miss her smile, I miss her noise. I miss her when I see that empty chair, when I eat alone. I even miss arguing with her.'

'I know you do Maggie.'

'It's every parent's dream to watch their child grow up, to be happy, get married, have children, he took that from me John.'

'I know he did Maggie, I'm so sorry.' John said as he tried to comfort her.

Chapter Thirty-three

Although it was Friday and Liz's day off, she had scheduled an appointment to see a new client. She had promised Claire, who often mothered everyone in the office, she would take another day off during the week in exchange. Claire looked in Liz's dairy and told her that Wednesday was free at the moment, and she was going to put a line through the day so that no one could schedule anything. Liz understood Claire's interference came from a caring place, so she just responded with, 'Thanks Mum' and they both exchanged a smile. Liz's other reason for coming in on her day off was she knew Karen had an appointment with Sally that afternoon, and she was keen to get an update.

Liz's new client had consumed her thoughts entirely during the session, thankfully leaving her no time to dwell on what was happening with Nathan. She had been very concerned for her new client's welfare and had spent most of the session working on a safety plan with her. The client's partner would never allow her to go out of the house with all of their four children alone. He would insist she left at least one of the children at home with him. He knew she would never leave him unless she had all of the children with her. If all the children needed to go out, then he would come along with her.

This was a worrying situation. Liz had confirmed the local women's refuge would be able to keep her safe, even if they didn't have a bed for her and all her children, they would find her one. They had been strategizing for most of the hour building a solid plan that included where she could go and how she was going to get there. The plan also included getting her hands on documents, important personal items, and changes of clothes for her and the children into a safe place, without his knowledge prior to her leaving.

She told Liz she had one friend she knew would store the items for her, and she had been putting some cash aside for a while. He would know if she tried to take money out of their bank account, so the only way she could get money without his knowledge was to purchase things, and then return them for cash. Liz suggested she get a spare set of car keys cut and to hide them where she could get easy access to them in a hurry. She already knew when she had an opportunity to run it would have to be swift with only the clothes on their backs. Liz made another appointment to see her next week, knowing full well she would worry about her in the meantime.

Liz had just walked back into the office after having lunch at a local coffee shop. Karen had been looking for her for the last 30 minutes. She asked Liz to come into her office, as she had something important to share with her. When Liz walked into Karen's office, Sally was already waiting there, with the most enormous smile on her face.

'You're not going to believe this. I don't even believe it,' said Sally shaking her head.

'What's happened?' enquired Liz with her heartbeat thumping in her ear.

Karen jumped in before Sally had a chance to say anything. 'It's Nathan, Sally's ex, he's been charged with the rape murder and abduction of that young girl in Lake Swan, apparently he confessed to it.'

'We're safe now, they're not even going to let him out on bail.' Added Sally almost to herself.

Raising both her hands to her forehead and shaking her head, Liz was totally confused with this new information as she spurted out 'Wait a minute. I don't understand. You said he confessed. What to murdering her?'

'Yes, the police called me earlier today, apparently he said it was an accident, that he didn't mean to do it, and then he just panicked and tried to hide her body in the lake,' said Sally sounding surprised. 'He even took them to where he buried some of her clothes and his DNA and fingerprints were all over them,' Sally continued as she kept looking from Karen to Liz.

Liz sat down slowly on one of Karen's chairs with a look of bewilderment on her face. She sat there for a few seconds not saying a word. Her mind was racing, trying to process what she had just been told. 'I don't believe it. It's a miracle,' she said to both Karen and Sally.

'Well, I wouldn't go that far,' said Sally, 'but it does mean my daughter is safe from that predator. And if he's found guilty, not only will he go to prison, he'll be put on the sex offender register as well. That girl was only fifteen.'

Liz got up from the chair and gave both Sally and Karen a hug. She walked back to her office and shut the door and wept with relief. Wiping her tears, blowing her nose, and pulling herself together she sat down quietly. Shaking her head, she still couldn't believe it. It felt strange, like some kind of divine intervention had occurred. As if some higher power had been watching over her. But of course, she did not believe in any of that crap, because if that was the case why would her children have been taken from her?

Liz tried to work on a report, but there was no way she was going to be able to concentrate on anything for the rest of the day, so she gave up and to Claire's surprise went home early.

Chapter Thirty-four

18 months later

Accompanied by her husband John, a very pregnant Margaret walked into the court room to hear the sentencing. Two weeks ago, after a week-long trial, and after only two hours of deliberations the jury in a unanimous decision had found Nathan guilty of the abduction, rape, and murder of Justine.

Nathan had gone through several solicitors by the time of his trial, not wanting to listen to their advice. The DPP hadn't charged him with pre-mediated murder, they didn't believe he'd planned to murder anyone, but it was no accident either. Although the evidence was overwhelming, Nathan had decided to plead not guilty. His original Lawyer had advised the not guilty plea in the hope of a plea bargain deal for a lesser charge. But Nathan wouldn't listen to any plea deals, he didn't believe he was guilty of anything, still claiming it had been an accident, that she had told him she was eighteen and that she had gone with him willingly. Fortunately, the evidence didn't support Nathan's story.

Margaret had provided a written victim impact statement a week ago for the judge to take in consideration when sentencing Nathan. It had taken her several attempts to write her statement. She wanted the judge to sentence Nathan not for the life lost, but for the life that would never be. She wanted him to know that Justine was a funny, bright, and trusting young girl with her whole life ahead of her. And that Margaret's life would always be in two parts, before Justine and after Justine.

After she had written her statement, she told John she didn't want to be cruel and hateful towards Nathan, as that would just make her bitter and twisted. Anger just eats away at you until there's nothing left. Nothing

"""

would bring Justine back. She could never forgive him for what he had done, but she needed to forgive herself for not protecting her. John just gave her a knowing smile and a big hug. He loved Margaret so much his heart was bursting with emotion. He held in his tears and just kissed her on the top of her head. 'You've nothing to forgive yourself for,' he whispered.

DS Andrews and DC McDonald were sitting on Margaret's right side waiting to hear the sentence from the Judge. Karen and Sally sat with trepidation at the back of the court, as they had throughout the whole trial. Liz had decided to join them today for the sentencing. They were holding hands as the judge started to speak. Nathan stood quietly in the dock looking at his hands and shaking his head as the judge used words like 'heinous' and 'monstrous' to describe the crime. As the Judge proclaimed a life sentence of at least twenty-five years to be served the crowd in the court collectively sighed and looked at Nathan. He would also be on the sex offender's register.

Nathan looked towards the back of the court directly at Sally and shook his head in disbelief. Then he noticed the person sitting on her right. It disturbed him. He looked right at her with a queried look on his face. He recognised her face, but from where he wasn't sure.

The end.

Acknowledgements

Thank you to the team at The Book Reality Experience for helping me bring my dream to a reality.

Thank you to my husband for his belief in me and his never wavering support. To my daughter Kate and the friends who ploughed through my first draft and provided valuable feedback and encouragement. To Greg who allowed me to pick his brains on Western Australian policing. Lastly to the survivors of sexual assault, sexual abuse and family violence for your courage and resilience. I hope I have done you justice.

About the Author

Lorraine Stephens was born in South London and emigrated as a child with her family to Western Australia in 1970.

She is a retired social worker who has spent more than a decade working in child protection, mental and community health, family and sexual violence. She has a degree in both Psychology and Social Work. Lorraine has been married for more than 40 years and has three children and a grandchild.